Bresly

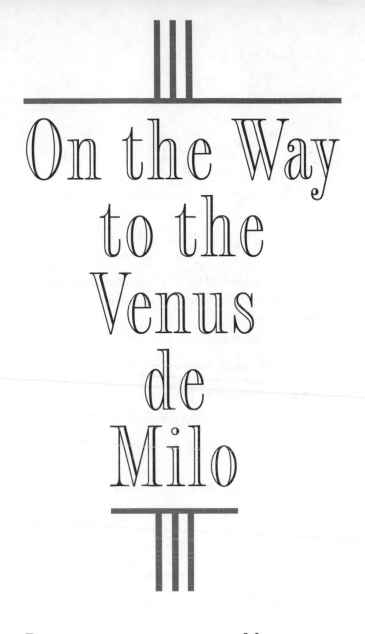

On the Way to the Venus de Milo

Pearson Marx

Simon & Schuster

New York London Toronto
Sydney Tokyo Singapore

SIMON & SCHUSTER
Rockefeller Center
1230 Avenue of the Americas
New York, New York 10020

SIMON & SCHUSTER and colophon are registered trademarks of Simon & Schuster Inc.

Designed by Paulette Orlando

Manufactured in the United States of America

1   3   5   7   9   10   8   6   4   2

Library of Congress Cataloging-in-Publication Data

On the way to the Venus de Milo / Pearson Marx.
p.   cm.
I. Title.
PS3563.A75705   1995
813'.54—dc20   94-25976   CIP
ISBN: 0-671-88335-6

Acknowledgments

Thank you Tom and Lois Wallace, Claire Wellnitz, and Eric Steel—for support and encouragement.

Thank you Linny, Cynthia, Kim, Lisa, and Gloria—for love and "lumps."

Thank you Alicia, for everything; Robert, for letting me adore you; and, especially, Amy—friend, mentor, inspiration.

To my mother and father, with love

...tears shed by one eye would blind if wept into another's eye.

Djuna Barnes

PART
I

1

Estelle woke Harry the morning of their twentieth anniversary with breakfast in bed: eggs, juice, and a rose that trembled as she lowered the tray to his lap. She said, I love you, watching him eat. He said, I love you back. She called him several times at work that day to say how much she loved him. Me too, was all he said, because there were people in the office and he couldn't talk. She greeted him at the door that evening in a black silk negligee, her black hair stiffly curled. She kissed him, and her eyelashes smelled of alcohol. Where's Lisanne? he asked. With a smile that would have been a leer on any other woman's face, she explained that she had sent their daughter to a friend's for the night. I didn't know Lisanne had any friends but me, he almost said—but didn't. Piloting him down the hall and up the stairs, she asked him tenderly how his day had been. Great, he began, that Lancel stock is booming. . . . She silenced him just outside the bedroom with a finger to his lips. Twenty scented

candles ringed the bed, twenty teardrop flames all shuddering. Frank Sinatra sang loudly, I did it *myyyy* way.
Why don't you undress, she said, and disappeared, returning moments later with a bottle of chilled champagne and
the silver bowl he had won in a club tennis tournament
filled now with a scoop of caviar. Why haven't you undressed? she said, putting the champagne and the caviar
down on the bedside table, then coming toward him, taking off his jacket, unbuttoning his shirt, easing his
trousers down to his ankles. Kneeling, she placed both
hands under his right thigh and jerked the thigh up, re-
leasing his foot from the shackles of the trousers. He staggered, and had to hold on to her hair to keep from falling.
Ow! she said. She rose, and kissed him, and pressed him
back onto the bed so abruptly he kicked over one of the
candles and burned his bare foot stamping out the little
fire. No harm done, she said, stretching out beside him to
pour him champagne, to spoon-feed him caviar. They
kissed—soaked, salty kisses. She raised her glass, To our
marriage. He raised his glass, To our marriage. She raised
her glass again, To our love. He raised his glass again, To
our love. Because I do love you, she said, so much. I love
you too, he said.

By midnight, he told Lisanne, I wanted to get in a car
and drive ten thousand miles.

"Hello, this is Lisanne, I'm not in right now, I'm probably
out giving a massage, but leave your name and number
and I'll get back to you as soon as possible."

Ellen Prawl slammed down the phone. So Lisanne was
a—a masseuse now? Her sister's cultivated voice still
stirred her. That that voice should ever have formed the
words, I'm probably out giving a massage, broke Ellen's
heart in two. That it should be forming those words over

and over again on a taped message broke Ellen's heart in—four? Ellen shook her head grimly, watching herself shake her head grimly in the mirror opposite the bed. She slowed the movement slightly, and softened her face, so that the grimness became sadness. Mrs. Prawl shakes her head sadly, she thought. Then: *Mrs. Prawl is vibrant in a pink and blue Ungaro.* Then: *Mrs. Prawl keeps her figure trim and lithe with daily aerobics classes and a sugar-and-salt-and-fat-free diet.*

Ellen raised her hands to her mouth, though she had not spoken aloud. Why couldn't she think without thinking about herself? Why couldn't she think about herself without adding to the *Harper's Bazaar* article she was always writing about herself in her mind?

Beside her on the bed, her husband Donald trembled and snored. Snores, her mother used to say, the most innocent sound in the world. Her mother had taped her father's snores, the red eye of the recorder burning through his sleep. She used to wake Ellen, and then Lisanne, in the middle of the night, so that they could watch him while he slept. Isn't he precious, her mother always said. Isn't he?

Who could stand it? Lisanne said to Ellen. Who could stand being loved that way?

Ellen wondered what Donald was dreaming about. She encouraged him to write down his dreams, but he said he never remembered them. Once she had heard him say, As I was saying, in his sleep. Once she had heard him say, Thus.

With a quick shove, she woke him. His whole body spasmed, and his eyelids fluttered open, and his eyes circled her angrily. "What the heck—?"

"I'm sorry to wake you, darling, but you've got to hear this." Ellen dialed Lisanne's number again and handed the phone to Donald. His face contorted as he listened. A

teardrop slid glistening from his left nostril down to the
dip in his upper lip. That drop seemed beautiful to Ellen,
so clear, and so rounded: you could look at the world
through it, she thought, and the world wouldn't change.
Then his tongue darted out and licked it away.

"I'll be damned!" Donald said. He too slammed down
the phone. "You know what it means—donchya?" He
was fully awake now.

"Well . . ."

"She's a hooker, damn it, a hooker! Your baby sister—
the hooker."

"I don't think—"

"You can be so naive, Ellen. What time is it?" Donald
pointed at the clock on the bedside table. It said 11:33.

"Eleven thirty-three," Ellen said weakly.

"Exactly!" His voice rose in triumph on the ZAC: egg-
ZAC-ly. "You think she's out giving a massage? At this
hour? No way! She's hooking!"

Ellen sighed.

"What amazes me, frankly," Donald said, "is that your
sister hasn't been murdered yet. All those strange states
she's lived in, all those strange towns . . ." Donald
seemed to think that anyone who lived south of Balti-
more was either a serial killer or a retard. "All those
strange jobs she's taken," he went on, "always dealing
with the public." Donald pronounced the word *public* as
though it were a loathsome animal, drawing his lips aside
like a prim lady's skirts. "Waitressing, and salesclerking,
and hostessing, and now—now *this*. It's a dangerous life
she's leading, you bet your ass it is!"

"Yes, yes, I suppose it is," Ellen agreed, though it was a
life she sometimes . . . no, *envied* was not the right word.
It was a life she wanted to watch on TV on the nights
Donald was away on business trips.

"So why hasn't she been murdered yet?"

Ellen considered the question seriously. If I were a murderer, she thought, Lisanne is the last person in the world I would choose. Because she wouldn't struggle, she wouldn't scream. Her gold eyes would be shining. They would light a pale gold path down her slim, swallowing throat.

Dr. Count Francesco von Cockleburg was once again showing Estelle the photos from his last trip to Rome. There were hundreds of these photos, assembled in handsome leather-bound albums. Although he traveled alone, he appeared in all of them—clearly, he had waylaid Romans on every street corner and forced his camera upon them. Beneath each photo, he had written the hour, the date, the place, his name, and his mood. (7:41 P.M. September 4th. Casanova Café. Dr. Count Francesco von Cockleburg. Morose.)

"Look!—there I am at the Villa Borghese. There's a prince standing right near me, just outside the frame. See here, this smudge—that's his shadow."

"A prince!" Estelle said.

"As you can see, I put on a bit of weight that trip."

"No! You're so photogenic."

"That's true. It's the cheekbones. I got them from my mother at birth, and I haven't been without them since." He looked up at her gratefully. "You always know just what to say to make a man happy. Don't you, dear lady?"

Estelle felt something begin to tremble in the trap of her heart. "But I mean it, Count," she said, "I mean everything I say."

Suddenly his face caved in like a poked pillow. His blue eyes strained. Her whole being rose fearfully to meet the touch of his eyes. "You remind me of someone," he said. "I can't think whom."

Who? Estelle was desperate to know. Who?
Someone beautiful? Someone loved?

Mrs. Rainey called at nine. Lisanne was just lying down
to dinner. (She always ate in bed.) Dinner was five but-
tered ears of sweet white corn. Mrs. Rainey did not iden-
tify herself. She did not speak at first. She sobbed. Lisanne
had never heard her cry before, but she knew that the sobs
could only be coming from Mrs. Rainey's . . . throat?
tongue? heart?

At seventy-two years old, Mrs. Rainey was the young-
est of Lisanne's few regular clients.

"What is it, Mrs. Rainey?" she asked. "What's wrong?"

"F-f-f-f-f-f—"

"Yes?"

"Frederick died," Mrs. Rainey with great effort choked
out.

"I'm so sorry," Lisanne said. She knew how much Mrs.
Rainey loved her dog, a Yorkie who trembled in the
palms of hands, and yapped at butterflies, and slept on
Mrs. Rainey's pillow. The yapping might have irritated
some people, but, as Mrs. Rainey said, "If I weighed two
pounds, I would yap at butterflies."

Mrs. Rainey had often gone out for no other reason
than the excitement her return would provoke in the dog.

"When did it happen?" Lisanne asked.

"J-j-j-just now." Mrs. Rainey started to sob again.
"Would you—could you—please—come over? He's in
the closet and I'm scared to—to— Please come over!"

"I'm leaving right now."

Mrs. Rainey lived forty-five minutes away, over on
Siesta Key. It was a long drive, but Lisanne loved driving.
Its dangers humbled and thrilled her. She was amazed by
all the people who seemed to be able to do it without brav-

ery, without fear. Young people, old people, stupid people, drunk people, crippled people, illiterate people, people who could not see without their glasses. Daydreaming mothers drove their children home from school, speeding past great sucking trucks on macadam that was often slick from rain. Perhaps they didn't know that one in a hundred people die on the road. But for Lisanne—anytime she arrived anywhere safely, she was aware that somewhere someone had died, somewhere red lights were flashing, crowds gathering. Someone had died so that, statistically, she would be spared. Someone had died—*for her.* In this way, any safe arrival anywhere filled Lisanne with despair and gratitude. To arrive safely seemed all that you could ask of God and the human race.

Lisanne rolled down the windows and thought, I could go anywhere.

Mrs. Rainey lived in a retirement complex called Sheltering Oaks. There were no oaks (not that the names of retirement complexes are meant to be taken literally). Lisanne found Mrs. Rainey pacing barefoot in her racy red silk robe outside her *compound,* which was what Mrs. Rainey called the small cottage: *Come into my compound.* Mrs. Rainey radiated distress as palpably as a siren, and Lisanne was surprised none of the other retirees had come to her aid. But then Mrs. Rainey only got along sporadically with the other retirees. Mrs. Rainey claimed this was because she was single . . . and a flirt. The wives *would* grow ruffled, they *would* draw their husbands away. "I can't help it," Mrs. Rainey said. "I've been a flirt all my life, and I'll be one till the day I die, which will probably be tomorrow."

"Oh, thank God you're here!" Mrs. Rainey said now. She stepped back, and the lamp in the doorway smeared a lurid light across her face. Lisanne had never seen her without her makeup before, without her polished cheeks, and reckless lips, and painted lids, and coated lashes. Naked, her face looked helpless and ashamed. But it looked alive. Lisanne felt her eyes swoop toward it, and she shut them. The face was not indecent, but Lisanne's eyes were. She put her arm around Mrs. Rainey's sharp shoulders.

"He's in there," Mrs. Rainey said.

"Frederick?"

"Yes, in the closet. He was in the closet all evening. I tried to coax him out, you know, with biscuits, and those liver treats he loved. But he wouldn't come. So I just assumed he sensed a storm coming. You know how frightened he was of storms. He always hid in the closet when it stormed. So I left him in there. Then when I went to fetch him for bed, I found him. On . . . my p-p-p-pink espadrille." Mrs. Rainey's voice had been soft but strong until this last sentence. The detail of the pink espadrille broke her down. "Think about it," she wept, "that pink espadrille was his deathbed. Oh why, oh why did he have to die alone?"

"That's the way dogs are, I guess," Lisanne said. "They crawl away, they dig their holes, they lie down in them. Your espadrille was Frederick's hole."

Mrs. Rainey seemed unsatisfied. "I think it's because he wanted to spare me," she said, "in his noble, gallant way. Oh Frederick."

"Yes, it is a kind of nobility," Lisanne said. She made a move to open the door. Mrs. Rainey held her back, clawing at her arm.

"I'm afraid to go into the compound," she said, hanging her head. "When I picked him up, when I realized he was . . . dead . . . I dropped him. That's the worst of it," she said, "that I couldn't bear to touch him. My poor little Frederick. How hurt he must be. Because he knows, oh yes, he knows."

Lisanne was going to tell Mrs. Rainey that what she had found in the closet *was not Frederick.* She stopped herself, not sure if this was true.

"Wait here," she said.

She went inside, pausing in the kitchen to get a plastic Ziploc bag and a large silver serving spoon she saw stuck in a bowl of Jell-O. Then she went into the bedroom, and over to the closet, tiptoeing, as though she might startle something: herself, of course. Mrs. Rainey had dozens of pairs of shoes, neatly arranged in rows. They all seemed inviting, and Lisanne wondered briefly what had attracted Frederick to the pink espadrille in particular. He lay half off it now, askew from when Mrs. Rainey had dropped him. She laid a finger on his chest, as if to wake him. It struck her as wrong, somehow, to pick him up by his head, or by his tail, or by his tiny paws—so she spooned him into the bag.

"Let's bury him," she said to Mrs. Rainey.

"But where?" Mrs. Rainey averted her eyes from the bag.

"Anywhere you want."

"Maybe here," Mrs. Rainey said. "No, maybe there . . . in that flower bed. Do you have a shovel?"

Lisanne lifted the spoon.

"What about worms?" Mrs. Rainey asked anxiously. "Will the worms get him?"

Lisanne hesitated. "Not for a while. I've sealed the bag pretty tight."

"I suppose it's just his body," Mrs. Rainey said. "But still—it's *his* body."

Lisanne sank to her knees in the flower bed, crushing alyssum, bruising lilies and gaudy gladioli. She began to dig, the silver spoon glinting in the dirt. "It's so sad," Mrs. Rainey kept saying, "so damn sad." She said, "You see, I always thought he'd outlive me." She hummed softly, then sang "Amazing Grace." Mrs. Rainey's voice was high and sweet and cracked, and it made Lisanne shiver. She felt the yearning in it as coldly as a gun at the nape of her neck, driving her forward: live, live, live, live, live. . . .

"How did you know it was me on the phone tonight?" Mrs. Rainey said. "Am I the only old woman you know who would call you crying?"

Lisanne stayed late, massaging Mrs. Rainey, who was afraid to go to sleep. "Pamela took my pills," Mrs. Rainey said bitterly. Pamela was Mrs. Rainey's daughter. She had flown down from New York last Friday, taken tennis lessons and, apparently, Mrs. Rainey's pills, and then flown back on Sunday. The massage table was set up in the living room. Framed photos of Mrs. Rainey hung on all the walls—a photographic ode to Mrs. Rainey's youth. They gleamed like fishtail scales in the dim light. Mrs. Rainey, tall and proud and statuesque and laughing at the camera. Mrs. Rainey, with assorted short men. Mrs. Rainey at a table in the Peppermint Lounge . . . leaning against a Rolls-Royce . . . lying on a lawn. Mrs. Rainey in a pensive moment on a pebbled beach. "As if anyone that young and blond and beautiful could have anything to think about," Mrs. Rainey said of herself in that picture. She always spoke of the woman in the photographs as if the woman were an enviable and slightly contemptuous stranger. The most recent photograph was taken over twenty-five years ago, on Mrs. Rainey's forty-fifth birthday. She was slicing a cake, she was shimmering in blue chiffon. "I remember how she danced a tango at that party," Mrs. Rainey said. "She danced it reluctantly. She was loved by all the greats, the kind of great they don't make anymore. And—would you believe it?—she was never satisfied."

Mrs. Rainey had been a showgirl, a starlet, a femme fatale. She had been unhappily a wife, unwillingly a mother. She had been defiant and selfish. And why not? Lisanne thought, looking at the beauty in the photographs.

"Does my body ever frighten you?" Mrs. Rainey said, as Lisanne kneaded her back, her thin, speckled haunches. Her hands parted the old loose flesh. "Does it ever disgust you?"

"Oh Mrs. Rainey," Lisanne said. She remembered what her father told her years ago, when she was fourteen, when she was shy and thin and awkward, when she used to think: If I saw me, I'd hate me. Her father said, Be thankful you're not a great beauty. He said, To be a great beauty is to be a disappointment.

"It's pretty damn fishy, if you ask me," Donald said. "I mean, he's been hanging around your mother an awful lot," Donald went on, "sniffing around her like she was some kind o' bitch in heat."

"Donald, really . . ."

"Sniffing around her like she's some kind o' bitch in heat," Donald repeated happily. He was always happy in a state of outrage.

"I gather he reads poetry aloud to her," Ellen said, "Byron's, Keats's, and—his own."

"And what a load o' crap that is!"

Donald was standing at the stove frying a ten-ounce steak—a bedtime snack. He wore only his boxer shorts. Through the thin blue cotton, Ellen saw that his buttocks were eloquently quivering. In outrage, Donald's face did not necessarily redden, his voice did not necessarily rise, but, inevitably, his buttocks quivered.

"Poetry!" Donald said. "Poetry, my ass! If you ask me, he's a fag—a fag or a gigolo. And frankly, in this case, I'd prefer the former."

Donald believed that any man who read or wrote poetry was a fag—a fag or a gigolo. Any man who wore
turtlenecks was a fag or a gigolo, according to Donald.
Similarly, any man who spoke French was a fag or a
gigolo (unless he was a native-born Frenchman). Any
man who went willingly to the opera (being dragged by a
wife didn't count) was a fag or a gigolo. Donald was furious when he found out that Ellen had encouraged Donald
Jr. to take flute lessons . . . because any little boy who
took flute lessons would surely grow up to be a fag—a fag
or a gigolo.

"And what kind of a friggin' name is *Cockleburg,* anyway?" Donald said. He flipped the steak onto a plate and,
without bothering to sit down, began to cut and eat it. As
always, he chewed so fast and so furiously that Ellen
feared he would choke. During their long courtship, Ellen
had learned the Heimlich maneuver. She had in fact had
to use it on Donald fifteen to twenty times in their thirteen years of marriage. Back in the days of their courtship, the mere thought of losing Donald had made Ellen
burst into tears. The thought alone no longer had this effect on her. She would have to lose him literally to burst
into tears now.

"Cockleburg," Ellen said. "Cockleburg, Cockleburg,
Cockleburg. Doesn't the name make you think of some
grim town in the middle of nowhere, surrounded by
toxic-waste dumps? Take the last exit and turn left—to
Cockleburg!"

"It's probably not even his real name!" Donald said angrily.

"Who'd make up a name like Cockleburg?" Ellen said.
"You can't go home again, not to Cockleburg. And if you
could, would you even want to? All the grass withered,
the trees dying, the sewage in the streets . . ."

"You know, I could have predicted this," Donald said,

"the minute your father died. In fact, I did predict it. I knew, sooner or later, some gigolo would slide up to your mother on a trail of his own mousse and flatter her out of a fortune. I'm frankly surprised it's taken this long."

Estelle had been a widow almost twelve years.

"So you think he's after her money, then?" Ellen said. She herself thought so, but she asked the question anyway because she knew it would inflame Donald. There was something exciting about Donald's wrath—when it wasn't directed at her, that is.

"Your money, babe," Donald was saying, "it'll be *your* money someday . . . and Donald Jr.'s. That is, if the old broad doesn't give it all away."

"Mine and Lisanne's," Ellen reminded him.

At the mention of Lisanne, Donald's buttocks began to quiver again, jumping like eggs in boiling water. "She probably makes more dough hookin' than I make at the firm!"

"Donald, please . . ." Why was she so thrilled when Donald insulted her sister? When he insulted her mother?

With a visible effort, Donald contained his outrage. Inch by square inch, his buttocks stilled. "All I can say," he said, "is that I, Donald Patrick Prawl, will not stand by and watch some oily gigolo screw you, and I mean literally *screw* you out of your inheritance!"

"How can you be so sure Cockleburg's intentions aren't honorable?" Ellen asked. "You haven't even met him. Maybe he's genuinely attracted to Mom."

Donald barked out a short laugh. "Come off it, Ellen! She's a sixty-two-year-old woman."

"And a very beautiful one," Ellen said.

"Beautiful like a—like a"—Donald groped for an appropriate simile—"like a tree. You wouldn't want to fuck a tree now—wouldja?—no matter how beautiful it was. Not unless it had twenty mil in the bank! Ha! Ha ha ha!

Ha!" Donald laughed heartily, in spite of his outrage.

"Donald, what a vile thing to say," Ellen said placidly. She made a mental note of her contentment: *Mrs. Prawl enjoys many a cozy moment with her husband, the important Mr. Prawl, in their bright, white spanking-new remodeled kitchen.*

No, she was not unmarried, she was not unwanted, she was not unloved, she was not alone. . . .

"Let's face it," Donald was saying, "life doesn't begin at sixty-two, not for a woman it doesn't!"

"But it doesn't end, either," Ellen said.

Just then, Ellen observed a thumb-sized cockroach scuttling purposefully across the counter toward her arm. Ellen jerked away, and sat rigidly, staring at the roach, who had paused, as if to stare back at her. She shuddered, sensing something taunting in the creature's gaze. Weren't they supposed to be afraid of humans? Well, most humans, maybe—but not her. Perhaps this was the same roach who had outrun her the other day. She had chased him three laps around the kitchen table with, ludicrously, a carving knife, which she had seized instinctively (it was the only weapon handy). After the roach made his triumphant getaway under the fridge, Ellen had sat slumped at the table for a full fifteen minutes, full of a strange despair.

She was torn now between the desire to alert Donald to the presence of the roach so that he could masterfully kill it and the fear that he would use it against her for months to come as yet another example of her "crappy" housekeeping (one of the constant themes of their marriage).

She was grateful to the roach when, abruptly, it sheered off the counter, down the dishwasher, and out of sight.

"I'd keep a close eye on your mother, if I were you," Donald was saying. "Drop by day and night, day and especially night," he was saying. "Don't let her alone with that gigolo, if you can help it."

"What am I supposed to do?" Ellen said. "Camp out in her hallway?"

"Yes," Donald said. "What else have you got to do?"

Ellen stiffened. What else did she have to do?

Every day Mrs. Prawl walks her son to and from St. Bernard's, though he has asked her not to, saying it embarrasses him. Then: *Mrs. Prawl is a tireless fundraiser on behalf of many socially prominent charities; executives flinch when their secretaries tell them Mrs. Prawl is on the line, demanding money again. . . .*

"Thank God summer's coming up," Donald was saying. "Maybe we can persuade the old dame to leave the city a couple of weeks early." Estelle always spent the summer at the house in Bedford. "At least in the country she'll be out of walking, I mean *slithering*, distance of that damn Cockleburg."

Donald had now finished his snack—always a difficult moment for him. Ellen tracked his finger as it twitched back and forth, back and forth across the emptied, blood-smeared plate.

She had a sudden, urgent desire to hear her sister's calm, low, unlucky voice. She would try her again before she went to sleep.

2

Around five o'clock, wherever she was, in the Carolinas, or in Georgia, in Louisiana or Florida, Lisanne thought of her mother. Because when she was a child, at five o'clock, always, she watched her mother get ready for her father. It hadn't mattered that her father was coming home later and later. Five o'clock was the hour the preparations began.

First, her mother would run her bath. While she undressed, Lisanne gripped the tub's slippery lip. As the bubbles swelled and frothed, she felt the nakedness bloom behind her. Sometimes she got into the water with her mother, the smell of vanilla rising from the bubbles.

After the bath, they went into the dressing room. Mirrored doors slid open on closets filled with every imaginable kind of dress, for every imaginable kind of woman: pale, fluttery sundresses; black-tie-dinner dresses with flopping bows and crackling taffeta skirts; long, lacy antique dresses; scratchy, tailored ladies'-lunch dresses. . . .

What are you in the mood for? her mother would ask her.

The chosen dress would float down over her mother's head, and Lisanne would button it up, her fingers creeping up the still-moist back. Oooh, that tickles, her mother would say, and hold out goose-bumped arms.

Then Lisanne would sit down beside her on a bench in front of the vanity table. There were dozens of paints and glosses and powders in pretty pots and tubes and jars, ranging in martial rows. Her mother's hands would flutter over them, and dip and rise and rub and smooth. Her hands seemed to Lisanne the only knowing thing about her. Her mother's eyes were the dark gray of smoke against night sky. She lined them in black. Her lips were sharply carved, slick with wine. She patted them dry, and painted them bright blue-red. She never wore foundation. There was no shade white enough to be her blue-white skin.

Lisanne loved her mother's face. It was proud and predatory as the face of an empress on an ancient coin. It was made to laugh while watching gladiators tear each other to pieces.

You should have had that face, her father told her.

Then her mother would brush her thick black hair and wind it in a knot at the nape of her neck. She would turn her head to check it in the mirror, showing her sharp profile. She would stand and stretch, and her glass beads would glimmer and ring.

Do I look all right? her mother would say.

You look fine.

Many times, Lisanne wanted to ask her, Haven't you ever thought of being cruel?

• • •

Ellen and Estelle spoke on the phone every day, usually in the morning while they had their coffee. They spoke even on the days they met for lunch, or afternoon tea, or dinner, or, more frequently, to shop for Ellen. The daily phone call had been a part of their lives since Ellen had first left home, twenty years earlier, to go to boarding school.

Almost always, they spoke of Ellen. Even in the years when her father was sick, when her father was dying, they spoke largely of Ellen—especially Ellen's new boyfriend, that impressive Princetonian Donald Patrick Prawl: how to seduce him, how to entrance him, how to enslave him, how to torment him, how to make him propose. Ellen would ask about her father, but her mother didn't seem to want to talk about him. She would immediately bring up Donald. There were moments when Ellen felt guilty for talking about herself so much. These moments passed.

Ellen was living in Boston at the time, waiting for Donald to finish business school. She considered moving back home. "But think of all the women on that campus," her mother said, "all the grad students, all the young professors" (Ellen had thought of them), "not to mention the coeds" (*coed*—the word alone chilled Ellen's heart). "I don't think it's a smart idea for you to leave Donald alone up there," her mother said, "do you? An attractive and popular man like that?"

As it was, she came home almost every other weekend. And after all, her mother did have Lisanne to keep her company.

After her mother made herself up, they went downstairs to the kitchen. What do you think he'll feel like tonight? her mother would ask, and Lisanne would say steak, or duck, or chicken. And her mother would take the steak, or duck, or chicken out of the freezer to thaw. She would turn on the oven. She would slice the vegetables and set them in a pot, ready to boil at the sound of a footstep.

They would settle in her mother's sitting room, the room opposite the front door. Here you could hear the elevator as it rose, the door as it opened and closed. Except for the bar along one wall, and the stereo, everything was blue and unbruising: the carpet thick, the table round, the bureau draped in fabric. Now Lisanne opened the first bottle, poured the first glass. Now she put on one of her mother's blues records: Willie Dixon or Etta James, Mama Yancey or Bessie Smith. She had noticed that music seduced her mother into sadness more quickly and completely than silence.

Then she would lie on the blue carpet, and do jigsaw puzzles, or her homework, while her mother reclined on the velvet sofa, her blanketed legs a mermaid's tail, and read: Blake and Shelley, Byron and Keats, Rimbaud and Rilke and *Vogue* magazine.

Lisanne watched the glass of wine as it rose to lips that were long and lean as muscles.

One morning in April, during their daily phone call, Estelle mentioned to Ellen that she had received a lovely letter from a dear old friend of Harry's, a Francesco von Cockleburg.

"I never heard Dad speak of anyone by the name of Cockleburg," Ellen said.

"I gather he's been living in Paris for the last thirty-six years," Estelle said. "I've asked him to dinner on Thursday, and I was wondering if you and Donald might like to join us."

Donald had a tennis game, so Ellen went alone. Intending to read his letter before he arrived, Ellen showed up half an hour early—unnecessarily, as it turned out.

Francesco von Cockleburg, poet, critic, scholar, linguist, tympanist, was late.

Ellen began to hope he wouldn't show up, but no—the letter was a masterpiece of self-congratulation. He wouldn't waste that effort.

"He sounds terribly smart, doesn't he?" her mother said.

The letter was addressed to her father: Mr. Harry Wolfe. The postscript read, "And I long to meet at last your bride, the incomparable Estelle of legend."

"How dear an old friend could he be," Ellen said, "if he doesn't know that Dad's been dead for twelve years?"

"He lost touch," her mother said.

They awaited the thinker in the library. Usually her mother entertained visitors in the high-ceilinged living room that overlooked Central Park. For a man of Francesco von Cockleburg's intellect, however, she felt that the library would be more appropriate. The thinker would step into this room, and with a grateful twitching of his nostrils, inhale the smell of books. He would sink into its welcoming gloom and dip his scholarly face in the cool shadows.

At last the doorbell rang, and Estelle with a radiant smile rose from the red brocade armchair. She tottered slightly, having finished a third glass of wine in the hour they'd been waiting.

The wooden doors swung open, and in staggered a man, disheveled and lacerated. Blue-white hair sprang up from his brow in a frizzled half-moon. His eyes were silvery-blue, vitreous and wildly staring. He wore a purple velvet smoking jacket and tight gray flannels. He was bleeding from the lip or nose. He reeled across the room and fell to his knees in front of Estelle.

"Shall I call the police?" Ellen said.

The man lifted his arms, then flapped them. He seemed to be fugling something.

"Mr. Cockleburg?" her mother said.

"Doctor!" he gasped.

"Ellen, call Dr. Charney," she said.

The man shook his head. "Doctor!" he gasped again. "*Dr.* Cockleburg!"

Estelle was confused. "You want a doctor?"

"No, Mother," Ellen said. "I believe he's referring to his academic title."

Estelle bent and heaved him by his shoulders over to the sofa. "Do lie down, Dr. Cockleburg. Ellen, fix the doctor a drink while I go fetch some towels and ice."

Ellen went next door to the bar at the back of the sitting room and poured a tall glass of scotch. Cockleburg looked as if he could use it.

His head rested on the sofa's arm. Estelle was sponging his face and holding a bag of ice to his nose. He let out a long, low groan that trailed off into rasping sobs.

Ellen gave her mother the scotch. She lifted the glass to his bloody lips. He gulped most of it down, then spat out a mouthful. It jetted up like whale spume and splashed onto the slope of his chin.

"I beg you, dear lady," he said, "dear lady, I beg you—forgive me."

"Dr. Cockleburg, calm yourself," Estelle said. "There's nothing to forgive."

"But my tardiness," he said, "my deplorable disarray . . ."

"What happened to you, anyway?" Ellen said.

"Ellen!" Her mother looked at her sharply. "Let the poor man rest!"

"Depravity," he said, "depravity for which, alas, I was not on the qui vive." He paused heavily, then went on, "Ah, the cloacal city. I am not used to its ways."

"There, there, Doctor," said Estelle.

It took him a while to recover sufficiently to tell them the story, yet when he spoke, his voice was sure and silky—and suddenly accented, mostly French, with a bit of German thrown in to roughen the g's and c's.

As the day was fine, he'd decided to bike the seventy blocks uptown from Gramercy Park. He was a superbly conditioned athlete—such a distance was nothing to him. At 60th Street, he veered over to Fifth Avenue and turned off into Central Park. He'd had a yearning for verdure. Just before the reservoir, on a stretch of deserted path, two vulgarly dressed youths leapt out from the bushes and set upon him—with sticks! The suddenness of the fustigation unseated and unmanned him. Though trained in the ancient arts of ninjitsu and jujitsu, he was simply too stunned to react. At this point, Estelle seized the doctor's hands. Yes, with sticks!—they beat him to the ground and to his horror began to dismantle his bicycle. He loved that bicycle. Just then a pentad of joggers, thanks to a merciful Providence, approached. One youth sounded the alarm, while the other youth abruptly hurled the front wheel of the bicycle high into the air. The doctor's dazed eyes tracked the spiraling sphere in its descent from the heavens. The youths disappeared into the bushes whence they came. Two of the joggers helped him to his feet while the three other joggers hunted the fallen wheel. Carrying the pieces of his bicycle, he then painfully limped the few blocks to Estelle's building.

Prone before Estelle lay a wounded man. With tender fingers, she smoothed his blue-white afro. He made a thrashing attempt to rise.

"Dr. Cockleburg, don't even think of moving. You must rest here till you regain your strength."

Estelle turned now to Ellen. "Darling, do you think we should call the police?"

"Yes, do!" said the doctor. "Those hooligans . . . they ought to be apprehended."

"They're long gone by now," Ellen said.

The doctor stirred. "You're right," he said, "but—'The Wanton Boy that kills the fly, Shall feel the Spiders enmity.' "

A long silence ensued, during which Ellen sensed his reluctance to footnote. Finally, he added, "Blake, 'Auguries of Innocence,' 1800–1808."

During the first bottle, her mother grew animated. She would look up from her book at Lisanne with moist, flirtatious eyes and ask in an eager voice How school was going, and Who the most popular girls were.

You ought to throw a party, Lisanne, she might say. We could get clowns in, and magicians, and maybe even a band. Wouldn't you like that?

She often planned parties for Lisanne during the first bottle.

During the second bottle, she grew sad. Her hands would tremble, and her head would bow.

Why are you so quiet? she might say. I worry about you sometimes, Lisanne, you're so quiet.

She often remarked on Lisanne's quietness during the second bottle.

During the third bottle, she grew angry, twisting and untwisting her blanketed legs. Lisanne would half-turn her back, looking away from her mother toward the door.

Look at me when I'm talking to you, Lisanne, her mother would say. Why don't you ever look at me when I'm talking to you?

Lisanne would get up from the floor, get another bottle, pour another glass.

Because the goal was to get her mother past the third

bottle by the time her father came home. Because during the fourth bottle, her mother always fell asleep. And then Lisanne and her father would go out to dinner.

Now Lisanne would stand over her, look down at her, and smile.

She would say, But I *am* looking at you, Mother.

She would think, You're in the pass-out phase—*just pass out.*

Two hours after his dramatic entrance (Ellen told a sickened Donald later), the doctor summoned the strength to move—down the hall to the dining room. Estelle had roasted a capon, boiled broccoli, and baked potatoes—though she worried that this simple repast was unworthy of the doctor. He must be quite a gourmet . . . all those years in Paris . . . But no! Capon was his favorite fowl, the doctor swore, broccoli his favorite green, potato his favorite root. "I'm so glad," Estelle said.

He was mortified, however, to sit at her table in his maculated state. Though not a gourmet, he admitted to a streak of dandyism. Estelle made Ellen go upstairs and get one of Harry's old sweaters.

She had saved all his clothes in a big box she kept at the back of her closet. It hulked there in the calm behind the troops of pumps and sandals. Ellen chose the ugliest sweater she could find—a V-neck the green of mold.

It was strange to see it on a man again. From the way it fit Dr. Cockleburg, Ellen got a sense of her father's body. He was so shrunken at the end; she had forgotten how tall and broad he had been. The sweater bagged out over Dr. Cockleburg's shoulders, it fell down below his hips, clinging to the hump of his majestic rump. Only the sleeves, reaching to just beyond his elbows, were too short.

What long arms he has! Ellen thought. They swung down from the tiniest torso she had ever seen, a squat triangle that barely accommodated his nipples. He was all neck and hip.

He took off his bloodied shirt before putting on the sweater, so now there was nothing between his flesh and Ellen's dead father's relic. Thick tufts of grizzled hair sprouted in the V. I should have gotten him a crewneck, Ellen thought.

Estelle led him to the head of the table, supporting him with her arms. He made a great eye-rolling, cheek-twitching, nostril-flaring show of his suffering.

"Shall I carve?" he asked.

"Please," Estelle said. "It's so nice having a man to carve."

Ellen lowered the capon in front of him.

"I'm generally a thigh man," the doctor said, "unless of course you two ladies—?" The blade of the carving knife he held aloft dripped red in the candlelight.

"No, no," said Estelle, "take *both* thighs."

"Yeah, go ahead," Ellen said bitterly. She herself would have liked a thigh.

Estelle spooned broccoli onto the plates.

"Well spooned!" The doctor nodded his approval.

"Why, thank you!"

"This is lovely, lovely, lovely," he said. "For me, a solitary bachelor, a rare treat indeed. Would it be presumptuous of me to propose a toast?"

"Not at all."

"Well, then—I drink to you, Estelle, my gentle nurse." His blue gaze swerved to her. "And to dear, dear, dear Harry." The blue gaze swerved to the ceiling. "And to the fair offspring of that union." It swerved to Ellen.

Ellen stared back at him.

His brows were startlingly black beneath all that white

hair, combed down now. With his long aquiline nose and his full, steeply curved, pink lips, he made Ellen think of a corrupt Venetian priest. He must have been in his early fifties, but his olive skin was too young for his hair. It shone as though freshly licked.

"I was so shocked when you told me on the phone the other day," he was saying to Estelle, "about Harry. I apologize again for my letter. You must have thought it so g-g-g-ghoulish."

"Well . . ." Ellen said.

"I left for Paris just after he'd met you. We kept in touch for a little while. He used to send me photographs of you. He was a man besotted, a man possessed by love."

"Really?" Estelle said.

"Oh yes, and I could well understand his obsession as I studied your photographs. *Mon Dieu,* how those photos gave me pause. They seemed to hold out all the promise of young American womanhood. The clean Yankee lines of your face—oh, Estelle, if you only knew how your face made me pine—pine for the simple land I had left!"

Ellen's gorge rose at this speech. "May I ask what you were doing in Paris?" she said.

He chortled, a rich, buttery sound. "Dreaming," he said, "dreaming those dreams that bookish youths will dream. Also, I had family in Paris, a count on my mother's side. The title passed to me at his death, though that's neither here nor there. . . ."

"Do you prefer to be addressed by your academic title," Ellen said, "or by your aristocratic title?"

"Well, actually my friends call me Count—Count Coco—though to the world I am simply, humbly, *Dr. Cockleburg.*"

"I hope you'll let us call you Count," Estelle said.

"I would be honored." He inclined his head in courtly

fashion. "You know, you remind me of someone, Estelle, though I can't think whom. Someone I knew in Paris, I would imagine. Because your face is actually more European today—isn't it?"

Yankee or European, her face was aglow. Usually she got paler as she drank. Ellen noticed she was on her fourth glass, not including the ones she'd had while they waited. The count, as Ellen now thought of him, ate like a pig but hardly touched his wine.

"I'd like to see those photos," Ellen said, "if you still have them."

"I suppose I must." He pivoted his head on that enormous neck. "Come to think of it, they were clippings, cut from gossip columns."

Ellen had never seen her father so much as glance at a gossip column—never. "Were there any letters?" she asked.

"Yes, of course. Though in your father's case, a picture was worth a thousand words. He was a lusty, hearty, kind, dear man, your father, but a scribe? No."

"I'd like to see those letters."

"Would you? Well, I'm afraid much of my stuff is still in storage. I've only been back a few weeks."

"You must find New York so brutal compared to Paris," Estelle said, "especially after your ordeal today. But please don't judge us too harshly. It's not so much a brutal city as a city in pain. Sometimes when I walk down the street . . . I can hardly bear the suffering I see."

"Madame, how could I judge harshly," he said, "a city which you call home?"

"Oh Count." Her eyelids fluttered. "That's kind of you. I've heard so much about the gallantry of Frenchmen. All true, obviously."

"But he's American," Ellen said.

"American, French, Icelandic, Zulu," he said, "I trust

all men, no matter what their origins, to celebrate beauty where they find it."

What a voice! Ellen could hear the tongue in it, thick and moist and muscular, leaving on each word it formed a viscous trail.

"Why did you leave Paris," she asked, "Doctor—I mean, Count?"

"For—personal reasons," he said, his long, greenish teeth gnashing into a second drumstick.

"Oh?" She leaned toward him.

Her mother looked away.

"It's a wonderful city," he said slowly, "but it became painful for me."

"Then don't speak of it, Count," Estelle said. "Here, have another baked potato."

"Thank you, dear lady, I think I will." He held out his plate, wiped clean but for the bones.

"We are so happy to have you here," she said.

In sleep her mother's anger was consumed again by sadness. Now the sadness seemed the living thing and her mother only the random object around which it had coiled itself. In sleep her mother's sadness seemed no longer abject but infinitely powerful, and Lisanne was afraid of it.

She would shut the sitting-room door on it, and then the front door, and then her eyes. She would lie on the cool tiles of the foyer floor, by the elevator, and still feel it, her mother's sadness, through wood and stone and eyelids, obscuring her like a skin of scum on the surface of a pond.

• • •

They repaired to the library after dinner for coffee (Ellen told a sickened and then violently outraged Donald later). Coffee, and more wine, in Estelle's case. A fire roared in the grate, though the night was warm. The count reclined like an odalisque on the sofa, lying on his side with his top knee angled and his great buttocks tilted upward. He held his coffee cup with delicately splayed fingers.

"Do my ears deceive me?" he asked. "Or do I hear a distant barking?"

"Your ears do not deceive you, Count," Estelle said. "Since Harry died, I've become something of a dog lover. I wasn't sure if you were, so I took the precaution of secluding mine up on the terrace. Though harmless, they are sometimes, well, disconcerting to the uninitiated."

Estelle had twelve dogs, all mutts, all unwanted, lost, or abandoned—and all appalling, Ellen thought. At the beginning of every summer, for the last eleven years, her mother had stopped by the pound and saved one mutt ("one *innocent* mutt," was how Estelle put it) from death row. She would have saved them all, Ellen believed, if Donald hadn't forbidden it—and quite rightly. "You'll be known as mad, Estelle," he told her, adding only half-jokingly, "I don't want my son's granny to be known as the mad old woman of Bedford—eh?" As it was, her mother had quite a reputation. Strangers were always dropping dogs off on her front lawn—old dogs, sick dogs, deaf dogs, three-legged dogs. . . .

"Oh, all we French adore dogs," the count was saying. "The Parisians even bring their dogs out to dinner with them. Ironically, I never had a dog until the last few months of my thirty-six years in that gay, dog-loving capital." Abruptly, his expression and tone turned mournful. "Poor, dear creature," he said. "She is noble, she is gallant, she is brave. In no way does she demean her ancient pedigree. And yet"—he sighed—"and yet I fear she languishes. Yes, I fear she pines—for fresh air, for glebe, for rousing canine fellowship. I fear indeed she may sicken and die. And who can blame her? Why, even the cockroaches recoil from my bleak, bachelor flat!" He shook his head.

"Don't you walk her?" Ellen asked.

"Frankly, the filth of the New York City streets seems only to depress her further. Anyway, it's not enough."

"She's a large dog, then?" Ellen said.

"Not large in body—but large in spirit, large in heart . . . both slowly breaking, alas." His vast slab of throat convulsed as if with swallowed sobs. "I must I must I must I must I simply *must* find a way to get her into the country—or forfeit her life."

Estelle had been listening transfixed to this tale of canine woe. Now, at last, earnestly, urgently, she spoke: "Well, then, Count, I absolutely insist that you and your pet—"

"Queen Elizabeth," he said, "named thusly in tribute to her dignity."

"—that you and Queen Elizabeth join me and my dogs in Westchester this summer."

"Dear lady, my heart swells at this generosity," he said, his hand over that organ, "but we couldn't, we wouldn't, impose, intrude. . . ."

"Do it for Queen Elizabeth," Estelle said.

"Not even for her," he said, "that light of my life, now tragically flickering out. No, not even for her."

"Well, then, do it for Harry"—and she swung upon him a look of the most abject supplication.

There was a long silence. Cockleburg bowed his head, then raised it, as if in mute hosanna. "For Harry," he said.

"Oh, Count, I'm so thrilled," Estelle said. "We usually leave at the end of May. So you must come by anytime after that. For as long as you like."

"The end of May?" Ellen said. "But it's only the beginning of April. Will the Queen be able to survive without glebe that long?"

The count was slowly folding himself into a sitting position. "What a splendid evening," he said. "Estelle—a joy to meet you at last. And Ellen—unexpected bounty. I didn't even know you existed."

"Same to you," Ellen said.

"You're not leaving?" Estelle said, alarmed.

"I'm afraid I must. Queen Elizabeth is probably ululating with loneliness even as we speak."

"But are you feeling strong enough to go all the way downtown?"

"After that succulent capon? I am a man renewed!" He rose cautiously to his feet. "Ugh-guh!" he groaned. "I must have sprained my ankle. But it's nothing," he added.

He made a move to pull off the borrowed sweater.

"Take it, Count," Estelle said. "You must. I've set aside your clothes to dry-clean."

"You are too generous."

Reaching into his pocket, he suddenly twisted up his face and spat out a curse. "*Merde!* My wallet!"

Ellen's heart soared. Here comes the punch line, she thought.

"It must have fallen out of my pocket when those two ephebi in their savagery knocked me to the ground."

Ellen found this hard to believe, given how tight his pants were.

"*Merde! Dieu! Merde!* This is indeed a blow." He had the distracted air of a man talking to himself—or pretending to.

"Dear Count, let me lend you some money, then." Estelle reached for her purse.

Carelessly, she peeled off a bill.

Cockleburg's hand lowered over it and closed. Then he

raised his hand and returned the bill to her purse.

"One dollar," he said. "For the subway. I will accept not a dime, not a nickel, not a penny, not a pound, not a yen, not a ruble, not a franc more."

"I think I have a token," Ellen said.

"Count! The subway? At this hour?"

He lifted a hand. "I fear I must beg of you one last favor."

"Anything."

Ellen knew she meant it literally.

"I left my shattered bicycle in a pile in your foyer. Would it be all right if I came by to pick it up later in the week?"

"Of course. Come by anytime."

He angled his tiny torso floorward and kissed Estelle's hand.

For a second Ellen feared he would kiss hers too, but he only shook it.

"Once again, thank you for an enchanting evening. You are sirens, mermaids in my sea."

With that valediction, he limped out into the hall and was gone.

3

When Lisanne got home from Mrs. Rainey's, there were two loud hangups on her machine. There was a pitiful message from Mr. Lumkin, one of her other clients: "My hip is real bad, honey. Two boys knocked me over in the mall tonight. I guess they didn't mean to, but they about killed me. Anyway, I couldn't stop screaming. Is there a chance you could squeeze me in for a treatment first thing in the morning?" The image of Mr. Lumkin flat on his back while people stepped over him to get to Baskin Robbins made Lisanne sweat. Not so much the writhing limbs as the screaming mouth. And not so much the screaming mouth as the forgiving eyes: *I guess you didn't mean to, boys.*

And then, to her surprise, there was a message from Ellen. Ellen's calls always thrilled her, and not just because they occurred so rarely. It sometimes seemed to Lisanne that when she was a child, her entire relationship with Ellen had consisted of her, Lisanne, listening to

Ellen talk on the phone to other people.

When Lisanne was seven Ellen was fourteen—and she had been popular for ten of those fourteen years. She had been liked in her short life by hundreds of people. She had her own phone, with a private line, and every night she spoke into it by the hour. The mouthpiece smelled of Ellen, of Jontue, bubble gum, and lip gloss.

At fifteen, Ellen went away—first to boarding school, then to college, then to Boston. She spent her visits home either out, getting dressed to go out, or on the phone. Lisanne was fascinated by her sister's different voices. There were the voices she used to talk *to* boys: a high whinnying one by day, a sultry purring one by night. And then there were the voices she used to talk *about* boys. The triumphant voice narrated: "After dinner he took me back to his house and made me look at dreary photos of him kayaking." The nasty voice described: "He'd be cute if it weren't for the boils on his back. I know you can't see them, but still—you know they're there." The knowing voice analyzed: "He's obviously intimidated by the fact that I'm number one on the tennis team, and a star of the glee club." And the sly voice strategized: "Maybe I should turn him down Saturday night, pretend I'm busy. But then again, maybe I should go, wear the red dress, give him the old pow-pow-pow."

Lisanne sat on the edge of the bed and lit a cigarette and listened to her sister's message.

Hi . . . this is Ellen. It's twelve-thirty. I wonder where you could be at this hour. Maybe out massaging? Anyway, the reason I'm calling is because I'm, well, sort of down. Maybe you don't think I have a right to be down, but I'm not down about *myself.* I'm actually down about Mom. So, when you get in from whatever it is you're doing . . . give me a call.

Lisanne's ears of corn lay on their plate on her pillow where she'd left them, shriveled and hardened. The world was full of symbols that did not even have the decency to be obscure.

After her 10 A.M. aerobics class, Ellen decided to stop by her mother's. During the buttock-firming exercises, she had begun marshaling the arguments she would use on her mother to get her out to the country early.

It was a beautiful, clear day, bright enough for the city to look clean, but not hot enough for it to smell. Even the homeless people seemed cheerful for once. In her brisk, high-stepping, arm-swinging, fat-burning stride, Ellen marched up Madison Avenue, propelled by goodwill. The strange unease of the night before had left her. She passed, with a nod and a smile and a compliment, several matrons with whom she was friendly. She couldn't help observing that not one of them looked as great as she did.

Mrs. Prawl is a dutiful wife, Ellen thought, *a doting mother, a concerned daughter, a loyal sister. And her inner thighs are firm.*

If her mother had not hated spring, Ellen might have said to her: Why not go to the country, Mother, where you'll enjoy these fine days so much more? But her mother shrank from fine spring days. She said they opened like eyes—blue, reproachful eyes—and she defied them with thick curtains. Her mother's rooms were always dark, always airless, all through April, all through May.

It must be the couples, Ellen thought, the young, hand-holding couples who appear in spring, running to the park with their kites, their Hula-Hoops, their balloons. It must be the couples that get to her.

They were enough to get to anyone, even a married woman like Ellen.

Her father lay dying on days like this. Ellen remembered walking home from the hospital and being knocked to the ground by one of these couples, the sun soothing after the cold light in her father's room until the couple bent over her and blocked it with their anxious faces, their bobbing red balloons.

Why not go to the country, Mother, Ellen might say, where you won't have to be reminded of youth and beauty and hope and love, and all the other things gone forever from *you*, Mother.

> *"And there she lullèd me asleep*
> *And there I dreamed—Ah! woe betide!*
> *The latest dream I ever dreamd*
> *On the cold hill's side."*

With a long sniffle and a loud snort, Dr. Count Francesco von Cockleburg fell silent.

"Don't stop, Count," Estelle said, "you read so beautifully."

She opened her eyes and saw that his eyes were blinking. Her breath caught. With a sudden movement, she closed the distance between them on the sofa. She laid her hand over his hand, which rested on "La Belle Dame sans Merci," open on his lap.

"This reminds you of something?" she whispered. She herself had been thinking of Lisanne. She had felt Lisanne staring up at her from where she used to lie on the blue carpet. *Her hair was long, her foot was light, And her eyes were wild.*

"All lovely things remind me of something," Cockleburg said, "something or someone I've loved." He sighed. His long, fine hand throbbed like a heart beneath hers and went still. "Just now, I was thinking about Harry," he said, "his vibrancy, his great unquestioning love of life."

"Oh yes," she said. "Oh yes."

"To me, a shy, a bumbling, bookish youth, he was like a god—so tall and proud and golden, with his pucks and sticks, his rackets and balls."

"Oh yes," she said. "He did love sports."

"But what I admired most about him was his—his kindness. He was so handsome, so charming, so quick— it's easy to forget that he was kind, too."

"I don't forget," Estelle said. "I never could have loved—I never could love—anyone who wasn't kind."

Ellen knew something was wrong at the sight of Gunter's face. The tiny doorman had lurched halfway up the street in his eagerness to greet her: "Boy oh boy, am I glad to see you!"

Gunter was a frank—indeed, an obsequious—admirer of her mother's. "You're the nicest lady in the building," Ellen had heard him gush to Estelle, *"hands down"* (raising and lowering his tiny chapped hands for emphasis), "and, you got the nicest hairdos too, *hands down"* (again raising and lowering his hands). He was always finding excuses to desert his post in the lobby and go upstairs to her mother's apartment. With breathless solemnity, he hand-delivered her mail, her packages, her dry-cleaned dresses (though these were, technically, the duties of the elevator men). None of this was surprising, of course, given that her mother routinely—and obscenely—over-tipped him. Ellen had remonstrated with her about this repeatedly. "Really, Mom! Fifty dollars? To bring a news-paper up in the elevator?" "But I feel so sorry for him," her mother would say, "poor little man! Did you know he once tap-danced on Broadway?"

Gunter now escorted Ellen to the elevator. In his shuffling gait, and gray, wizened face, there was no trace—no memory even—of gay terpsichorean youth.

"What is it, Gunter?"

"Oh, missy"—Gunter never acknowledged Ellen's married state—"there's a man up there!"

"Up where?"

"A man *up with your mother.*" He listed toward her to whisper these words. Ellen feared he would collapse upon her bosom (which she swiveled out of reach of his brow). He reeked of alcohol. "And he was rude to me! Came in this morning, didn't say hello or nothin', didn't even wait to be announced!"

"This morning?"

Gunter nodded heavily.

"When did you last see this man?"

"When did I last *not* see him!" Gunter cried. "He was there all afternoon on the Sabbath day, he was there on Monday, and on Tuesday, too. But I can't ever get a good look at his face, with *all that hair,*" he added mockingly. "I saw he was wearing high-heeled shoes, though. And limpin' in 'em. And that was enough for me. I tell you frankly, I don't like the look of him." Gunter grew increasingly animated as he spoke of his rival. "He brought her flowers this morning," he went on, "the ugliest flowers I ever did see—or smell!"

Ellen darted past him and sprang into the elevator.

In the foyer, beside the pieces of its predecessor, there stood a brand-new, gleaming, black ten-speed bicycle. The knobs and gauges at its handlebars looked complex and formidable enough to fly it to the moon. Threaded through the spokes of the rear wheel was a fat red satin ribbon. Taped to the seat was a pink heart-shaped card on which Ellen read the following:

To my dear Count,

Please, please do accept this humble token of our friendship. May you enjoy many years of sunny days of riding through the park without being beaten to places where you will be welcomed as warmly as you will always be welcomed here.

Ellen pushed open the front door (which was never locked) and stood still in the hallway, her ears straining through silence—ominous silence. Dear God! could they be upstairs?—upstairs *in the bedroom?* Donald, she knew, would not have hesitated to burst in upon them *even there*—but she, Ellen, somehow lacked the stomach for this.

Then suddenly, the count's voice pulsed toward her from the sitting room.

" 'I saw pale Kings, and Princes too, Pale warriors, death-pale were they all, They cried, "La belle dame sans merci hath thee in thrall!" ' "

So he was reading poetry to her again—and before noon. If it hadn't been so pathetic, it would have been absurd. Still, it could have been worse—much worse.

Ellen crossed the hall to loom, a sour duenna, in the doorway.

" 'I saw their starved lips in the gloam / With horrid warning gapèd wide. . . .' "

Ellen cleared her throat—so violently she forced up phlegm.

The two middle-aged, almost elderly, people looked up at her in alarm.

"Why, Ellen!" Her mother rose and trotted toward her. "I didn't expect you . . ."

"Obviously."

". . . but it's lovely to see you." Her mouth cringed into a smile.

"I was in the neighborhood," Ellen said grimly. Then: "So—I see you have a new bicycle, Count."

"The bicycle of my dreams!" Cockleburg began.

"I did think it was so *you*," Estelle said.

"Of my dreams," Cockleburg repeated. "But one which I cannot, will not, accept."

"Count! You must!"

"I think the count is absolutely right, Mother!" So he had a little honor after all.

"You are so thoughtful, dear lady, so munificent, and I will treasure the gesture always." His voice broke. His glistening brow sank almost to his chest.

"You hurt my feelings, Count." Estelle had tried for an arch tone, but her voice came out wounded.

"Mother, honestly!"

The count now raised his head. "But I could borrow it!" he exclaimed. "If that would make you happy, dear lady, I could certainly b-b-b-b-borrow it!"

"Could you?" Tremulously, "Would you?"

"I could and I would! I can and I will!"

Ellen turned to Estelle. "Could I talk to you for a minute?"

Estelle smiled. "You could and you will, Ellen."

"I was just leaving," Cockleburg said. "Dear lady, a joy to see you, as always. And you too, Ellen." He swooped into a bow, and hobbled from the room.

Ellen waited until the front door closed behind him— barely—and then said loudly, "What a ludicrous little man!"

Estelle held Ellen's gaze for a long moment. Her face was not angry, not sad, but set. "You don't know him," she said.

Neither do you, really, Ellen wanted to say, but her mother had spoken so coldly she knew that further attacks would be futile. Ellen had not only never known her mother to say a bad word about anyone, she had never known her to listen to a bad word about anyone.

She drew a deep, calming breath. "I have a favor to ask you," she said, knowing that of all the sentences in the English language, this was her mother's favorite. "The city's starting to get to me, and I feel like I could use a change of scene."

Ellen lay in bed, filing her nails, with a green clay mint mask tingling on her face. The morning had drained her. The phone rang. Ellen sighed and picked up. "Hello?"

"Ellen, of course you have a right to be down!"

"Lisanne!"

There was an awkward silence. Any silence was awkward to Ellen. She leapt into it. "Don't think I don't know how lucky I am, Lisanne. My duplex, my husband, my Volvo, my servants, my darling child . . . not to mention my"—she almost said *beauty*—"my health, and the fact that I'm an American citizen."

"Still, Ellen—"

"I know. It's just that when I think of all the poor women of the world, the lonely, single, infertile, ugly, unhealthy, foreign women, I guess I feel like I just don't have the right to be depressed."

"Still, Ellen—you're a human being. Aren't you?"

"I suppose so," Ellen said, moved by her own sympathy, which extended to *all* the women of the world, save a hundred or so, among them Princess Di, *Vogue* models, and the wives of billionaires. Thinking of Lisanne, Ellen found herself giving five-dollar bills to homeless people. She enjoyed, now and then, borrowing her sister's virtue, as she would, say, a sweater—just to see how it looked on. Perhaps it was pity for Lisanne that made Ellen strive for nobility and generosity whenever she spoke to her—or rather, that made her strive to avoid selfishness and self-absorption, self-pity and self-indulgence. Or perhaps it was shame. Certainly Lisanne never accused Ellen of any of these qualities. It was just that Lisanne herself was so selfless—weirdly so, Ellen thought. She never spoke of herself; she listened. She never looked at herself in mirrors or on blades of knives or in people's glasses. She never seemed to think of herself. She never tried to improve herself. She never even groomed herself. She was like the Little Match Girl, staring through windows into other people's warm, full lives—except that, unlike the Little Match Girl, Lisanne didn't seem to want to come in from the cold. In some ways, she reminded Ellen of those pale, dirty, dark-eyed girls from her college days, girls who wore baggy black clothes and drank black coffee and lip-read Sartre and de Man; girls who sang songs of protest, songs of freedom, to their own guitar accompaniment, outside the library; girls who were not popular, like Ellen, but *cool;* girls whom Ellen had sometimes sensed sneering at her through their coils of cigarette smoke.

Though, to be fair, Lisanne never sneered.

"You sounded so forlorn in your message," Lisanne was saying, "I was worried about you."

"Well, thank you." Ellen was pleased. "May I ask what you were . . . where you were last night?"

"I stayed late at one of my clients'," Lisanne said, "this sweet sad little old lady. Believe it or not, her lap dog dropped dead on a pink espadrille."

Believe it or not? Ellen did *not.* "Since when have you been a masseuse?" she asked.

"For a couple of months. I thought Mom would have told you. I got my license in the fall."

Estelle rarely spoke of Lisanne to Ellen. Ellen had assumed they weren't in touch. She felt oddly betrayed that they were. There's something sneaky about those two, she thought, with a surge of anger—those two seemingly simple, guileless fools.

"So then—speaking of sad little old ladies—you must know about Mom's . . ."

"Mom's what?"

"Mom's suitor!" Ellen said dramatically. There was another long silence.

"But that's wonderful," Lisanne said.

"*Wonderful?*" Ellen said.

"I just thought"—Lisanne hesitated—"I've always hoped that Mom would meet someone, and fall in love again, and be happy."

"So have I!" Ellen said. "But I had in mind for her some rich, respectable, divorced businessman, maybe. Not the vile little pauper she's taken up with. Because, believe me, Lisanne—he is vile. And anyway, surely Mom can be happy at her age without a lover. I mean, she has Little Donald, doesn't she? She has Little Donald to focus on."

"Are they *lovers?*" Lisanne whispered.

"Not yet"—here Ellen's voice swelled—"and they never will be, not if Donald Patrick Prawl and I have anything to say about it!"

"Who is he?"

"He just appeared out of nowhere a few weeks ago, claiming to be a long-lost childhood friend of Dad's, which I don't believe for a minute. Dad would never have been friends with such an odious little creature. He calls himself a count—Count Francesco von Cockleburg. Donald's convinced he's a fortune hunter—*gigolo* was the word he used—and so am I! He's a good ten years younger than Mom, which means he'll probably outlive her—and get all the money, of course. Our money!" Ellen stopped herself, recalling that this was not a wise tack to take with Lisanne, who, perversely, enjoyed being poor (or pretending to be poor). "But the money's not the point, obviously," she said. "The point is, I'm worried about Mom. I'm worried she'll get hurt. I just don't think I could bear to see her hurt." Ellen forced a quaver into her voice.

"Ellen, you're so good," Lisanne said.

Ellen's heart leapt.

"So good," Lisanne went on, "the way you take care of Mom, the way you watch out for her."

"Well, someone has to do it," Ellen said. "You know how vulnerable she is."

"Yes—I do."

Ellen was finding it painful to move her mouth. She had left the mask on too long; it had hardened like concrete on her face. "Lisanne, hold on a minute," she said, and went into the bathroom.

Lowering her face to the sink, Ellen noticed, poking straight out of the drain at the lip of the sink, two stiff, black, glistening antennae, as long as the hairs on her head.

It was the roach again—and Ellen was relieved to see it alive and well. That morning, she had scraped some crusty, brown, shell-like slivers from between her teeth. She had feared that the roach had somehow crawled into her undefended open mouth while she slept, and that she'd eaten it.

Only now did she remember that in a rare indulgence, she'd had a handful of almonds before she went to bed.

When Ellen returned to the phone Lisanne had hung up. Ellen dialed her number. There was no answer, not even a taped one. Lisanne had disappeared again into silence—just like that.

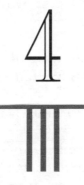

Exile. At the time, it seemed like a beautiful word, a word like *coffee*, or *solitude*, a word that makes the thing it names worth trying.

At the time, her mother's eyes seemed always to be on her. Lisanne trained herself to be perfectly still under her mother's eyes. It was like being still while slugs slid over you.

Lisanne pitied her father, helpless in his hospital bed, a feast for those eyes.

And yet he wanted her there day and night.

Before the operation, they shaved his head. Lisanne had read that hair is the body's way of pointing out what's vulnerable, but her father's head in its nakedness looked barren and indestructible as the earth photographed from the moon.

The first time her mother saw it, she burst into tears. She would not look away.

Leave him alone, Lisanne thought. *Just leave him alone.*

There was nothing in the world as obscene as her mother's eyes. Her mother's eyes were responsible for all the suffering they saw.

Lisanne went out into the hall. It smelled of old people's perfumes, of disinfectants, dark damp places, throats.

Already she'd begun to unfurl her father's life like a flag in her mind.

She was glad that she had stood back from each moment, watching it hatch into a memory.

Ellen was coming home from Boston almost every other weekend. When she was not talking on the phone to Donald, she was talking to her mother about Donald. Eventually, she would talk about her father, and then cry in her mother's arms.

Lisanne would look on, thinking: Don't give her the satisfaction, Ellen, *don't give it to her.*

At the time her father was dying, it seemed to Lisanne that her mother had never been happier. For it was now—wasn't it?—now in the purity of her one hopeless desire that she was learning to submit, now that she was flowing into her truest, deepest hours.

It was at this time that Lisanne began to buy atlases and road maps, at this time that she began to whisper the names of towns to soothe herself to sleep, long lullabies of names like Belle Chasse and Byhalia, Florian and Glenmora, names like Echo and Eros, Enigma and Ash, names like Violet and Vidalia, Cross Roads and Esperanza, Petal and Pearl and Flowery Branch, Dewy Rose, Deep Step, and Rising Fawn, Maiden and Eden, First Hope and Shallotte, Many, and Slaughter, and Kill Devil Hills. . . .

•   •   •

Estelle was unlucky with her caretakers. One by one, they died, or went crazy, or were corrupted. First there was chain-smoking Dan, diagnosed with lung cancer a month into the job. Then there was Mitch, who hanged himself from a beam in the garage, then Gregory, whose heart gave out in the garden. There was Duncan (nicknamed Drunken), who ran over three of her dogs within three weeks. Two summers ago, Estelle and her sister-in-law, Lady Perdita, came home from a walk in the orchard *trembling*—Estelle in shock, Lady Perdita in fury. Billy Boy, the Vietnam veteran, had fired his gun in the air and called them—bitches.

The first Friday in May, Ellen in one car, and Estelle and her dogs in another, drove up from the city to discover the yard overgrown with dandelions and the paintings and silver gone. Estelle hesitated to call the police. There was a chance she had sent them in for cleaning or repairs and forgotten about them. Estelle could never find her car in parking lots. She left her coat behind in restaurants on the coldest nights. She came home from shopping, fixed a snack, and shut her packages in the refrigerator. She was always putting things down—and losing them forever. She had faith in her own absent-mindedness to explain all manner of strange disappearances, of which there had been many since she'd hired Lester Lipp, this last caretaker.

By that evening, though, she was forced to acknowledge that Lester himself had disappeared.

"Is it something about the job?" she wanted to know.

"No, Mom, it's something about you," Ellen said. "If only you'd listened to me on this."

But her mother, usually so pliable, was stubborn about her caretakers. She chose the most pathetic applicants she could find, the lost, the desperate and down-and-out, the ones with twitches and gimp legs—and no references.

She gave them the job because it allowed her to feed them, and shelter them, and give them money. She left them alone in the luxurious caretaker's cottage eight months of the year. She paid all their bills and let them charge what they wanted on the accounts in town. (Gregory, the glutton, had spent a fortune at the gourmet shop; Drunken, a fortune at the liquor store.) They kept up the grounds when, and if, they felt like it. Estelle never asked anything of them but that they enjoy the country air, the heated pool, the tennis court. Look at all we have, she'd say to Ellen, with a wave at the orchard, the terraced lawns, the gardens, the woods, the pond, the big blue-and-white stone house where Harry had grown up. Look at all we have to share.

Donald and Little Donald arrived just before dinner. When Donald heard the news about Lester, he said, "Didn't I tell you, Estelle? Didn't I beg you to fire him?" He wagged a finger at her.

Donald, Ellen, and Estelle were sitting in the living room having cocktails. Naked patches where the paintings had been paled the yellow walls.

"That servant was so unattractive," Donald went on, "so"—he groped—"so *flashy*."

Just then Mrs. Nipe, the cook, waddled into the room with a plate of shrimp. She was smiling hugely, and Ellen suspected she'd been listening at the door. Mrs. Nipe was Dan's widow. She lived with a fireman paramour on the edge of the property in a house Estelle built for her after Dan's death. Once she had been trim and pert in hot pants. Since the fireman, she'd let herself go. With a fierce burning passion, Mrs. Nipe hated Lester—as indeed she had hated all the caretakers who came after her husband. She lived to denounce them. She was always gathering evidence against them and laying it at Estelle's feet—like a cat with corpses. Estelle shrugged sadly—and did nothing. Mrs. Nipe stepped lightly in her muumuu now, as she passed round the shrimp. Lester's thievery and disappearance had left her giddy with triumphant vindication. Much as Ellen deplored the cook's slatternliness, she could not help but share in her mood of triumph.

"That devil's probably halfway to Mexico by now!" Mrs. Nipe said, indicating with a dirty thumb the blank spaces on the wall. "I'd get the police on his tail sooner, rather than later, if ya get my drift, Mrs. Wolfe."

"You mean—?" When the full import of the cook's words sank in, Donald grew mighty—mighty in his outrage. Ellen thrilled to the telltale quivering, clearly evident through seersucker, as he rose to pace before the coffee table. "You mean you haven't called the police yet? Good God, Estelle—are you mad? That Homer alone was worth—" Donald paused to nod a dismissal to the cook. With palpable reluctance, Mrs. Nipe exited.

"Maybe he'll bring them back," Estelle said. "Maybe he's just, you know, borrowing them."

"Like a museum?" Donald lifted his lip and released his loud, galloping laugh.

"I don't care about the paintings," Estelle said. "It was the decorator who insisted I get them. Anyway, they're insured—aren't they?"

"That's hardly the point, Mom," Ellen said.

"I suppose I'll miss that big silver salad fork, though." She laughed.

"This is no laughing matter, damn it," said Donald.

"Donald's right," said Ellen.

Estelle fell silent. She poured herself another glass of wine—her third—though these days, she tried to limit herself to two before dinner, two at dinner, two after. . . .

"I'm calling the police this instant," Donald went on. "There's such a thing as principle."

"I couldn't agree with you more, dear," said Ellen.

"I don't want to get anyone in trouble," Estelle said. "That poor little man, he always seemed so lonely, skulking across the lawns like a lost soul."

"Skulking, yes," said Ellen. "I never saw him mow them."

"Loneliness," Donald said. "Isn't that the hallmark of the sociopath?"

While Donald called the police (his voice *booming* into the phone across the room), Ellen raised the question of—the new caretaker. "I mean, I'm assuming you've fired Lester."

"I hadn't thought about it, actually," said Estelle.

"Why don't you let me handle it?" said Ellen. "I'll put an ad in the paper first thing Monday morning. I suppose I'll have to interview *lots of young men*. For I feel very strongly that the next one should be young. You always choose the oldest, most decrepit specimens, Mother. No wonder so many of them drop dead."

"Now that you mention it, there is someone I have in mind," said Estelle, "someone I know from the hospital."

Estelle volunteered three times a week at the hospital where Harry had died.

"Not a doctor?"

"No, no, of course not. I'll tell you about him later, if he says yes. I'm going to ask him next time I go in to work."

"Is he young?" Ellen asked. "Is he single? Because we wouldn't want any children crawling around by the tennis court day and night."

"He's young, yes," said Estelle. "About your age, I should think. And single—now. But he has a child."

"Well, then, I vote no."

"Little Ian," said Estelle. "He won't be crawling around much. He lives at the hospital."

• • •

"Presents!" came a sudden piercing scream. Little Donald hurtled into the room just as Big Donald hung up the phone. "I wanna open some presents—*Now!*"

Little Donald was adorable this evening in tiny jeans and a tiny navy blue sweater. Blue, red, and green were the only colors Donald allowed the boy to wear. Any other colors were—faggy. Ellen loved to shop for her son almost as much as she loved to shop for herself, and chafed at this strict rule. But the one time she violated it, with a pair of orange overalls too winsome to resist, Donald had been apoplectic in his outrage. "What'll it be next, Ellen?" Donald had said. "Barrettes in the lad's hair? Tutus, and ballet slippers on the lad's feet?"

Little Donald was tugging at Estelle's skirt. "C'mon, Granny, gimme some presents. Gimme some presents—*now!*"

"Donnie, you can't have any presents, you know that," Ellen said. "And I think it's outlandish of you to expect your grandmother to produce them every time you see her."

Ellen was irritated that the child had not greeted her with a hug. They had been separated a whole day! But then, Little Donald hated hugging, had always hated it, even as a toddler. This was a bitter disappointment to Ellen. What was that warm, sweet, constantly eating and shitting little body for, if not for hugging? But every time Ellen approached him with that give-me-a-hug-now-damn-it look in her eye, the child darted away like a hunted fawn. In a wild moment, Ellen had considered drugging him: surely, in a coma, the child would hug! Donald beamed with pride when Ellen complained to him about Little Donald's dread of physical affection. "You ought to be pleased, Ellen. He's a fine, stalwart,

manly little man." And Estelle told her not to worry.
"Some children are just like that," she said. "Remember
Lisanne?" Ellen remembered. Lisanne had been so lovely
as a child, so little, so slender—and yet, somehow utterly
unstrokable, like a baby goldfish. "I used to clutch my
hands together to keep from touching Lisanne," Estelle
said.

"But Granny told me she'd have presents for me!" Little Donald swung his black, lashless eyes on his mother.
They glittered with hatred—Ellen shrank before them.

"Donnie is right, Ellen," Estelle said sheepishly. "I did
tell him I'd have presents for him. And you know what?"
She smiled down at her grandson. "I do!"

"See, Ma!" jeered the child. Then: "Give 'em to me,
Granny. Give 'em to me—*now!*"

"That's the way to tell her, Donnie! That's the way to
tell her!" Big Donald slapped his big thighs in delight. "I
like to see a show of spirit in the lad," he said, with a majestic patriarchal nod in Ellen's direction.

"Spirit?" Ellen said angrily. "How about rudeness?
How about greed? How about sneakiness?"

Little Donald giggled—odiously, Ellen thought.

"Lay off the kid," said Donald.

"Yes, Donald"—Ellen now addressed her son—"*sneak-
iness.* You went behind my back, didn't you? And asked
Granny to get you presents. Because you know that
Granny can't say no. Isn't that right, Donald?"

Little Donald giggled again.

"Why do you have to go and ruin a nice evening,
Ellen?" Donald said belligerently. "Why do you have to
do it? What drives you, Ellen? *What drives you?*"

"But what about the punishment?" Ellen said. "We dis-
cussed this, Donald. You agreed with me."

"I did not *agree* with you," he said. "I went along with
you to avoid a scene."

For Little Donald's ninth birthday, on September 15, Donald had gone against Ellen's better judgment and given the child a pellet gun. A few days later, the principal of St. Bernard's called to say that Little Donald had been caught shooting younger boys in the hallway. One five-year-old had been seriously injured in the calf, another in the nates. Donnie was suspended for a week. (He would have been expelled had Big Donald not been chummy with several members of the board.) Appalled, Ellen had taken away not only his pellet gun but all the other presents he had received that birthday. On top of this, she made him write a letter of apology to each little boy he had shot. (The letters went like this: "Dear X, I'm sorry I shot you. Because I shot you, she took away my gun and my skateboard. Because I shot you, she took away my train set," etc., etc.) On top of that, she had insisted that Donald receive no new toys for a full year (except for Christmas). Big Donald had grudgingly supported the confiscation of the gun and the other presents, and the writing of the letters, but at this last injunction he protested: "You go too far, Ellen! He was just acting like a man, by God! Those other kids were wusses!"

Still smiling, Estelle now returned with an armful of beautifully wrapped and beribboned packages.

"Mother, put those away," Ellen said firmly. "You know the deal." (Ellen had told her mother about the moratorium on new toys.) "Donald can have them on September fifteenth."

Her smile finally faltering, Estelle stood still in the middle of the room.

Little Donald's mouth began to tremble.

"Why don't you give the kid a break?" said Donald. "Hasn't he suffered enough?"

Here Little Donald whimpered in agreement.

"Please, Ellen," said Estelle. "I just got him a few simple things. One of them is even—educational! It would give me so much pleasure."

"Please, Mommy!" said Little Donald. "Please oh please oh please oh please oh please oh *please!*"

Ellen thought about the time Little Donald had the flu, how hot his cheeks had been against her hand. She thought about the night he woke her screaming with his nightmare of the green men, and all the other times he had let her comfort him. She thought about how her body had contained his, and she was flooded with a tenderness that had nothing to do with love. Her love had to take its revenge in escapes of hatred, but this tenderness would never have need of revenge.

"Okay, sweetie," she said, "but let's at least wait until after dinner."

"*No!* Give 'im the presents"—Big Donald spoke in his most commanding voice—"give 'im the presents. Give 'em to 'im, Estelle. Give 'em to 'im—*Now!*"

Little Donald let out a shriek of triumph.

Ellen looked away, out the window at the orchard. Darkness lowered over those tangled branches. She closed her hot, bald eyes. In a far, far distance, she heard the sounds of happiness.

Because I am a crappy housekeeper, she thought. Because I ruin evenings.

Lisanne stopped in Savannah on her way home. She could have driven on through the night, but she loved the old city, and wanted to see it again. She loved it for its melancholy, and for the way it seemed tired in its beauty, and reproachful.

She got a room at the Hyatt, a room with a king-sized bed and directly in front of it a TV with six movie channels for her "viewing enjoyment." She sat in the armchair

by the window and smoked cigarettes, and looked out at
the slow brown river, the low bruised sky. At her feet, like
a faithful dog, lay her big black suitcase, half empty, sagging in its center, filled with everything she owned. She
had accumulated in her travels only what could be thrown
out, or given away, or lost, or left behind. Every day she
wore blue or black jeans, with a white shirt or T-shirt, or
one of two black sweaters.

She had left home twelve years ago, almost to the day.
She left the morning after the night her father died. She
had not waited for the funeral. The idea of the funeral
had been repellent to her: Look how beautifully I mourn.
Ellen in particular had made her sick, wearing her grief
as though it were a flattering new outfit, thrilled that the
trauma of watching her father die had taken off ten
pounds. Lisanne knew what Ellen was thinking. She was
thinking about Donald. She was thinking: Donald will
have to ask me to marry him—now.

And her mother? To Lisanne, there had been something obscene and promiscuous in her mother's sadness,
in the way it seemed to mingle and couple with all the
dirty little sadnesses of the world. It was like a river
bloated with garbage, fed by a thousand streams. Studying her mother the night her father died, Lisanne came up
with this image: a tick, swollen and sated with sorrow.

Down the hall in a drawer in her room, cherished as
letters from a forbidden lover, were her train schedules,
her road maps and atlases. Under her bed was her packed
black suitcase. She told no one she was leaving. She did
not want her leaving tainted with tears and farewells. She
preferred the neatness of a note on the kitchen counter:
Don't worry about me. At the last minute, she decided
not to take her car, the BMW her father had given her on
her sixteenth birthday. It was too big, too red, too *much.*
She would get on a train and ride to any town with a

beautiful name. She wanted her hands free.

I am leaving home, she said to herself, over and over, as though the words were a song. And then, all the next day on the train: I have left home . . . I have left home. . . .

With my black suitcase, she thought, as she looked out at the Savannah River. And with no fear, and with no shame, neither fear, the eyes, nor shame, the tail. There were things she could do then she could never do now. Without fear, without shame, anything is possible. She wondered why it is that hatred is the purest source of energy, purer than love, purer than joy, purer even than anger, pure as fire, burning everything else away.

And yet the hatred itself is always corrupt.

Just before dark, she rose, rode the elevator down to the lobby. She went out onto Bay Street, and then wandered on into the old part of town, through Johnson Square, and Wright Square, and Telfaire Square. Through square after square of clipped glossy grass lined with houses, cream and blue and carmine and flushing rose facades laced with wrought iron, furred with vines, sills spilling flowers, trees shadowing windows. And everything milky in the streetlights. She met no one. She saw no one, no one at the doors, no one on the balconies, no one on the steps.

This is what surprised her most about America when she first left home: the emptiness of the streets of its towns, with now and then, in a yard, a small, blond child.

It was as if no one lived here—and yet she felt herself seen.

After a while she turned back toward the river, walking until she reached the statue of the Waving Girl. Beneath the Waving Girl's bronze windblown skirts was the plaque that told her story: how her lover left her and was lost at sea, and how she had still waited for him. How she had come down to this shore every day for the rest of her life to wave in every ship.

Well, they called her the Waving *Girl,* but she had died an old woman—a ludicrous old woman, Lisanne thought when she first saw her, her first time in Savannah almost twelve years ago. It made her angry then that they had built a statue in her honor. It was like honoring everything that made women ludicrous, that made them weak.

Looking at the statue now, Lisanne wanted to cry—not for the Waving Girl, but for herself, her lost merciless self.

She got back to her room at nine. The great TV gaped at the bed in which she would not be able to sleep, she knew. She checked out and drove. Mississippi John Hurt took turns with Howlin' Wolf and John Lee Hooker on the tape deck—her mother's music, restless and dark. Lisanne could only listen to it when she was on the road, in between places; or after midnight, in between days.

In North Carolina, the fog lowered, so thick you could reach out your hand and stroke it. In Virginia, the rain started and never stopped. She had been home ten times in twelve years, and every homecoming was the same. There would be her favorite dinner. There would be wine. There would be cool, clean sheets on the bed, and fresh towels in the bathroom. Flowers would fill her room, Lisanne knew, lilies and orchids and white roses; sprigs of baby's breath; and twelve-apostle flowers, with their purple petals, their forgiving yellow eyes.

5

Lisanne was running up and down the length of the pool, throwing tennis balls in the water. With massive splashes, the dogs leapt in to retrieve them. Estelle sat on the diving board, clapping her hands and yelling encouragement ("Go, Jimmy! Go, Brando! Get it, Monroe!")—like a half-wit child, Ellen thought. This game had been going on for an hour. "Give it a break!" Ellen said. "I think I saw that fat one pee in the water," she said. "It's hardly inviting for the rest of us!"—meaning herself and Donald.

She was ignored.

Ellen had never learned the names of her mother's dogs. "That fat one" was how Ellen referred to all of them—not effectively, as all of them were fat. Estelle's great joy in life was to feed them. They came to her starving, sharp-ribbed, cowering from prior abuse. Within a matter of weeks, they were happy, healthy, vibrant dogs. Within a matter of months, they were happy, morbidly obese dogs. Her mother meekly agreed when Ellen urged her, in the name of decency, to put the dogs on a diet, but they did not get any thinner. Obviously, her mother was feeding them behind her back. Two nights ago, Ellen had gone downstairs to the kitchen for a glass of water—and caught her mother in the act: a great ham out on the counter, the refrigerator door open, her mother bathed in its sickly light, twelve unblinking pairs of eyes riveted to her.

"Have you no self-control?" Ellen wanted to know.

Estelle blushed. It was hideous on her white, harsh-angled face. She hid her greasy hands in the folds of her bathrobe. "There ought to be support groups for people like me," she said. "Dog Overfeeders Anonymous."

"Don't joke, Mother." Ellen spoke sternly. "You'll kill these animals if you don't get a grip on yourself."

Not that this would be such a bad thing.

Ellen hated dogs. She had been nipped on the nose by a neighbor's dog as a small child, but that was not why. It was their messiness, for one thing, their slobbering and shedding on your clothes. It was their smell. It was all the crimes you could commit against them and get away with. It was their silence. It was the way you could read anything into their eyes: love, pity, contempt, fear, reproach. Her mother had not had dogs when Ellen was growing up, thank God, because her father was allergic to them. The summer after he died, Estelle, without a word of warning, adopted her first three dogs.

And who was aiding and abetting her mother, slicing the ham into slabs for her mother to fling?

Lisanne.

"How can you encourage her?" Ellen demanded. "It's sick—feeding dogs until they puke!" Because they did puke—often.

"Leave her alone," Lisanne had said, not unkindly.

Yes—*like you did,* Ellen thought now, watching Lisanne laugh, as the dogs splashed and panted and drooled and peed, and her mother clapped her hands.

When Lisanne was not playing with Estelle's dogs, she was gardening with her, or taking long walks with her, or playing tennis with her, or arranging flowers with her, or just sitting quietly, reading or watching TV with her. In her past brief visits home, if she had made these gestures at all, she had made them at an obvious cost, with a tight smile, and a look of pained concentration in her eyes. Ellen had seen this look in the eyes of old women at the supermarket, peering into tiny purses, counting out their last few coins to pay for a can of soup. Now Lisanne was making the gestures ardently, almost helplessly, like a lover uncertain of her beloved. Even Donald, who had only been up from the city since last night, had noticed the change.

What does she want? Donald had said. *What the hell does she want?*

Lisanne had arrived home unannounced, unexpected, almost a week ago, and already Ellen couldn't wait for her to leave. It was her longest stay in the twelve years she'd been gone—and yet she showed no signs of the old restlessness.

Ellen thought it was fowl, that cawing that slammed against the hills above the pond and reeled back over the lawn in dizzy echoes. If you come from the city, you can ascribe any number of terrible sounds to nature.

It began just as they were regathering around the pool after lunch. The cries seemed to circle Estelle's voice as she read aloud from her latest romance novel. She liked bodice-rippers, the ones with the feverishly alliterative ti-

tles *(Sweet Savage Surrender, Tender Torrid Triumph)*, the
ones set in eras when men were free to tame women in
the true, manly way—through abduction and rape. Ellen
found these romances too absurd to be in any way arous-
ing. The sex scenes filled her with a sort of queasily enter-
taining amazement, the kind she used to feel at college
gymnastics meets watching fat girls flip across the bal-
ance beam. But Estelle was addicted to them. She had
started reading them after Harry died and now consumed
as many as ten a week.

Estelle's voice dove into a baritone when she recited the
hero's lines: " ' "Do not fight me, little spitfire," '
growled Rolfe the Relentless masterfully, ' "for I will
take ye here in the dirt, in the mud, whether ye like it or
nay, though my men look on and though wild boars snort
in the woods yonder." ' "

"Will you listen to those goslings!" Ellen said. "I wonder what they're cackling about?"

"Those aren't goslings, dear," said Donald, "they're
ducks. And they're cackling because they're mating."

"Whatever they are, they sound like they're in pain to
me." Estelle laid down *Pirate's Proud Passion* and rose to
her feet.

"Everything sounds like it's in pain to you," said Ellen.

Estelle's ponytail slapped against her neck as she ran
across hot concrete.

"I assure you, they're only mating," said Donald.

"I thought mating was supposed to be pleasant," said
Estelle.

"Not for all the species, dear," said Donald.

His mouth settled into a complacent, squirely smile.
Ellen could not remember the last time she'd seen him in
such a good mood. She supposed he was basking in the
success of his trout. The prize catch of a recent fishing

trip, it had been proudly served up at lunch. Ellen was still sick from the few bites she had forced down—but Lisanne had gone back for seconds, and, ostentatiously, thirds. "What fabulous trout," Lisanne kept saying. What foul trout, Ellen kept thinking. Foul, foul trout.

Little Donald had not shown up for lunch, as he had not shown up for breakfast that morning, nor for dinner the night before. These last couple of weekends in Bedford, he'd been spending eight to ten hours at a stretch prowling the property for "bad guys"—playing posse, he called it—armed to the teeth with toy guns. "And if I see a bad guy, Mom," he explained the game, eyes aglitter, "I fire a single warning shot—pow! And if he keeps moving, I shoot to wound—pow pow pow! And then I move in for the capture, and if he tries to resist, well, then, I shoot to kill—pow pow pow pow pow pow pow pow *pow!*"

Big Donald had applauded this demonstration: "Ho ho! that's the way to give it to 'em, lad, that's the way!" "But there are no bad guys, honey, at least not around Bedford," Ellen said (both Donalds here rolled their eyes at her naïveté), "and it would mean a lot to me if you'd take a break and join us for lunch, at least. I've missed you, sweetie, being out here all week long without you."

Making no promises, Little Donald huffed off—at which point Big Donald exploded: "Give the kid some air, God*damn* it! What are you trying to do? Suffocate him?"

"But he could get hurt out in those woods," Ellen said, "he could fall, or get lost."

"Nonsense!" the father boomed. "If he wants to be out on his own, acting like a man, why can't you let him?"— as though lunching with family was somehow unmanly behavior!

Lately, Ellen worried that Donald's homophobia was

pushing the lad into—sociopathy. Donnie had become more obsessed than ever with guns and killing. He no longer permitted Ellen to read aloud to him, as she used to, a chapter a night from *Little Men*. Instead, he stayed up way past his bedtime studying magazines like *Mercenary Monthly* and *Guns and Ammo*.

Estelle was climbing the steps. One hand to her brow, sailorlike, she stared down at the pond that shimmered at the end of the lawn.

"I don't see anything," she said. "But it sounds like someone's calling, 'Help! Help!' "

"Mother, really!" Ellen spoke sharply.

Estelle returned to *Pirate's*. " 'He was a murderer, yea, an outlaw and a rebel and a killer and a thief, yet his kisses were sweetly searing, the faint irritation of his mustachios intoxicating. "Ride me," he groaned thickly, and though he was a murderer, yea, a rebel and an outlaw and a killer and a thief, she needed no urging. Head flung back, breasts thrust forward, mouth agape, she rode him hard!' "

Estelle was giggling by the time she finished this passage. She looked demented—her face was not constructed for giggling. Lisanne stared up at her from her towel on the deck and shook her head.

"Mother, remember all the poetry you used to read?" she said. "I just don't see how you can stand such trash."

"Because it *is* trash," Estelle said.

Ellen was enjoying Lisanne's dismay. She recalled her own dismay the first few times her mother asked her, years ago, to stop by Doubleday and pick her up a new batch of romance novels. Let's do Wild Indian Braves this week, she would say. Let's do Highwaymen-Who-Are-Really-Bastard-Sons-of-Dukes. Ellen now viewed her mother's romance reading as a useful distraction. The

novels kept her mother safe at home, out of trouble—out
of singles bars, for example. And at least Estelle had a
sense of humor about them, sort of.

"Good God, now what on earth is *that?*" said Donald,
gesturing from his chaise.

Ellen looked up to see, whirling in frenzied circles at
the top of the hill, a small fluffy black-and-white ball.

"It's a rabbit!" cried Lisanne.

"That's no rabbit!" said Ellen. "That's a—a—a—"

"A shih tzu!" Estelle finished for her. She was halfway
up the hill, she was up the hill, she was on her knees, she
was cradling the creature in her arms.

"A *shih tzu?*" Donald said. "Why, I had no idea shih
tzus roamed wild in the woods of Westchester! I wonder
how they manage to feed themselves."

"Donald, don't be silly," Ellen said. "It's probably just
another unwanted pet, dumped on our doorstep."

"Jesus, it's not even June yet," Donald said. "This is really getting to be too much."

Stirring in their holes under the bushes, all twelve
mutts seemed to shrug in bafflement. They clearly did not
recognize the shih tzu as one of their own kind—as a dog.
Or even, frankly, as animate.

Estelle disappeared over the curve of the hill. Ellen,
Donald, Lisanne, and the dogs rose as one and followed
her in a careening zigzag to the pond. She had set the shih
tzu down, as if to let it lead her to—to what?

In a rapid, unfaltering gallop that left them wheezing
to keep up, the shih tzu made a beeline for the westward
shore of the pond. It seemed to move in a cloud, leglessly,
the long skirt of its coat streaming magnificently behind
it. Only the high plumed tail betrayed its species, and
that—barely. Ellen surmised that he, or she (for the clue
to its gender was decorously obscured), had been recently groomed. The stench of cheap perfume swirled all

around it, and four red ribbons, though sadly askew, still clung on—two at the brow, two at the hip. The mutts, in contrast ever more monstrous, fanned out in its wake like the retinue of royalty. Ellen noticed they'd begun to snort and pule, jolted from their customary torpor. All twelve pairs of canine eyes were trained unswervingly upon the shih tzu's rear. Every now and then, lunging ahead, the two fattest males would narrow the distance, only to reel back, perhaps in awe, perhaps in giddiness from the perfume.

They came upon a family of ducks among the lily pads. Clearly these ducks had already done their mating for the year. Stepping daintily around puddles, the shih tzu ignored them, circling the pond, then veering off to the left. They trailed its tiny, surging rump into the darkening, tangled green. In the days of Dan, the most active of the caretakers, paths carved through this wildness. Now they were thickly overgrown. But, dodging clumps of shrubbery, leaping over fallen branches, the shih tzu did not slacken its pace. Relentless. Implacable. Unstoppable. These were words that came to mind—for this, plainly, was a shih tzu with a mission, a shih tzu *possessed*. Though no myrmidon by nature, Ellen was silent in the face of such single-mindedness. And the dogs—they seemed to recognize in the creature, if not an actual dog, then still, a natural leader.

With a sudden, bloodcurdling yap, the shih tzu, as if shot from a cannon, charged off the choked path, and for one brief terrifying moment, disappeared from view.

"Shih tzu!" Estelle called. "Shih tzu! Shih tzu!"

She fell silent, and the silence all around her flooded with agitated life.

And then they heard a low, moist, sucking sound. They flailed toward it.

"There!" Donald pointed.

At the edge of a bed of poison ivy, they saw the shih tzu, its head haloed with flies, its shoulders lowered over a paleness smearing the shadows.

Estelle screamed.

Ellen gasped.

For it was Cockleburg!—Cockleburg, prone in the frondescence, Cockleburg, muddied and bloodied, Cockleburg, wordless, but still, unmistakably—

Cockleburg!

"That's not the new caretaker, I hope," said Donald. "Dead on arrival! Estelle, you've really outdone yourself this time."

6

Lisanne was standing over the kitchen sink, rinsing a coffee cup, when the battered blue Comet shot into the yard. A man climbed out, stretched, turned, and began to walk toward the kitchen porch. Lisanne ducked out of view beneath the sink; she didn't want him to catch her peering at him through the window like a suspicious concierge. It didn't occur to her that she had every right to peer: he was a stranger, after all, a stranger approaching her mother's house.

Lisanne would have worried about offending her own ax murderer.

Her brief glimpse of him had been unnerving. From a distance, he looked like a male version of herself. He was wearing what she was wearing: a white T-shirt, jeans, and flat brown boots. They had the same coloring: tawny, with a blaze of bronze. They even had the same hairstyle: a long ragged braid slung over the shoulder.

His legs were slightly bowed, she had noticed. She had

always associated bowed legs with good things: athletes, cowboys, whores with hearts of gold. . . .

She heard three quick knocks and looked up from where she crouched on the floor. He was standing at the screen door, gazing down at her. She rose awkwardly.

"I'm Adair Quirk," he said. "Is Estelle around? She's expecting me."

His voice was low, and slow, and open at the edges. It made Lisanne think of caramel and, at the same time, of animals dead on desert roads.

"Are you the new caretaker?" she asked.

"I guess so," he said, "though I told Estelle I don't know much about flowers."

"Come in," she said. "Wait! On second thought, I'll come out."

He looked at her, amused—as though she thought him too low to admit into the house. Lisanne blushed. The truth was, she didn't want to subject him just yet to the cold, keen eye of Mrs. Nipe. Lisanne could hear Mrs. Nipe sucking down smoke in the laundry room next door to the kitchen. The loss of her husband to lung cancer had not cured the cook of a three-pack-a-day habit.

"I'm Lisanne," she said, piloting him out of view of the laundry-room window. "Estelle's daughter."

"Melissa Anne," he said. "Your mother speaks of you often."

His tone was mild, but Lisanne sensed an insinuation coiled behind it. She wondered not about what her mother had told him, but about what he'd guessed from what she'd told him: Oh yes—Melissa Anne, the younger child, the favorite child, the one who lied, and stole, and left when she was needed most.

"Mom's not here," Lisanne said. "She's at the hospital."

"I didn't know she worked on Sundays."

"She doesn't. It's a different hospital, over in Mount

Kisco." Lisanne hesitated. "A guest of hers was shot in the buttock."

"Just a flesh wound, I hope?"

Lisanne nodded.

Estelle, Donald, and Ellen had made the pilgrimage to the hospital to visit Cockleburg—Estelle in compassion, Donald and Ellen in suspicion masquerading as compassion. Cockleburg was recovering splendidly. He was due out in less than a week. Estelle called Lisanne with hourly bulletins on the state of his buttock. The doctors were all agog at its gibbosity—indeed, it was to this gibbosity that Cockleburg owed not only his life but the future use of his limbs as well. For the great gluteal globe had curved up in that dire moment to intercept the bullet from its deadlier mark—the spinal cord. "We must give thanks for that," Estelle said. With every call, she inquired as to the well-being of the shih tzu, Queen Elizabeth—this being a source of the gravest anxiety to the fallen nobleman. On his bed of pain, piteously, he moaned for her. His first words out of surgery had been, "Majesty! Majesty!" (apparently, his pet name for his pet). Lisanne assured Estelle that the shih tzu's wish was her command, and that every conceivable comfort was being provided her. The shih tzu was upstairs watching TV in the air-conditioned sitting room.

"I guess I should show you to your house," Lisanne said.

"Show me around first," Adair said.

Lisanne led him down stone steps, past the tennis court, and around the hedges. It was a hot, sunless, low-skied day, and the air was clotted with swirling gnats. His eyes were almond-shaped like hers, the heavy lids so glossy it looked as though the gnats would stick to them. Lisanne noticed a few faint pocks among the freckles on his cheeks. They walked on into the garden.

"Roses," he said, pointing. "I know those. I've sent them. And tulips," he said, pointing. "I know those. And daisies," he said, "if you had daisies, I'd know those. And poison ivy. Your basic fern. Christmas trees. Four-leaf clovers. I know all of those," he said. "And Spanish moss." He laughed, a high, manic laugh that did not go with his voice. "I know what not to eat in Mexico," he said, "and General Lee's last words. And a woman who's now with a man who drinks the equivalent of eleven baked potatoes a day."

"Who's that?" Lisanne said.

"Some agent out in Hollywood. I'm told he drinks them in a sort of milkshake, for energy—and potency."

"I mean, who's the woman?"

"My wife," he said. "My soon-to-be-ex-wife."

"You seem to know a lot of things," Lisanne said.

"But not much about flowers," he said. "And nothing at all about shrubbery. Shrubbery. Of shrubbery I am truly ignorant." He seemed to relish the word, for he said it again: "Shrubbery."

"Well, there are books about that," Lisanne said.

"Your mother knew I needed this job," Adair said. "And she knew how ill-qualified I was for it. But she did everything she could to make me feel like I'd be doing her the favor if I took it. She even went so far as to warn me that the job was cursed."

They ducked beneath the pleached trellis, and into the shade of the dying oak, split open in a storm. Lisanne remembered that storm, and the tornado that had trailed it into the pale sky. Her father had been away somewhere. She and her mother had hid under the big bed upstairs, her mother forgetting in her fear, or not knowing, that the basement was the safest place to be. They passed the hammock swaying between the elms, and Ellen's old playground, the rusted slides and swing sets shrinking, it seemed, year by year. They came out onto the great lawn. Lisanne felt her heart dragging itself along the floor of her chest. Everything is haunted by me here.

"It's beautiful," Adair said. "Just like your mother promised."

Lisanne helped him unload his car. It didn't take long. He had brought with him only one suitcase, a guitar, a tape deck, a box of books and tapes, and a garbage bag he said was full of photographs.

Dr. Count Francesco von Cockleburg was released from Mount Kisco Hospital on Saturday afternoon, a week almost to the hour after being shot, if not as good as new, then about as good as old.

Ellen, Donald, Little Donald, Lisanne, and Mrs. Nipe were gathered outside the house (as per Estelle's request) to greet him when he arrived. They stood in an orderly line in front of the kitchen porch—like the staff of a Victorian mansion, Ellen thought, waiting to curtsy to their lord's new bride. Adair, the strapping, unkempt caretaker, got out of the car first, then Estelle. Together, they hoisted the count out of the back seat, and helped him halfway across the yard; at which point, gently, bravely, proudly, he shook off their hands and continued the rest of the way leaning only upon his new cane, an elegant (and extremely expensive, Ellen happened to know) antique with a carved onyx dog's head—a get-well present from Estelle.

"Dear Count," Estelle said, when he had tottered to a halt. "My family, as you can see, is eager to welcome you."

"I *do* see!" the count said fervidly. "And I am honored to the very core, the very marrow, of my being!"

Here Donald swung upon Ellen the first of many baffled, and then bitter, glances. Ellen gave a little grimace and a quick shake-shake of her head in reply.

"Ellen, of course, you already know," Estelle said.

"And to know her, I vow, is to esteem her. Which I do—greatly." Clutching tightly the knob of his cane, Cockleburg convulsed into a painful bow—*from which he did not rise.* Catching Estelle's anxious eye, Adair sprang forward to assist the genuflecting nobleman into the upright position.

Little Donald began to titter nervously. Ellen jabbed him into silence with a cocked elbow.

"Meet Donald Patrick Prawl, my son-in-law, whom you may recall—"

"Dear lady, you speak in verse—in charming rhyming verse!" Cockleburg beamed at Estelle, who paused in her introductions to beam back.

"—my son-in-law, as you may recall, from his visit to you in the hospital last Sunday."

At this cue, Donald stepped forward out of the line. Cockleburg acknowledged his step forward with a frank and manly smile. The two men—the businessman and the nobleman—shook hands, man to man, *hombre a hombre.*

"Dimly I recall you, Donald Patrick Prawl you!" Cockleburg playfully rhymed, "When o'er my bed of ag, your face flapped like a flag!"

"*Ag?*" Donald said.

"Ag," Cockleburg said, "short for *agony,* for which I blush to admit I could not find a rhyme—in time."

"I see," Donald said, though clearly he did not. "Well, let me take this opportunity, Cockleburg—"

"Count Cockleburg," said Cockleburg, "or Doctor, or Doctor-Count, or Count Francesco—whichever you prefer."

"All right then, *Count* Cockleburg," Donald resumed, his face reddening, "let me seize this opportunity to tell you that I, Donald Patrick Prawl, as the master of this house, will not rest until I have found—found, and brought to justice," he added darkly, "the vile coward who shot you in the back!"

"The back*side*," Ellen said, and smiled in spite of herself.

"Donald Patrick"—here Cockleburg extended a trembling hand, which Donald reluctantly shook and quickly released—"Donald Patrick, I beseech you, contain your wrath. Vengeance is mine, sayeth the Lord—and I couldn't agree with Him more. So let's leave this little matter in His immense and capable hands—*d'accord?* And let me also say, briefly, simply, and, I hope, movingly, that the warmth of the welcome I am receiving here today makes not only the wound itself, but all the suffering it has caused me—and will no doubt continue to cause me—worth it."

"So you don't intend to sue?" Donald said slyly.

"Sue?" Cockleburg drew back, affronted. "That is not the way of the von Cockleburgs!"

"Well, I'm glad to hear that, Count," said Donald, in a sudden burst of bonhomie. "And I'm sure my family will join me in hoping that the remainder of your stay here in America will be pleasant."

"I hope so, too," said the count, "as it will be the remainder of my life."

"You mean you're not going back to France?" Donald said.

"Of course," Cockleburg said.

Donald was visibly relieved.

"To visit," Cockleburg said.

Donald was visibly disappointed.

"For America is my home now," Cockleburg went on. "It was home during my boyhood years, and it will be home during these, my twilight years."

"Twilight years?" Estelle said, with mock indignation. "Why, Count, you're in the very prime of life!"

"Dear lady!" He kissed his hand to her.

"You mean, you were born here?" Donald said. "You mean, you're *American?*"

"*Oui,*" said the count. "But my mother—*ma mère*— was French-born."

("Well, then, why the heck does he speak with that crazy gay accent?" Donald would ask Ellen later. "I suppose the accent was passed to him at birth through the placenta of his French-born mother—*sa mère,*" Ellen answered.)

Donald was silent now, though. Grimly silent. He stepped back into the line.

"And this is my little precious, my little pride and joy, the sweetest little boy who ever drew breath," Estelle said, in the high, lilting voice she used when speaking of, or to, her dogs and grandchild, "my little grandboy, my little Donald."

"Aw, Granny," Little Donald said, recoiling from this eulogy.

"*C'est un bon enfant!*" Cockleburg said in tones of rapture.

"Now, Donnie, will you give a nice big hug to this dear friend of mine, Count von Cockleburg? He was also a dear friend of your grandpapa."

"God rest his soul!" Cockleburg thundered out.

Li'l Donald shied a little closer to Ellen, who affectionately ruffled his lank black locks. Her hand came up slick with grease. Good God, when had the child last washed his hair?

"Don't make the boy hug, Estelle," Donald said angrily, "don't do it to him, damn it!"

"Hey, hey, I think I have a little something for you, *cher!*" Cockleburg said, groping in his pockets.

"What?" Little Donald darted eagerly forward.

"*Voilà!*" With a dramatic flourish, Cockleburg pulled out—a packet of Sweet'n Low. A soiled, crumpled packet of Sweet'n Low, which, with a benevolent smile, he handed to the speechless child.

"Is that his idea of a joke?" Donald asked Ellen in a hissing aside.

Even Estelle was taken aback. "Why—why, how thoughtful of you, Count," she said, faltering.

At that moment, Ellen noticed Lisanne and Adair exchange identical grins. She had the distinct feeling that they were laughing not at Cockleburg, but at *her*—her, and Donald, and Little Donald, her poor duped child. The hot rays of Ellen's outrage briefly swerved from Cockleburg to Lisanne. How lacking her sister was in decent family feeling! And what a cad the new caretaker was, to be sure!

"And this is Lisanne," Estelle said, recovering herself, and continuing with her introductions, "my younger child, the free spirit."

"Well, her spirit may be free," Donald whispered to Ellen, "but her body sure as hell ain't!"

"I'm so pleased to meet you, Count," Lisanne said, shaking his hand.

He held her hand, Ellen thought, a moment longer than was necessary. "*Enchanté!*" he exclaimed.

"And last but not least," Estelle said warmly, "is Mrs. Nipe, who has been with us for years, and who is like a sister to me."

"Pleased, I'm sure," Mrs. Nipe said—regarding the guest with palpable hostility.

"Pleased, *I'm* sure," Cockleburg returned gallantly. He quarter-wheeled round to Estelle. "How justly proud you must be, dear lady, of your lovely family! How comforting to know that you are not alone in this world, all alone, like—like some of us," he finished sadly.

"Oh Count," she said. She reached for his hand, and gave it a long, tender squeeze. Her shining eyes said: You are not alone.

"And now," Cockleburg said, "if you'll forgive me for abbreviating this truly heartwarming welcome, I must make haste—to greet my Queen."

Once again, Adair and Estelle joined forces, helping the count up the porch steps into the house, Ellen, Lisanne, and Donald following. The shih tzu was awaiting Cockleburg in the living room. "Would it be too much, dear lady," he said to Estelle, "to beg for a private moment with her?"

"Take as long as you like, dear Count," she said.

The living-room door closed upon him. "Majesty, Majesty, Majesty"—the count moaned. And then the howling began, a sound like nothing they had ever heard, the sound of despair that had no beginning—but had this end.

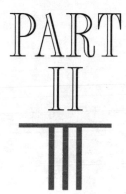

PART
II

7

"We need to talk," Ellen said. "Alone."

She invited Lisanne, formally, to have tea with her in the empty guest cottage down the driveway from the big house. It was Monday. Donald and Little Donald had gone back to the city after dinner the night before. Estelle had driven in to the hospital that morning with Adair, she to do her volunteer work, he to visit his son in the same ward. Cockleburg was presumably doing what he was always doing: napping or eating.

When Lisanne arrived at the appointed hour there was no tea—and no need for it, clearly, nor for any other stimulant. Ellen was rapidly pacing up and down. The cottage seemed barely large enough to contain her body, and her body barely large enough to contain her wrath.

"When it doesn't add, it doesn't add," she said. Lisanne knew by her inflection that she had gotten this expression from Donald.

In the nine days since Cockleburg's release from the

hospital, Ellen said, her initial suspicion had blazed into outrage. She had tried, she said, to give the man (if that's what you could call him) the benefit of the doubt. She had tried in vain.

Estelle had begged him to stay the full length of his recuperation, "which," Ellen said, "I'm sure he'll drag out for weeks." She had sent Adair into the city to pick up Cockleburg's things: his books, his portfolio of poetry, his black ninja's robes, his kettledrums, the shih tzu's grooming kit. . . . Aghast, Ellen had watched as he moved himself and his dog (if that's what you could call it) into the guest room *across the hall from Estelle's bedroom.* Ellen suggested that he take the guest cottage so that he could have more privacy—this suggestion he had sinisterly rejected. She watched, skeptical, as one by one, with many manly protests, he declined Estelle's offerings: the Louis XV writing table for his room, the Brooks Brothers nightshirts, the five-hundred-dollar orchid plant. She watched, triumphant, as one by one, overcome by Estelle's insistence, he graciously accepted—or, rather, "borrowed"—these offerings. She overheard, appalled, his request that Estelle read aloud to him from *Remembrance of Things Past.* She stood by, sickened, as Estelle did just that.

Friday night was the final straw. Estelle had returned from the city with a tin of Beluga caviar (Cockleburg having hinted he had a craving). Ellen and Donald had hurried downstairs for cocktails, only to find the tin empty, the fish eggs consumed, Cockleburg's lips greasy with them. "I'm afraid I've finished the caviar," he said, "but here, have some saltines."

"What exactly is it," said Lisanne, "that you think doesn't add?"

"Nothing adds," Ellen said.

She continued to doubt his friendship with their father.

She doubted that he had even *met* their father. All that was just a ploy—didn't Lisanne see?—a fiendish ploy to meet their mother. She doubted that he had ever lived in Paris. She was beginning to doubt that he even spoke French. She doubted his degree. His title wasn't worth doubting, it was so patently fraudulent. She doubted, frankly, the validity of his wound.

"You cannot deny," Lisanne said, "that a bullet did indeed pierce his left buttock?"

"I believe he did it on purpose," Ellen said.

"You mean—?"

"Yes"—stoutly—"I believe he pulled the trigger himself. And Donald agrees with me. In fact, he thought of it first."

"But why on earth—?"

"To get attention! To lower our guards! To legitimize himself!"

"Surely there are less painful ways—"

"I fear he's read Mother," Ellen said. "I fear he's read her all too well."

The official explanation of Cockleburg's wound held a poacher responsible. He had dropped by on a spur-of-the-moment visit, found the house deserted, circled round and down to the pond in search of his hostess—and there been felled. Estelle did not allow people to hunt on the property, but Adair, only days into the job, had made some shocking discoveries about his predecessor. Lester had had a thriving business going: renting out the cars and the pool and the tennis court and even the house, selling the gasoline (they kept a big tank in the garage), letting the neighbors fish and hunt for a fee. . . .

"Not that Mother's hard to read," Ellen said. "Any five-year-old could see right through her. And for a man like that, a man steeped in deceit . . ." Her voice trailed off, then surged up again. "I bet he has files and files on rich widows," she said. "I bet he's spent the last year in some dingy little room in some dingy little suburb plotting and scheming, choosing his prey. And now he's slithered forth to make his move. He'll eat her for lunch and spit her out. If those dogs of hers had any sense, they'd tear him and his shih tzu to shreds. But they don't have any sense. And neither does Mother. But I do! And I'm counting on you, Lisanne. We must save her. We must get rid of him. Not only for her sake, but for the sake of our poor dear dead father, now spinning in his grave!" She stood still in the middle of the living room and raised a clenched fist.

Yes, Cockleburg knew a good thing when he saw it, Lisanne thought. No, he was not the kind of guy to turn down a free meal. This much had been obvious, she gathered, from that first night he'd limped into their lives. But to Lisanne, he seemed too absurd to be the formidable enemy that Ellen described. Any fool can be cunning, any fool can be mean—but evil? To Lisanne, true evil was a beautiful, a dark and terrifying, a rare thing. Cockleburg's accent, his title, his pedantry, his pretensions, his stutter, his bathos, his shih tzu—all these disqualified him. They were affectations, certainly—but calculations? If so, he had miscalculated. Estelle was the least snobbish woman in the world. She cared nothing for titles, nothing for degrees. These were only barriers to her pity, barriers to be beaten down.

Ellen had resumed her pacing. "It's not that I begrudge Mother a little romance," she was saying, "a little fun, a little happiness. Of course not."

No, of course not, not so long as you believed she'd never get them, Lisanne thought—and went cold at her own uncharitableness. She did not ever want to do it again, think the worst of anyone; and again she felt her heart struggle up as if to pluck it out, that cold, dry eye in her mind that would not close, would not soften, would not weep.

"No one," Ellen was saying, "has been more vocal than I in encouraging Mother to find a man. But that's what I meant—a *man*—a nice, respectable businessman, for example. Not this *snake*. And he's so homely, on top of everything else. I mean, I thought gigolos were at least supposed to be good-looking."

"Maybe he's not a gigolo," Lisanne said.

Ellen seemed not to have heard her. She flung herself onto a chair. "I never thought it would come to this," she said. "Tomorrow I have an appointment at Elizabeth Arden for a waxing. And I'm afraid to go."

"Afraid? But why?"

"I'm afraid to leave Cockleburg alone with Mom, that's why! So if you could keep an eye on them while I'm gone, Lisanne, it would really be a load off my mind."

"Sure, but I doubt it's necessary—"

"Please, Lisanne." Ellen spoke as solemnly as though she were asking Lisanne to take care of her child in the event of her death. *"Or I won't be able to go to my waxing."*

"All right."

"And try not to worry, darling," Ellen said. "I'll think of something."

The next morning, at breakfast, Ellen thrust into Lisanne's hand a copy of a letter she'd just sent. "I thought of something," she said, "someone who'll send him running."

Lisanne was upstairs in her room, sitting in the armchair by the window that looked out over the lawn. In this room, she had spent her first seventeen summers, seventeen summers that had left no trace here. Lisanne noticed that her mother had placed on the bookshelves, along with the usual flowers, some of Ellen's old dolls, Ellen's old club tournament trophies, even some of Ellen's old yearbooks.

Lolling across the brass headboard of the bed was one of Ellen's old teddy bears. Lisanne found she could not look it in its button eyes, which hung loosely on black threads, and seemed to be weeping.

She was writing another letter to Mrs. Rainey—"Dear Mrs. R., I think of you"—when she heard shouting through the open window: "Avaunt! Avaunt!" Lisanne looked out. It was—

Cockleburg!

This was the first sign of him she had seen all day. He appeared harmless enough; in fact, he appeared to be in distress. She wondered where her mother was—probably still in bed with her romance novel, *The Duke's Doxy*. Lisanne had knocked on her door an hour ago to ask if she wanted to take a walk. "Desiree has just been captured by the Duke!" Estelle said, her face flushed. "Could we do it a little later?"

Lisanne went downstairs, through the back door, and out onto the terrace. The gray flagstones dropped off into curling cotoneaster. Stone urns marked the steps down to the lawn. Halfway to the pond, she saw the bust of Cockleburg (for his lower half was blocked from view by the dogs who ranged about him). He had raised his walking stick in an attempt to drive them away.

"Avaunt!" he kept shouting. "Can't you see she needs privacy, damn it? Avaunt, indelicate creatures, avaunt!"

Just as Lisanne began to run to his aid, Adair rushed out through the arch carved in the hedges that bordered the lawn. He was whistling. Immediately, with a chorus of servile barking, the offending animals slunk toward him. So commanding was his whistling that it was all Lisanne could do not to slink along with them. Adair

herded all twelve mutts through the arch and shut the little gate behind them. He wore loose khaki shorts, slung
low on his hips, and no shirt. Lisanne felt herself helplessly staring. After Mrs. Rainey and Mr. Lumkin, there
was something almost frightening about a body so perfectly formed. She thought of the heroes of her mother's
romance novels, with their well-corded necks and mighty
chests, their flanks forged of steel and their calves like
young tree trunks, their muscles "hewn as though by
God Himself, that master whittler" (a phrase Lisanne's
mother had read aloud over breakfast that morning).

Cockleburg was gasping his thanks to the caretaker
when Lisanne drew near. Attached to his hand by a long
red leash, resplendent in a red sweater and a red tartan
collar, was the shih tzu, Queen Elizabeth.

"It's a calamity," he said, "one which I would never
have predicted, though I know her better, in some ways,
than she knows herself."

"She's such a charming little dog," Lisanne said po-
litely.

"Charming, yes," agreed the doting master, "charming
even in her affliction. For not one word of complaint has
she uttered—*not one word*—through all her ghastly suffering. *Entre nous*," he said, lowering his voice and limping closer, "she is woefully costive. Were her coat not so
long and velutinous, you would see for yourselves the terrible tympanitic distension of her stomach. Why, I could
hardly get her sweater on, she's so bloated!"

"This is awful," Lisanne said.

"Awful," Adair said.

"She's so refined, you see, so fastidious, so highly bred,
that she has been unable to"—he paused—"to relieve herself in these strange surroundings."

"Not once?" Lisanne said. The shih tzu had been with
them now over two weeks.

"Well, once or twice," conceded the count, "in a dusty corner of our bedroom, behind the wardrobe, hidden from hot, prying eyes—and then only in the darkest hours of the night." His blue eyes blazed as though with bravely unshed tears. Indeed, in his emotion, he even let his accent slide—across the continent of Europe, over to England, and up into Scotland. Yes, Lisanne definitely detected a faint Scottish burr insinuating itself among the Gallic and Germanic inflections.

"The few times we've ventured out," he went on, "dear Estelle's dogs converged upon us in the most aggressive and importunate fashion. As you saw! Though kind-hearted, well-intentioned, *gemütlich*"—he spat out this word with a spray of spittle—"*gemütlich* animals in their way, they are simply—and please don't take offense at this, Lisanne, I only speak the truth—simply *uncouth*. Yes, uncouth. Grossly insensitive, I might go so far as to say—though through no fault of their own, I hasten to add. Because it is of course otiose to expect of low-born mongrels any understanding of or sympathy for a creature like the Queen—a creature of such ancient and aristocratic ancestry that I daresay her genealogy goes back even further than my own."

"I would have thought she'd have welcomed the company," Adair said.

"Company, yes! Playmates, yes! Rousing canine fellowship, yes, yes, yes," said the count, his voice rising. "But not the vulgar attentions inflicted upon her here. For your dear mother's dogs, Lisanne, could never hope—I know this now—to consort with her as equals. With the most gelid hauteur, she has repulsed their every advance. And I can hardly blame her. And yet, I can hardly blame *them*. Their fascination, though lamentable—indeed, catastrophic—is understandable. Few can resist Her Majesty's fatal allure. Fatal," he repeated. "I mean that literally. *Fatal to her.*"

"Poor Queen," Lisanne said. "I wouldn't be able to go myself, with twelve strangers staring at me every time I tried."

"Ah!" breathed the count. *"Mais vous comprenez exactement!"*

Suddenly the shih tzu, with a wild rolling of her bulging eyes, strained at the leash. "Silence!" commanded the count (*seelawns*—in the French pronunciation). "Distance!" commanded the count (*deestawns*—again in the French pronunciation).

Adair and Lisanne stepped back. They looked on in horror as the shih tzu hunched over into the defecatory squat for several long, tense moments—then spasmed—then screamed.

With no results.

"Yet another tenesmus!" cried the count. "I can stand it no longer. *Il faut téléphoner* the veterinarian!"

Adair and Lisanne rejoined the anguished nobleman.

"May I make a suggestion?" said Adair.

"Speak, for God's sake!" he said. "Now is not the time to stand on ceremony! Speak, man!" he exhorted him. "Speak!"

Adair spoke. "My wife had a dog, Jezebel, who had a similar problem. And her trainer taught us that dogs respond to subtle verbal cues. What you must do," he said, "is chant rhythmically these words—"

"What words?"

"These words: poo poo."

"Poo poo?" doubtfully.

"It's worth a try," said Lisanne.

The count hesitated, but he was a desperate man, a man without the luxury of scruples. Adair and Lisanne retreated again, and watched as he began to wamble with his shih tzu over the grass. "Poo poo!" he repeated in a tremulous falsetto, "poo poo!" for two minutes—three, four, six, eight, ten minutes—until the very birds seemed to join in the refrain.

At last, his efforts were rewarded.

The count limped over to them—the shih tzu stepping highly now, and tossing her head in the ecstasy of her release.

Solemnly, Cockleburg bowed to her savior. "Twice today, you have rescued us," he told Adair. "Yes, you!—you, with your thaumaturgy! And though I wouldn't presume to speak for *her*, I—I, at least—am your slave forever."

Adair laughed. "Well, I'm always on the lookout for a new slave," he said, but though he addressed Cockleburg, his eyes were on Lisanne.

Why are you looking at me? she thought. She felt somehow poured into his eyes, clear as water, poured, measured, and contained.

She turned away and hurried back up to the house. She met her mother in the hallway.

"I saw you all from my window," Estelle said, "and I was just coming down to join you. How kind of you, Lisanne, to walk with the count. I do so hope"—she hesitated—"it would make me so happy if you and the count became friends."

"I like him," Lisanne said, suddenly wanting to, and surprising herself—because she did. He was absurd, of course, but he seemed perfectly in control of his absurdities. She had a sense that they'd been missing the point—Ellen, Donald, and Estelle, too, in a different way. It occurred to Lisanne that he did not intend to be taken literally.

"Do you, darling, do you really?" Estelle said.

. . .

On her way home from her waxing, Ellen stopped by
Doubleday on the usual errand for Estelle. When she had
first started buying bodice rippers for her mother, there
was only one shelf of them to choose from. Now the romance section extended two full aisles. As always, three
or four plump, drab women were canvassing the gaudy
rows. They ranged in age from adolescence to late middle
age, but there was something interchangeable about
them. Whether out of shame, or delicacy, or indifference,
they never acknowledged one another, not by word or
smile or glance. Shoulders lowered, heads thrust forward, they squinted at the titles, wearing the glazed, frenzied expressions of binge eaters in bakeries. Ellen never
failed to speculate (with a secret little thrill) about what
had driven them here; about who had failed to love them,
who had failed to admire them, who had failed to notice
they were even there at all. Ellen knew that her beauty,
her proud, upright posture, her grimace of distaste, dis-
tinguished her from these other customers. But just in
case, she always murmured as she joined them, "Now I
wonder which ones Mother would enjoy!"

She was ignored.

Today Ellen felt an unfamiliar, humbling throb of compassion for these women. For suddenly she saw them
clearly—their husbands, fat men in shiny suits, with
moist, mean mouths. And suddenly she was there with the
women, in their silent rooms, while in a thousand dark-
ened gymnasiums the lucky ones danced—the golden-
haired, laughing prom queens. Where did I go? she
wondered, for she herself had been those prom queens—
all of them. Then: Where have I been? she wondered.
Hadn't they been waiting all along for her, these lonely
ones?

Compassion—it was such a gassy feeling.

And on the covers of these novels, in impossible, un-fleshly colors, the heroines all swooned, prostrate at the booted feet of their lords. They had long, tangled hair and high, heaving bosoms. They were proud and haughty, their spirits as high as their bosoms. That's what they needed: to be pushed onto the ground and taken, there in the dirt, in the mud. That's what they needed: to be taught the lesson of love.

Lisanne went back to her armchair. She couldn't read, couldn't finish her letter.

She thought of her first train ride, her first flight away from home. How romantic she had seemed to herself . . . though there had been nothing romantic about the journey.

An hour out of Penn Station, the air in the train had soured. Lisanne clawed at the windows that would not open, then dipped her face deep in her collar, making a mask of her black sweater. But there is no escaping air. She imagined she could see the odors swirling through it, in glistening lengths, all slithering out of humid holes. Every human sound had a smell, every cough, every sigh, every prayer, every breath. When she closed her eyes, Lisanne could hear them, the other passengers, under the shriek of the train, breathing in and out in snorts and pants and phlegmy gusts. To have to breathe in this air that the bearded man beside her had breathed out seemed to her an obscene intimacy. To have only two choices, through the mouth, so that she could taste his life, or through the nose, so that she smelled it, was unbearable.

Holding a hand to her mouth, Lisanne rushed out to rinse herself clean in the cool dusk, standing between the shuddering cars until a conductor ordered her back to her

seat. Although she had bought a ticket to Miami, wanting to go as far south as she could go, no one was forcing
her to stay on that train. But Lisanne would not have gotten off for anything. She was enjoying her disgust too
much. Humanity—it didn't disappoint her, it didn't let
her down. Lisanne sometimes thought that all the flights
that followed that first flight had been nothing more than
an attempt to recover the safety of that perfect, passion-
ate disgust.

I've got to get out of here, she thought, and went downstairs and out across the front lawn. It was almost dark,
the day flowing into deep blue pools around her. Lawns at
dusk always made her melancholy, and now she knew
why. It was the way they seemed to promise, Nothing's
changed, and nothing ever will.

A quarter mile down the road, she felt her heart contract in faint alarms, and though she walked faster, she
did not look back. She was used to this feeling of being
watched, or followed.

"I've got to get out of here," she said aloud, as if to convince herself. And because her heart wasn't in it anymore,
she began to run, a sound rising in her ears like the baying
of hounds.

It was her breathing.

When she reached the bridge above the stream, she
rested, leaning out over the railing. Turning around, she
saw a man walking toward her. By his bowed legs, she
knew it was Adair. She had to fight the impulse to hide
behind the roadside fringe of trees. A passage from one of
her mother's romance novels flared up in her mind:
"Lady Twilight thrashed in the Viking's massive arms,
like a wildcat she thrashed, yet even as she thrashed, fair
Twilight knew she was lost. . . ."

Lately her mother had been reading aloud to her from
her novels at every opportunity. Now, against Lisanne's

will, the lurid images had insinuated themselves in her imagination.

Adair stopped beside her on the bridge. He took a pack of Marlboros from the pocket of his jeans, lit one, and handed it to her.

"How did you know I smoked?" she said.

"I could hear you wheezing all the way down the road," he said, lighting one for himself. "So how much longer are you going to be around?"

"I was just wondering that," she said. "Not that it's any of your business."

"Because I'm just the caretaker?" he said.

"That's not what I meant."

"Or because you never tell anyone when and where you're going?"

He was making fun of her now. He knew too much about her. Lisanne stamped out her cigarette. "I think I'll head back now."

He kept up with her effortlessly. "You might try the West next time around. From what I hear, you've pretty much done the South."

It was the only part of the country that had ever interested her. Her mother's music, she supposed. Those songs of the Delta—they could still make her shiver.

"Go West?" she said. "Like your wife?" How easy it was to be nasty, after all these years. Like riding a bicycle, you never forget.

"Like my wife," he said evenly. "It was the desert that drew her. Junellen was fascinated with the desert. Once, when the weatherman said, 'The winds are coming up out of the desert,' she held out her arm for me to see the goose bumps. She used to make me say it, 'The winds are coming up out of the desert.' That was poetry to her. She said she wanted to live in Death Valley. But then when she finally got to it, she was disappointed. She wanted it to be emptier, smoother, golden . . . more like the Sahara. She was upset because things grew there."

Lisanne was trying to imagine Junellen's face. She wanted to ask what she looked like, but was afraid to.

"Or you might consider Europe," Adair said, in his mocking vein again. "Gay Par-ee, for example. Romantic little cafés, harmonica players on every street corner, dashing poets in berets. I could command my slave, Bonhomme Cockleburg, to show you around."

"I can tell you've never been to Paris," Lisanne said.

"Not yet," he said. "And then, of course there's always the Down Under. And from there, it's just a quick flight to the South Pole."

As Adair went on, listing the countries of the world, Lisanne felt something buckle and go down inside her. It wouldn't be enough now to go to a place where she knew no one. She would have to go to a place where she wouldn't know herself, a place where there would be no memories at all.

Abruptly, Adair fell silent. His hand on her arm was gentle and warm— even welcome—before he took it away.

But she hadn't given him permission.

> How can I express in words the way you impact
> me? You make me feel like a superman. I can't
> wait to come home to you at night. Sometimes
> I wonder if there are any other men who are as
> fortunate as I am. The answer to this is no. For
> you are one sexy, special lady. I'M REVVED!

Ellen was reading the love letters at the front of a book called *Rev His Engine*. "Tired of sobbing alone on Saturday nights? Stop sobbing and start strutting—straight to your mailbox for love letters like these! Throw out your hankies and discover how the secrets in this book can transform your life—and bring him to his knees!" Frankly subtitled *How to Make Your Man Your Slave,* the book guaranteed its readers not only a daily batch of love letters, but also moonlit walks on the beach, candlelit dinners, boxes of bonbons, breakfasts in bed, hugs, kisses, secret glances, and tenderly peeled grapes.

Ellen had picked up the book on impulse on her way out of Doubleday that afternoon.

Walking home, she had stared at the women she passed on the street who were younger and more beautiful than she. Thirteen in twenty-five blocks, she counted: one every two blocks! This was way up from one every six blocks just a few months ago—and it could only get worse. Ellen found herself stroking the new book in her bag as though it were the part of her that needed soothing. Such books were trash, of course, but maybe—

"God*damn* it!" Donald yelled from the kitchen. A mucus-thickened, gurgly "God*damn* it!" Followed by a second "God*damn* it!"—higher, smaller, clearer, shriller, *thrilled*—trilled out by Li'l.

It was nine o'clock. Father and son were making fudge together. While cooking with a recipe fell under the rubric of Forbidden, Faggy Activities, cooking without one was okay on occasion (preferably plain, hearty, salty, manly beef-and-organ dishes; no soufflés, quiches, or cream puffs; nothing that required herbs). Just to be on the safe side, Big Donald always made a big, manly mess—and left it out, in manly fashion, for Ellen to clean up.

"What is it?" Ellen called from the bedroom.

"God*damn* it!" came the answer. "God*damn* it!" (basso and soprano)—and then a pounding of pots on countertops, and a single cymbal smash of glass.

The author of *Rev His Engine,* April O'Boyle, grinned aggressively in her book-jacket photo, the big eternal teeth thrusting out of a wrinkled face. The bio beneath boasted of her "fifty-two-year-long love affair with her husband, Billy O'Boyle"—to whom the book was dedicated.

"As for my credentials," O'Boyle bragged in her Foreword, "I have degrees in astrology and sexology, but that doesn't really matter. More important is that I have been married for *fifty-two years of ceaseless joy* to the same man and I have seven happy, well-adjusted children. Most important of all is that I *still rev my husband's engine!!!*"

Loathing O'Boyle, and loathing herself for what made her read on, Ellen—read on.

O'Boyle offered up harrowing accounts of the trials and torments of women who were less deserving than she. "It just boggles my mind how many of you so-called liberated ladies have not the foggiest notion of how to get a man, let alone keep a man, let alone keep his engine revved."

"Get her, Daddy! Get her, Daddy!" Little Donald sang.

"If you want a man, then be a woman," O'Boyle wrote in the chapter titled The Bull, The Cow, The Pig, The Sow. "For as the bull needs the cow, and the pig his sow, so too needs the man the woman."

Being a woman meant, if not having a man, then at least wanting one badly. Start with that. It meant loving that man unconditionally—or, as O'Boyle flatly put it, "What you see is what you love." (And if you don't love him unconditionally, O'Boyle warned, *some other woman will.*) It meant complimenting him at least once a day (a five-page list of possible compliments was provided). It meant lining your halls, and circling your bed and bathtub, with candles—and lighting them every night. (Reading this, Ellen was thankful at last for the fire extinguisher Donald had given her on her thirty-fifth birthday.) It meant springing naked out of giant cakes and ape suits. It meant barging into his office in the middle of the day wearing nothing but a swirling purple cape. (Donald would kill her if she tried this.) It meant seducing him even if it was the last thing in the world you felt like doing. ("Remember: His animal needs must always come before your emotional needs.")

"And if none of this sounds like you," O'Boyle concluded, "well, then—*don't be you.*"

As Ellen read this last sentence, Big Donald appeared in the doorway, his neck and pajamas smeared with fudge. He was panting—with outrage? excitement? exertion? Without that revealing rear view, Ellen could not be sure. He was sweating so hard his face seemed shellacked.

"Goodness, darling—" she began.

"Ellen, what's your problem? Have you gone deaf—or what? Didn't you hear me yelling?"

"I just assumed you had everything under control, dearest," Ellen said. "You're always so in control in a crisis. I never feel scared when you're around because you're such a man." (*Rev His Engine,* Chapter Four, p. 132: "Compliment him on how in control he is in a crisis. Tell him you always feel safe around him because he's such a man.")

Donald lurched over to the bed. "I just saw the biggest goddamned roach I've ever seen in my life!" he said. "As big as—as big as—" Words failing, Donald held his hands up a yard apart.

"As big as—your cock?" Ellen ventured. (Compliment him on his roach-sized cock . . . ? No, this was not on O'Boyle's handy list.)

"That's pretty talk, Ellen!" Donald said angrily. Then, sotto voce: "Think of the lad!"

As if on cue, the lad bounced into the room and onto the bed. His pj's too were tarred with fudge. "Mommy! Mommy!"

"I heard, darling," Ellen said. "Were you terribly frightened?"

"At first, 'cause she was so big, and she just came out of nowhere, and flew right in my face—"

"No, you were *not* frightened," Donald said firmly. He gave Ellen a meaningful look. "The lad was not in the least frightened."

"So did you get it?" Ellen asked.

Both males drew in deep breaths:

"First we threw a glass at her."

"Then we swatted her with a spoon."

"We tried to drown her in the fudge pot—"

"—but she got away too soon."

Father and son took turns narrating the tale . . . a tale of bravery, of heroism, of proud men united in battle against a treacherous foe.

"She must have darted 'neath the dishwasher."

"We couldn't find her anywhere."

"Our land forces were superior—"

"—but she whipped our asses in the air!"

Father and son seemed to be awaiting applause. Ellen applauded. "Wow! I bet you chased it away for good."

Donald shook his head. "You can bet we haven't seen the last of that bug."

"She's making babies right now, I bet," said Li'l.

"I bet we get rodents next," Big said.

Ellen could see the exhilaration draining from his face. The moment of transcendence had passed. All soldiers must come home from the battlefield, home to their brides.

"No, the way you keep house, Ellen, rodents wouldn't surprise me at all. Rodents, and maybe even a few wild pigs. God knows this place is fit for 'em."

"Donald, the apartment is perfectly clean!"

"Yeah—on the days the maid comes."

"I wouldn't mind some pigs, Daddy," Li'l said. The Precious, Ellen thought—he's sticking up for me.

"At least pigs are big and fat and easy to shoot," the child added.

Big went on muttering darkly about pigs.

As the bull needs the cow, and the pig his sow . . .

Rev His Engine was a bestseller—and it was only one of hundreds of books just like it: *How to Make Him Commit, How to Keep Him Monogamous, How to Drive Him Wild in Bed, How to Find a Husband in Six Weeks*—all written by women, for women, while across the aisle, men were buying books on How to Succeed in Business, books on Building Your Own Canoe. . . .

We've been knocking ourselves out, Ellen thought. Ever since the first cavewoman strewed her cave with flowers and the first caveman came home from a hunt and didn't notice, we have been knocking ourselves out, and we go on knocking ourselves out.

While Big was tucking Li'l into bed, Ellen went into the kitchen and surveyed the damage. The milk carton floated, bloating like a corpse, in a windless lake of milk. Flung pots and spoons made hoops of light in distant corners. Glass shards tinseled the tabletops, and glittered on the tile floors, all this wreckage beautiful—beautiful, and tormenting.

Ellen reached for her broom.

Down the hall, her husband was reading a bedtime story to her child—something from *Soldier of Fortune*, it sounded like: " 'Stinger—This is the weapon that turned the tide for the Afghan *mujahideen* in their guerrilla war against Soviet occupation. As issued, a Stinger missile consists of an expendable missile round/launch tube assembly. . . .' "

Sweeping, Ellen thought of the women she knew. Not one of them ever felt appreciated enough, attended enough, admired enough. In all of them, there was that pulpiness at the core.

In all except Lisanne. She alone had never cared to be admired. Look at me—only her eyes had never made that plea. A hard, polished wholeness, like a pit or a pearl, set her apart, so that thinking of women, Ellen always thought of Lisanne last. Was it because Lisanne had this that she had nothing else, or because she had nothing else that she had this?

There were times when Ellen was comforted counting up all the things her sister didn't have. And then there were other times when she was comforted counting up the things her sister didn't want.

Someone was crying. The sounds of it woke her that first night, hauling her up like hooks. Estelle lay still, surrounded by dogs. Their breathing chests rose and fell in waves that rocked the bed. They were deep in dreams, their legs kicking through meadows of air. They slept on through the sobbing and crying as though these sounds belonged to silence, had always belonged, buried deep in it as the sounds of feeding worms.

When words are taken away, love and longing and despair all sound the same. Estelle was remembering a group of deaf retarded children she heard once keening in a subway station. They had cried in a kind of weird feral anticipation, and they kept it up until three minutes later another group of deaf retarded children appeared.

The next night, Estelle got out of bed and went into the hall and stood outside the door. The third night, she leaned against the door, and the fourth night she opened it. The fifth night, she entered with her arms outstretched and fingers tensed, as though gripping ropes of darkness. The sixth night, she moved closer, the seventh, close enough to see the nervous hands, pale movements on the blankets. Always, her feet clutched the same path, exactly here by the bureau, not there; exactly here on the threadbare throw rug. It was as though the sounds now formed a narrow plank she walked out over nothingness.

At the foot of the bed, she rested.

Estelle wondered what he was remembering. Dreams alone couldn't create such sounds, dreams alone wouldn't have the power. These were the sounds of memories.

He held the shih tzu crushed beneath his arm, and rolled her over with him as he tossed and turned. It couldn't have been very comfortable for her. Her black eyes were weary, even pained, but the little black bearded mouth was brave.

She always seemed slightly angry, as though she'd been expecting Estelle and had had to wait too long.

Since Harry died, there are days and days, whole days Estelle has forgotten. What she remembers are images, moments of suffering that did not involve her, but that somehow belonged to her. . . . A beautiful woman walking up Fifth crying . . . bludgeoned greyhounds piled high in fields . . . an old man sitting alone in the park . . . chimps strapped into spaceships . . . and one pig tied down and set on fire in a military experiment to determine how burns would affect a pilot's thirst: the hose of fire, the pig's quick-cracking skin and grateful drinking lips as the torturers hold a bowl of water.

8

Ellen held the phone an arm's length away from her ear. Her aunt's voice was not a pleasant thing to wake up to.

"*Frothila! Frothila! Titla frothila!*"

Lady Perdita was calling from England, and the connection was bad. But though static crackled, it could not muffle the mighty instrument of her voice. Always loud, it was raised in anger to a deafening and distorting volume. Between that and her aunt's thick British accent, Ellen could not make out a word she was saying.

It was clear enough, however, that she had just received Ellen's letter regarding Cockleburg.

"*Titla frothila! New kezin botit, titla frothila!*"

"I'm sorry, Lady Perdita, I can't quite understand you." Ellen always addressed her aunt by her title because her aunt insisted on it. Even Dave (Harry's younger brother), her husband of twenty-four years, called her Lady Perdita (or, simply, milady). The only people she permitted, and not without reluctance, to forgo this formality were her two children, Alaric and Oribel, who called her Mumsie. "Could you please speak more clearly?" Ellen said.

More clearly seemed to mean, to this maddened noblewoman, *more loudly:* "*Lizin tew me!*" she screamed.

"I *am* listening," Ellen said.

"*Frothila, I til yew! New kezin bowtit, titla frothila!*"

Straining, Ellen at last began to make out recognizable sounds: *Fraudulent, I tell you! No question about it, the title is fraudulent!* And there could be no doubt as to whose title she referred, her own title, which traced back to the Norman invasion, being above suspicion.

"Fraudulent?" Ellen said. "Well, the thought had crossed my mind."

Lady Perdita was born a Montresore, a fact that she was not shy of mentioning. The Montresores were among the finest families in all England—nay, the world! for what other countries counted? Her uncle-the-duke's country seat, Montresore Palace, was the finest in all England. But the duke was a miser, and Lady P. herself had no money, a fact that she *was* shy of mentioning—except to Estelle. She had gone through Dave's inheritance within months of their marriage. His modest salary as a helminthologist was hardly enough to maintain in style her pets (Lady P. bred King Charles spaniels, the finest dogs in all England—nay, the world!), let alone Alaric and Oribel, let alone *her,* proud fruit of a duchy! "*I know wot he's ahftah! I know exactly wot he's ahftah!*"

Harry had supported them all for years—Dave, Alaric, Oribel, Lady P., and the spaniels—and very generously, too, in Ellen's opinion. He paid for all their necessities, all their comforts, all their luxuries, even—but he refused to pay for Lady P.'s extravagances: for the thoroughbred horses she longed to ride, for the redecorating she longed to do, for the diamonds she longed to wear. . . .

No, these had to wait till later, till after Harry died—till two days after he died, to be exact. Yes, Estelle had okayed the horses and the redecorating only hours—*hours*—after the funeral.

Upon hearing this, Donald (then barely Ellen's fiancé) had given voice—and motion—to his outrage, as only he could. "Ballbuster!" he had yelled. "That damn dame's a ballbuster. And that husband of hers has got no balls at all! She's busted 'em! And if we don't watch out, she's gonna bust your mother's bank, too!"

As manager of Estelle's financial affairs, Donald had been in a constant state of outrage in the twelve years since Harry died. Estelle did not understand money, he often said. She did not care to concern herself with it, except to spend it on other people. She didn't look at the bills as they came—she just paid them. She kept no record of the checks she wrote—she just wrote them, signing them with her dribbling E.

Many times, Donald had tried to reason with her. He cautioned her against the $100,000 lent to an ex-partner of Harry's who swore he would shoot himself without it. ("Tell him to go ahead," Donald had said.) He had cautioned her against the college tuitions paid on behalf of various "dear old friends' " children; against the monthly donations to assorted charities; against the $30,000 car for her favorite godchild on his sixteenth birthday. Estelle had close to a hundred godchildren. People she hardly knew, hearing rumors of her generosity, asked her to be godmother to their children—sometimes retroactively. Recently, she was asked to be godmother to a nineteen-year-old! She said yes to all of them and recorded their birthdays and graduation dates in a special notebook. More than once, Estelle had handed Ellen a stack of birthday cards, addressed to godchildren, and asked her to mail them on her way home. More than once, Ellen had steamed open the envelopes and removed the enclosed checks before doing so.

Above all, Donald cautioned Estelle against setting up $1 million trust funds for Alaric and Oribel. ("That's money out of our son's pocket!" he told Ellen.) No matter how loudly his voice boomed out in protest, Estelle, in her soft, mild way, held firm.

And after all, it was her money.

"It ain't gonna last forever, not with in-laws like that," Donald said, "not even with *me* investing it."

No, there was no love lost between aunt and niece. But even the oldest enemies will unite to defeat a common threat.

"*Your dear motha has no judgment atahll,*" continued her ladyship, "*noon atahll. Shez helpliz—helpliz oz a chilled!*"

"I'm afraid I've often thought the same myself," Ellen said.

"*We simpleh cahnah—simpleh cahnah have such low pipple grubbin round!*"

"I couldn't agree with you more, Lady Perdita," Ellen said. "What exactly do you propose to do about it?"

"*I'm gowing to call your motha this instant and hov her book me a flight to New York two weeks from Friday—first clahss!*"

Estelle was waiting.

"And let the games begin!" she said. "Let them begin!"

With this pronouncement, she had marked the dawn of each new day for the last twelve years.

"And let the games begin!" as soon as her eyes opened, for some four thousand mornings, ever since she'd adopted her first three dogs.

"And let the games begin!" though often they had already begun—always with the same excitement, and the same gratitude, undulled by repetition, each dog bursting from the night of sleep as though from prison.

More often than not, it was the games that woke her. Not today.

"What is it?" Estelle sat up in bed. "What's wrong?"

They stood still, these mutts, in solemn semicircle, facing the windows, half-open over the lawn. All ears were cocked, all snouts were quivering.

"What do you hear?" Estelle said. "What do you smell?"

The bed lurched as Marilyn and Loren, then massive Marlon and Monroe, leapt off, charging the windows. They stood up on their hind legs to look out. Estelle rushed after them and pulled them away, fearing that in their frenzy they would jump.

Estelle left the dogs in her large dressing room, out of harm's way, and went downstairs to find Ellen. She was in the screened-in dining porch off the kitchen, eating breakfast with Lisanne and the count.

Estelle stood in the doorway. Newspaper pages turning, cereal spoons splashing up milk, made the usual soothing sounds.

"Dear lady!" Cockleburg half-rose, then fell back into his chair. The bun he'd been about to butter bounced onto the table. "Dear lady! What is wrong?"

Ellen looked once at her mother, then looked away.

Lisanne's eyes went back and forth between them.

"I-I-I-I—" Estelle began.

"Ellen, what's going on here?" Lisanne said.

"Hey, don't get mad at *me!*" Ellen said.

"Girls, girls, girls." Cockleburg spoke with rare authority. "Now is not the time for strife!"

Ellen glared at him—and then shrugged.

"I saw—" Estelle began again.

"What, Mother, *what?*" said Lisanne.

"What, dear lady, *what?*" said the count.

"Little Donald is playing with his BB gun," Ellen explained reluctantly, "and Big Donald is playing with him."

"A BB gun is not a toy," said Lisanne.

"I couldn't agree with you more." Ellen turned to address Estelle. "You know how I feel about that gun, Mom. After what happened this fall, I begged Donald to take it away from Donnie—for good."

"These American boys!" Cockleburg threw up his hands. "In France, the little ones are not so bloodthirsty."

Ellen's color was high. She went on: "Donald promised the boy he'd take him shooting before tennis camp began. I tried to interfere, but . . . Boys will be boys. Their weapon of choice was Donald's forty-five. It took me hours to argue them down to the BB gun." Ellen shook her head again. "I'm sorry, Mom. I was hoping they'd finish before you woke up. I know how upsetting guns of any kind are to you. Let's at least be thankful they're not using a real gun."

"But they're shooting birds!" Estelle said.

"Donald promised me they wouldn't actually kill anything," Ellen said. "BB guns can't kill, Mother, except at very close range. . . ." Her voice trailed off.

"So they're just leaving them there to suffer? That's even—" Lisanne stopped, glancing at Estelle.

Estelle gripped the door frame as the world began to spin—a single slow, drunken revolution.

After several unsuccessful attempts, Cockleburg had managed to push himself up—up, back, and away from the table. He now limped over to Estelle and wrapped his arm around her shoulder. She welcomed its weight that nearly drew her to the floor. He leaned so heavily upon her that she knew his wound must pain him.

"Someone make them stop," she begged. "I can't go out there."

"I already tried," Ellen said wearily. "Just wait it out, why don't you? I doubt they'll last much longer."

"Ellen, come on! With a gun in their hands, those two could last all day," Lisanne said.

Ellen didn't bother to argue.

Lisanne stood up. "I'll make them stop," she said.

"*No!*" Cockleburg shouted. "*No!*" He dropped his comforting arm, and stepped away from Estelle. They were all staring at him. "No," he repeated, quietly now. "Please allow *me*, dear lady, to perform for you this one small service." He inclined his massive stalk of neck. "*I'll* make them stop."

With a low bow, he goose-stepped from the room.

They remained, for a long moment, frozen in their places, Estelle in the doorway, Ellen at the table, Lisanne by the sideboard. Then, wordlessly, they followed—into the kitchen, down the hall, through the back door, and out onto the landing above the great square lawn.

Cockleburg, having descended the stone steps, was moving steadily across the grass toward the huntsmen. In his brisk, martial stride, there was no hint—no hint at all—of the usual claudication.

Estelle felt her heart begin to rise and fall, in giddy, swooping pendulums, like a child in a swing.

The Donalds, Big and Li'l, stood atop a hummock about a hundred feet away. They faced the pond, their backs turned to the watching women, the onward-marching count. They were dressed identically in full military regalia: green fatigues, helmets, polished knee boots; goggles, Swiss Army knives and water flasks hanging from their belts. They took turns with the BB gun, passing it back and forth like a bottle, and they slunk toward their prey in crouching, stealthy steps.

Big Donald had the gun now. He had tiptoed to the foot of a small blossoming tree on the left border of the lawn. He raised the gun, took aim at the lowest branch, and fired—pop!—a playful, breathy exhalation.

A robin dropped through the leaves, to spasm between his boots.

At which point father and son, returning to their hummock, bellowed forth a hearty cheer and clasped hands in manly fellowship.

At which point Estelle clutched Lisanne's arm.

"Why do they stay around?" Lisanne said. "Why don't they just fly away?"

The huntsmen remained blissfully unaware of the nobleman's approach until he was virtually upon them.

Although the women were too far away to make out the exchange of words (except for the few that Big Donald shouted), it was all too clear what transpired.

Cockleburg spoke first, gesturing toward the women.

Big Donald spoke next, shaking his head. "... *Men!*" the women heard him shout. Then: "... *God damn business!*"

Cockleburg spoke again, wringing his hands.

Then Li'l Donald spoke, stamping one booted foot, and then the other: a quick stamp-stamp, like the opening steps of the Virginia clogging dance.

Cockleburg spoke again, now extending his hand, as if to receive the gun.

Big Donald spoke again, holding the gun away from Cockleburg. "... *Men!*" the women heard him shout. Then: "... *Goddamn fags and gigolos!*"

For another long moment, Cockleburg spoke, obviously pleading with the huntsmen to cut short their hunt.

In response, Big Donald, having evidently sighted another bird, defiantly lifted the gun and pointed it, over

Cockleburg's shoulder, in the direction of the hedges opposite.

Thus was the stage set for a scene that Estelle was never to forget, a scene that she was to replay in slow motion, over and over, for the rest of her life.

Cockleburg now turned, as if in defeat, and took several rapid steps away from Donald. Whereupon he suddenly spun round, screamed for a good solid fifteen seconds (the hairs rose on Estelle's neck), and ran *back* toward Big Donald, who had lowered his arm in astonishment. Running with a speed Estelle would never have dreamed possible, his thighs churning, Cockleburg launched himself high into the air, twisted into a back flip, and landed smack in the middle of the hummock, in a high kick that sent the BB gun spinning out of Donald's hand. The dazed huntsmen tilted helmeted heads to track the arc of their weapon. As it descended, Cockleburg's arm shot out and stole it from the air. He then, letting out another hair-raising scream, lifted his free hand and, *in a single karate chop,* split the BB gun in two, and hurled the pieces to the ground.

Stunned silence from the huntsmen.

Absolute silence on the huntsmen's hummock.

"Jesus!" Ellen was sheet white.

"So he really is a ninja!" Lisanne said.

"But of course, darling!" Estelle tried to contain her exaltation. "He said so, didn't he?"

The count was making his way back up the lawn toward the swooning women. Just before the landing, he lifted to them a face that was humble as cupped hands.

He shook his head as Estelle began to stammer out her thanks. Wordlessly, he seized her hand and (standing as he was a foot below her) rose up on tiptoe and kissed it.

Then he mounted the steps. The women parted for him. Thus passed the paladin into the hall.

Silence, still, from the huntsmen.

Absolute stillness on the huntsmen's hummock.

Upstairs in Estelle's bedroom, Lisanne, passing the window in her pacing, glanced out and saw Adair.

"It's so rare," Estelle was saying, "to find a scholar trained in the arts of war."

He was gathering up the birds and dropping them in a black plastic garbage bag.

"So rare," Estelle was saying, "to find the man of letters and the man of action rolled into one."

Something about the way his bare back bent . . .

"I know you think I'm silly, darling," Estelle was saying, "and I *am,* but when he did that kick!—well, it made me think of Lord Stede in *Moonlight Madness.* Now Stede, as you know, was a poet and a pirate, too."

Unfortunately, Lisanne *did* know. Barely a month home and already she was on a first-name basis, so to speak, with her mother's favorite heroes. And while certainly Cockleburg had stunned and impressed them all with his flip and his kick, to compare him, a plump, blue-haired, middle-aged pedant, to the tall, dashing, laconic, steely-eyed rogue Stede was *a bit of a stretch.*

Yet it appeared that her mother was admitting him into the pantheon. Stede, Kade, Keen, Rolfe, Cap'n Blackheart, the Cherokee brave Burning Arrow, and now, alongside them—Cockleburg!

"Especially in that scene where Stede rescues Lady Storme from the villain, One-Eyed Jacko," Estelle went on. "It gives me goose bumps just to think of it!"

Adair slowly straightened, his hands on his back, and turned toward the house. The black bag sagged at his side. Lisanne ducked back behind the fluttering curtains.

"What is it?" Estelle joined her at the window. "Oh, I

see." She looked at Lisanne as she said, "If you can bear it, why don't you go down and help him?"

Lisanne stopped first in the kitchen, for a garbage bag, which she unfurled with a snap.

She approached him cautiously.

"Looks like the boys had a big time this morning" was all he said in greeting.

Lisanne went over to the left side of the lawn, as Adair was covering the right side, and traced out a connect-the-dots trail of fallen birds. She wished she had the spoon she'd used on Mrs. Rainey's dog, Frederick.

The third bird she picked up twitched in her hands and she flung it away.

Adair dropped his bag and came over. "What?"

"It's alive." She couldn't look at it.

"Lisanne, go wait for me back at my house." When she hesitated, he gave her a little push. "I'll meet you on my porch," he said.

His porch: it was a screened-in cube, opening off the living room of the cottage, built high on beams along a small, steep-sloping hill, cooled and green-lit and umbrella-ed by trees. Lisanne climbed steps from the grass and sank into a hammock strung up between the beams. She closed her eyes. She swayed there, lulled by air, embraced by the lowering branches.

This feeling could make you stupid. No wonder the birds had felt so safe.

At the sound of boots on steps, she tried to rise. Breezes curled around her like sleeping hands. This sadness must be peace, it was that patient, and that pure. In its still eye, unclouded by fear, she saw herself reflected.

It was like looking at an animal in a zoo.

"Wake up," she heard Adair say.

"So what did you do with them?" she asked him.

When he didn't answer, she knew: "You killed them."

"What did you think I was going to do with them, Lisanne? Heal them with my hands?"

She wasn't sure what she had thought. "You could have taken them to the vet."

He said, "I wasn't going to leave them crippled."

Crippled—the way his voice held that word, she remembered his son. She had almost forgotten he had a son.

"How did you do it?"

"Does it matter?"

"I should get going," she said. She rolled off the hammock, and stood, facing him. "Don't you have work to do?"

Her voice was taunting, and she knew her eyes were mean. Something buried in her rose, unfolded, and flexed: her meanness. Suddenly, she understood the odd thrill and release she felt around him. Here at last was someone her meanness couldn't touch. He had the strength of the brokenhearted. His one longing would protect him. It gleamed before him like a shield.

There was a reckless pleasure in being so disarmed.

Don't you have work to do?

"Not until I've had a beer," he finally said. "Stay a minute and have one with me."

"I never drink."

"Not even on special occasions?"

"Is this a special occasion?"

"Well, how about some iced tea, then?"

She hesitated, long enough for him to slide open the glass door and disappear into the cottage. He returned a few minutes later, carrying two tall glasses.

"Don't look so scared," he said, handing her one. "I didn't spike it—promise."

He sat down on the tilting brown sofa beside the door and watched her. She settled back into the hammock, though her body felt too wary for its cradling now. They sipped their tea in silence.

Suddenly Adair let out a low whistle. "Is it a bird, is it a plane, or—"

Cockleburg!

He had minced into view at the bottom of the hill with his shih tzu, Queen Elizabeth. "Poo poo, my beauty," they heard him chanting. He appeared unaware of his audience.

Adair said, "Fourteen species a day are dying out, and he doesn't care, so long as the shih tzu survives."

Lisanne leapt to the count's defense. "That's not fair. He had nothing to do with what happened this morning. In fact, he was the only one of us who had the guts to stop it."

Lisanne recounted for Adair, with accompanying pantomime, the tale of Cockleburg's heroism. "And then he did this incredible backflip and"—she kicked her leg up as high as it would go—"and kicked the gun right out of Donald's hand!"

"No!"

"I wouldn't have believed it if I hadn't seen it with my own two eyes, but yes—he truly is a ninja. I've asked him to give me lessons, as a matter of fact."

"Lessons?" Adair laughed.

"Go ahead, laugh," Lisanne said. "I'm going to get strong." She called down the hill to Cockleburg. "Hey, Count!"

He spun round. "Who goes there?"

"It's me, Lisanne!"

"Ah! Greetings, fair one!"

"And Adair!"

"Greetings, master!"

Cockleburg panted up the hill—suddenly, dramatically, painfully limping. Watching him jerk and drag himself along, Lisanne thought: *He's affected himself into muscular dystrophy!*

"I just finished a poem," he announced. "An epic poem. Thank you, Calliope! The epics always leave me frisky, longing for a gulp of air. So here I am," he said, "gulping. My, what a pleasant nook you youngsters have here! It does so jubilate my heart to see youngsters basking in the day!"

The poet was dressed for his gulp in a billowing blue-and-purple paisley shirt and crisp green linen trousers that strained to accommodate his steatopygia.

"Since you're feeling so frisky, Count," said Lisanne, "how about giving me a jujitsu lesson?"

"Nothing would please me more." The sensei inclined his head. "As the Queen has finished her business for the day, let us begin. *Maintenant!* I'll go change into my robes."

Lisanne turned to Adair. "Thanks for the tea."

"Have a good time," he said. "But don't get too strong."

9

By noon Saturday, the house was silent. Estelle was walking through the woods behind the pond with her mutts, Adair having cleared the old paths. Somewhere deep in the same woods lurked that tiny, tireless, self-proclaimed rooter-out-of-evil Donald Jr., playing his endless game of posse. Big Donald and Lisanne, in a rare pairing, had gone into town in search of a dop kit and a duffel bag for the boy, who was leaving for tennis camp in two days. Cockleburg was nowhere to be found, which meant he was probably writing a poem. ("If I don't write at least one poem a day, by God, I go mad," he said.) Ellen and Lisanne had listened outside his door during these Parnassian interludes. Cries of *"Mais oui! C'est sublime!"* alternated with muffled groaning.

So for once Ellen had the afternoon to herself. She was on her way downstairs to the pool to swim her daily laps when suddenly, from the direction of her mother's bedroom, came sounds that riveted her to the landing: a hiss, a howl, then a clatter—then a heavy thud.

"What the heck—?" Ellen flew across the hall and into Estelle's room. It was empty. In her alarm knocking over two chairs, she lunged to the door of the dressing room and flung it open.

A man lay writhing and coughing on the hardwood floor. It was Cockleburg.

Ellen screamed.

Cockleburg screamed.

Ellen screamed again.

Cockleburg screamed again.

Ellen cried, "What are you doing in here?"

"Help me, Estelle!"—rolling onto his back and rubbing his eyes. "Help me, Estelle! I can't see!"

It was then that Ellen noticed, on the floor beside him, the can of Mace she had given her mother on her fifty-fifth birthday. (Ellen: "Promise me you'll take this everywhere you go." Estelle: "Oh, but darling, I could never . . .")

It was made to look like a bottle of French perfume.

"For Christ's sake." Ellen stepped over him, to the sink, and moistened a washcloth. This she laid across his brow.

"Dear lady, your touch, as always, soothes me."

As always? "It's Ellen, by the way."

"El-el-el-el-ellen?"

"That's right. And I'm afraid you've sprayed yourself with Mace."

"B-b-b-b-b-b-but—I thought—the label said—Joie de Nuit—"

"I know. I gave it to her for protection."

"So this burning . . . this blindness . . . ?"

"It'll go away."

"All I wanted," he said sadly, "was the delicious scent of her 'pon me. For inspiration."

"To be honest, Count," Ellen said slowly, "you shouldn't

be looking through my mother's things when she's not here."

A silence fell. Cockleburg's breathing grew even more labored.

"Let's let this be our little secret," he said finally.

Did he actually think she would lie? To protect *him?* Ellen was about to protest indignantly.

"You see," he went on, "*entre nous,* your mother has enlisted my help on a *petit* project she's been working on—"

"I don't frankly see how sneaking through her toiletries could possibly—"

"Let me finish!" He lifted a limp hand. "I would cut off my left arm—or, for that matter, my left leg—or my right leg—yes, I would eagerly embrace life as a monoped—in fact, I would eagerly embrace death itself—"

"Get to the point."

"—*before I would betray your mother.*" The limp hand curled into a fist. "This being the rare, the *one,* exception," he continued, "for your mother specifically requested that I not breathe a word of our collaboration until we'd finished."

"Finished what? What?"

"Her novel. Yes, I burst with pride to reveal to you, Ellen, that your mother has pleaded for my help with a novel she is working on, and that to the utmost of my ability I have pledged that help."

Ellen had been crouching beside him on the floor. With a groan, she now collapsed upon her rear. "A *romance* novel?" she whispered.

For it had to be this. Ever since she'd started reading them, Estelle had flirted, only half jokingly, with the idea of writing one. Ellen had indulged her, even to the point of giving her a typewriter one Christmas. Not for one minute had Ellen believed that her mother would make this vague dream a reality.

"Exactement!" Cockleburg exclaimed. "And now you bring me to the crux of the matter. Not being familiar with that genre, I ventured in here—into this sacred inner sanctum of her muliebrity—for purposes of *research*. On that I give you my word of honor, Ellen. *My word of honor.*" He stretched out the long pink cradle of his tongue as though he meant for Ellen to scoop it up from there—the word of honor.

Ellen had to admit that her mother did keep her summer's supply of romance novels in stacks on a table in her dressing room. This represented, of course, only a fraction of her immense collection, which remained in the library of the New York apartment.

"I was wondering," said the count, "if, in my infirmity I might beg of you an enormous favor."

"And what is that?" Ellen said sourly.

"Help me with my research. Read aloud to me, Ellen, at least till I regain my vision."

Ellen didn't see how she could refuse her mother's guest. She took a book off the top of the tallest stack, roughly helped him to his feet, piloted him into the bedroom, and pushed him onto the sofa.

She sat facing him on the edge of the bed. "This one's called *Cap'n Blackheart's Revenge*," she told him. "I think it's one of Mom's favorites. Do you want me to start from the beginning?"

He nodded. "I'm interested in methods of exposition, in structure and narrative techniques, as well as theme and style."

Ellen turned to page one:

"On this glorious May day of 1797, Lady Blessing rose early, as was her wont, and skipped merrily across the meadows of her father's vast country estate. Every now and then, humming to herself a favorite hymn, the high-born maiden stooped to pick a flower, to breathe deeply of its heady perfumed fragrance, to press it to her proud upthrusting breasts. At seventeen years old, Blessing's beauty was as fair and fresh as any unplucked flower of the fields. . . ."

By Chapter Three, Blessing had been raped forty-four times and sold into white slavery to her father's sworn enemy—Cap'n Blackheart.

As Ellen read on, the count's expression grew increasingly pained. His eyes were covered with the washcloth, but his cheeks twitched, and his mouth trembled, and even his nose spoke eloquently of an inner turmoil. This was to be expected. He had said he was unfamiliar with the genre, and for a self-proclaimed poet/critic/linguist/thinker, Ellen could well imagine what a rude awakening *Cap'n Blackheart's Revenge* must be. But was his agony purely aesthetic? Ellen wondered. Was he questioning only the collaboration? If I were he, Ellen thought, I'd be questioning *a lot more than that.* After a particularly harrowing rape scene, she paused to say, "You know, that's always been a fantasy of Mom's," and smiled grimly as he shifted on the sofa. Ellen wanted Cockleburg to picture himself in the role of ravisher. She wanted him to ask himself: Is this what she wants? And if so, Am I up to it? And most important, *Is it worth it?*

Enthusiastically now, Ellen read on.

Suddenly, Cockleburg tore off his blindfold. "I see light!" he cried.

Ellen turned. There in the doorway stood Estelle.

"Count, are you—are you ill?" she said.

Ellen explained what had happened.

"Oh Ellen!" Estelle looked at her daughter reproachfully.

"What have *I* done?" Ellen said.

"Nothing!" said the count.

"I knew it wasn't a good idea to keep weapons in the house." Estelle was hurrying to his side.

"Nothing!" repeated the count. "Ellen has done nothing but aid and succor a nobleman in direst need!"

Flinging *Cap'n Blackheart's Revenge* to the floor, Ellen left them. Estelle was stroking his eyelids.

An hour later, Ellen was sitting at the kitchen table, gassy and despairing, before a bowl of cookie dough, when Donald and Lisanne pulled into the yard. She went outside to greet them. "Did you find anything nice?" she asked.

"We went to every shop in town," Donald said. "I've never seen so many faggy-looking duffel bags in my life— all pink and purple and flowered. Not a single plain, manly leather bag in the whole damn town."

"And how was your afternoon?" said Lisanne.

"Cockleburg blinded himself," Ellen announced glumly. She told them the story.

"God*damn* it! Don't you see?" said Donald. "It's another dastardly play for sympathy! That man will stop at nothing to worm his way into her heart. Next he'll be cutting off his own leg!"

"He actually said he might do that," Ellen said.

"Where are they now?" Donald asked.

"Upstairs," Ellen told him, "in her bedroom."

"You mean to say—you left them *alone?*" With a piercing battle cry, the outraged son-in-law charged into the house.

Lisanne seemed unperturbed, even when Ellen unveiled the secret of the romance novel.

"Don't you see what that could lead to?" Ellen said. I mean, he's skeptical now—but that could change. Can't you just see them trying out lines on each other, acting out scenes?"

Every word her mother had ever read aloud to her came back to haunt Ellen now. Cockleburg pressing her mother back upon the pillows, looming over her with the blood beating in his throat, in his guts, in his loins, even in the bunions on his feet . . . lust, thick and hot, swelling Cockleburg's sac, tightening it, weighting it . . . Cockleburg's manroot brutally carving out his own place inside her . . . her heart cartwheeling as Cockleburg's plunging sword penetrated her with its flaming blade . . . their desire rising up in towering waves, then smashing down in showers of sparkles, towering again and toppling, mounting and shaking and pulsing in the age-old rhythm . . . Cockleburg and her mother, exulting and spasming in every atom of every inch as the stardust whirled and swirled about them in an extravagant frenzy that shattered them almost into unconsciousness . . .

"Don't look so worried," Lisanne was saying. "Cockleburg is hardly the stuff romantic heroes are made of."

"Well, he's got the well-corded neck, at least," Ellen said.

Lisanne put her arm over Ellen's shoulder. "Listen to me, Ellen. She's not in love with him. She's just being kind, Ellen. She's just being herself."

Ellen woke that night to wine-drenched breath, to lashes crawling on her face. She opened her eyes. Her mother was bending over her in the darkness.

"I'm sorry I snapped at you today," she whispered. "I feel so bad about it. The count told me how wonderful you were to him. And I know you'd never hurt anyone. I love you." She said it like an explanation: I know you'd never hurt anyone *because* I love you. Her hands were rooting in Ellen's hair. "I love you, lambie. Go back to sleep."

She banged into the bookshelves on her way out, tripped over the fan, knocked over the tennis racket, all the while whispering, "Go back to sleep now, lambie, go back to sleep."

Beside Ellen on the bed, Donald began to stir and mutter: "Goddamn it . . . what the hell?"

Ellen looked at the clock on the bedside table. It was three in the morning.

She had left her mother in the living room two hours ago, drinking wine and playing backgammon with the count, rolling the dice with exaggerated waves of her arm—and laughing. Donald, Li'l Donald, and Lisanne had long since gone to bed. Only Ellen had remained, saying, "Honestly, Mom, is it really necessary to open another bottle at this hour?"

All through dinner, Estelle drank steadily, and laughed at everything Cockleburg said. "Oh, Coco," she would say, after each bon mot, each anecdote, each florid compliment ("Dear lady, this salad is as humbling and awe-inspiring as yourself!"). "Oh, Coco!"—laughing with her mouth open and full of food, giddy, stupid, *happy.* "Oh, Coco!"—laughing while the rest of them, Ellen, Donald, Nipe, and even Li'l, looked on, exchanging glances, first surprised, then embarrassed, then disgusted.

All except Lisanne, whose long eyes were inscrutable above her slowly curving smile.

Surprised, embarrassed, disgusted—and finally angry: *How dare you?* Ellen had wanted to smash that laughing face, then smooth it back to pity and despair.

She wondered how long her mother had watched her while she slept. She remembered her mother creeping into her room, waking her, gently pushing her down the hall to the master bedroom. "Look," she said, pointing, "*look*"—and her face was lambent with love. She was pointing at Ellen's father. He lay on his back in his baby-blue pajamas, his hands folded on his chest. His eyelids fluttered, and his legs jerked. His mouth was open, and he was snoring, deep shuddering snores—"the most innocent sound in the world," her mother said. She gripped Ellen's arm. "Isn't he precious? Isn't he?"

Who could stand it? Lisanne used to say. Who could stand being loved that way?

Estelle was all in white: white linen pants, a loose white blouse, a white straw hat tied with a white ribbon under her chin. She lay back on a white sheet, arms folded in wing curves, hands behind her head. Beside her, startling in shorts and a tunic of brightest cochineal, reclined Cockleburg. In an obvious nod to pastoral tradition, he was chewing on a blade of grass. He appeared to be reading from a volume open at his side. And beside *him*, in a pose of uncharacteristic abandon, flat on her back and spread-eagled, napped the lapdog, Queen Elizabeth.

They were picnicking in the shade of an elm along the mossy bank of the pond. An enormous cold roast capon (worthy of King Henry VIII) formed the entrée of their repast.

Lisanne peered out from behind a rock on the opposite shore. She had been sent here on a mission of espionage by the Prawls. ("Picnicking by the pond?" Donald said. "Next thing we know, they'll be wrapping it up in the bushes!") Lisanne had argued for a more direct approach. "I don't see why I can't just casually join them. I don't see why I have to sneak and spy."

The Prawls had exchanged incredulous glances.

"Don't you see, darling," Ellen said, "we need to observe them *au naturel,* so to speak—in the bush."

"Or in the bush*es,* if it comes to that," Donald added darkly.

"And we're depending on you," Ellen went on, "because you're so innocent. No one would suspect you of anything."

She, innocent? Lisanne was about to laugh—but Ellen had spoken without irony.

Finally, Lisanne agreed to the mission, not because she shared Ellen and Donald's sense of urgency, but because—she had to admit it—she was curious. And because she knew that if there was anything actually to report, she would not report it.

High on her hill, Lisanne had an almost bird's-eye view of the picnickers. At this angle, her mother seemed pinned, a white butterfly, to the sheet. Although Cockleburg, lying on his side, leaned toward her, he did not touch her. Estelle had lifted her head and appeared to be gazing into his eyes. At that moment, the two of them seemed haloed in happiness—a happiness, Lisanne sensed, that had all the depth and gravity of grief. She wondered what they were talking about. A poem? Harry? She knew they often spoke of Harry. She had overheard them, without meaning to, on the porch, in the garden, by the pool. They always fell silent at her approach.

A pair of binoculars swayed over Lisanne's heart. They hung from a strap around her neck, placed there by Donald ("These might come in handy") with all the pomp and ceremony of an Olympic champion's bemedaling. Keenly aware of her ludicrous position, Lisanne now raised the lenses to her eyes.

"Bird-watching?" said a voice behind her.

It was Adair. "You're silent as an Indian," Lisanne said. This was, in fact, how Ellen now referred to the caretaker. "That Injun," Ellen called him, provoked by his silent, lurking presence, she said, and by his braid.

"Someone ought to tie a bell on you," Lisanne said.

Adair was smiling oddly at her. He knew she was spying. Lisanne turned back to face the picnickers and again raised the binoculars to her eyes. Estelle's face was magnified to luminous loveliness.

And then a moment later Adair was looming over the picnickers and pointing at her perch on the hill. The picnickers shaded their eyes to follow his finger. Lisanne stepped out from behind the rock. "Hi, Mom! Hi, Count!" she shouted.

They waved and beckoned her down.

Adair had seated himself on the sheet beside Estelle. The drumstick on which he gnawed could not hide his satisfied smile. His eyes were the color of the smells in the air—deep, heated fertile greens and browns.

"Darling!" Estelle greeted her with open arms.

Lisanne stooped and kissed her brow. "I was just doing a bit of bird watching," she said, fingering her binoculars.

"Ornithology!" translated the noble pedant, ever unable to resist the opportunity for a choice sesquipedalian. "In my nonage, untold moons ago, I too indulged in that simultaneously soporific and tonic, steadying and transporting pursuit." He patted a spot on the sheet to his left. Kneeling beside him, Lisanne could only shudder at what the Prawls would make of this scene: the two couples gathered around the capon, like double-daters.

"I was just proposing to Adair," Estelle said, addressing Lisanne, "that we plant something—a bush, a tree, maybe a flower bed— something to, well, commemorate these gay summer hebdomads in which the count has honored us with his presence."

Gay summer hebdomads? Pedantry's catching like a virus around here, Lisanne thought.

"Honor?" boomed the count, in his most orotund

voice. "Honor?" in one lithe movement, on his knees. "All the honor here redounds to you, dear lady, to you, dear hostess. Yes, to you! Never before have I aestivated so blissfully. Your overwhelming hospitality, together with the peace and beauty of this villatic setting, have created a paradisal Cockaigne surpassing even my most febrile dreams. Ergo, if any commemorative vegetation, be it floral, frutescent, fructiferous, bacciferous, herbaceous, or arboreal, is planted, let it be planted, I say, let it be planted, I repeat, to you, dear lady. Yes, to you!"

"No, Count, I absolutely insist that it be planted to you," said Estelle.

"No, dear lady, 'tis I who must insist here—and insist I do, firmly, indeed implacably, I insist that it be planted to you," insisted the count.

"I agree with Estelle. I think we should plant something in your honor, Count." Adair lent his weight in this tug of war to the lady. "If not a tree or a bush, well, then, at least a weed. How about, for example, some cockleburs?"

"Ha ha ha ha, you japer!" the count cachinnated. "You're daft, my good man, quite simply daft! Ha ha ha ha!"

For all his bombast, Cockleburg had a lively sense of humor about himself. Lisanne guessed that the bombast was a form of self-deprecation.

After a slight hesitation, Estelle began to laugh with him.

"Now, Donnie," Ellen said, "are you sure you've packed everything? Toothbrush, toothpaste, Band-Aids—?"

The child nodded.

"For God's sakes, Ellen, he's not going to darkest

Africa," said Big Donald. "He can get all that stuff in Beaver Dam."

"—shampoo, conditioner—?"

The child nodded.

"Conditioner? I've never used that crap in all my life— and I ain't none the worse for it, either." Big Donald was inordinately proud of his luxuriant chevelure.

"—tweezers, cotton balls, sunscreen, astringent, moisturizer?" Ellen reeled off the items from a list in her Filofax.

The child nodded.

"Moisturizer? Ellen, what is all this faggoty crap? Next thing I know, you'll be stinkin' the lad up with perfume!" Big Donald unzipped his son's new duffel bag, pulled out the new dop kit, and, with a grimace of disgust, removed the moisturizer and threw it in the trash. Ellen didn't have the energy to protest.

"And remember, honey, if you get lonesome or homesick, you can always come home early," she said.

"The lad will *not* get homesick," Donald said. "The lad will *not* be coming home early."

That spring, when Donnie announced his desire to go to tennis camp for ten weeks, Ellen had been appalled. "That's virtually the whole summer! He can't go away that long! He's only nine years old!" Ellen knew that Donnie was his father's favorite companion; Donald was desolate if the child went away even for a weekend. And so she'd expected Donald to take her side—on this, at least. But no. "I don't want the kid to go, either," he said. "But a man's gotta do what a man's gotta do. Let's just be thankful he's not like that little sissy Angus—may as well call him *Angie*—Windburn, who's always clinging to his mama's skirts. I'm glad the kid wants to learn tennis"— obviously bolstering himself with his words—"tennis is a great way to raise capital. It's not like he's going off to needlepoint camp, for God's sakes!"

Or gun camp, Ellen thought, taking some small comfort in the fact that at least the boy would be separated from his arsenal. She would be the last to deny that he needed some new interests.

Still, now that the time had come to say goodbye, Ellen couldn't bear to let him go. She stared into his freshscrubbed, upturned face and found herself, as always, to her shame, looking for herself there—and to her disappointment, finding only Donald. He had Donald's tiny graceful ears, and Donald's spacious nostrils, Donald's buttery jowls and fat upper lip, and Donald's black, gleaming, but unfortunately rather close-set eyes. In the days of her early motherhood, wheeling Baby Donald's carriage through Central Park, Ellen had been stopped by a kindly-looking old lady who'd peered down at the infant and then exclaimed, "My! What close-together eyes it has!"

Eight and a half years later, Ellen still smarted from this insult. She'd hoped that the child's eyes would grow apart as he got older; alas, they had actually grown closer, and now formed a perfect little horizontal figure eight just above his nose.

Mother and son had, if anything, even less in common emotionally than they had facially. The lad's interests were Donald's. His reactions and habits and instincts and desires were Donald's. All, *all*, Donald's! It was as though some mad scientist had scraped a few cells off one of Big Donald's buttocks (where, God knows, there were billions to spare) and grown the child in a Petri dish.

Ellen thought of Lisanne, and of how she too had belonged completely to her father. And she realized, for the first time, the pain this must have caused Estelle. But at least Estelle had her, Ellen—the better end of the deal (if Ellen did say so herself).

"Let's get a move on," Donald was saying—no, *shouting*. "We're late! The kid's gonna miss his plane, Ellen, if you don't stop hangin' and moanin' and moonin' all over him."

Ellen sighed, and choked back a sob, and ducked down for one last kiss. The child bore the osculation stoically—or at any rate without the wincing that was his usual response to physical affection.

"I-I love you, Little Donald," she said.

"I love you too, Mommy," the child started to say—but these rare, sweet words were drowned out by the father's howl of rage.

"How many times, Ellen, how many goddamn times do I have to tell you? *Don't* call him *Little* Donald!"

"But he is little," Ellen whispered, "aren't you, honey?" she added, looking down at the child, who had begun to shift about.

"He is *not* little. He's a fine young man—aren't you, son? And anyway, if he were Tom Thumb, I wouldn't let you call him 'little.' You demean his manhood, Ellen, with your goddamn diminutives! Build the kid up, for chrissakes, don't put him down! Make him feel like a man, not a mouse!"

"I'm sorry," Ellen said.

"Don't apologize, Ellen—*just don't do it!*" With this command, the father swung round and stalked out of the kitchen and across the graveled yard to the Volvo that would convey him and his clone to the airport.

Little Donald flung himself into Ellen's arms—for the first, and possibly the last, time in his life. The gesture tore at Ellen's heart. "I do love you, Mommy"—he whispered this secret. Then he added, in his normal piping voice: "And tell the count to write me, okay?"

"I certainly will, darling," Ellen said, swallowing her
bile at this request. Much to her and Big Donald's dismay,
Donnie had developed a case of hero worship for their
sworn enemy ever since that Bruce Lee display out on the
lawn the previous weekend.

"Let him go, Ellen!" Donald roared from within the
revved-up Volvo. "Why can't you just let go?"

The child turned and trotted off to the vehicle—and
out of her life for ten long weeks.

Waving goodbye from the porch, Ellen blinked back
hot tears—the tears of a mother's sorrow, yes, but also
the tears of a wife's humiliation. Why did Donald have to
yell at her like that?—and in front of the child! And yet
even with the rage rising inside her, Ellen found herself,
as usual, making excuses for him. She had long ago realized that Donald had no idea how he sounded. Stone deaf
in one ear, he alone was unaware of the nerve-shattering
volume of his voice. A pampered only child, he grew up
with the sense that his tantrums were privileged—un-
challengeable as storms. Although Donald bullied, he
never betrayed. He lacked the discipline for betrayal, just
as he lacked the discipline to control his temper.

He's a better person than I am, Ellen told herself. If he
was fire, she was acid. They both burned, but Ellen knew
that for all her outward patience and docility, she was the
more dangerous of the two.

For there were moments, and this was one of them,
when Ellen hated her husband—a cold, corrosive hatred
that was a million molecules removed and refined from
Donald's crude, flatulent fury. Like the troll he had in fact
played in a long-ago elementary school production, Donald stamped and fumed—but he didn't hate her, and he
didn't deserve her hatred. At these moments, Ellen almost pitied him—and feared herself.

She remained on the porch, still waving goodbye, like a chicken with its head cut off, long after the Volvo had disappeared down the drive. Only a sudden prickly sense of being watched made her, at last, lower her arm. Warily turning, she scanned the yard. Adair was sitting on the stone wall, an enormous pair of weeding shears in his hands. Ellen felt emptied; she couldn't summon the anger he usually provoked. No, it wasn't anger that flushed her cheeks. She knew from his expression what he had witnessed and understood. And then he smiled in a way that made her conscious of the clingy coolness of her dress, and grateful for the way its blue silk greened her eyes, and gilded her hair. I'm not so old, she thought. I could leave. I could go anywhere.

Pushing seventy in dog years, the mongrel brothers Marlon and Brando were well past the first blush of youth. And yet, so potent was the Queen's allure, that these two senescent castrati were maddened by love. The merest whiff of this shih tzu and they began mounting everything in sight: sofas, chairs, trees, garbage cans, table legs, Donald's legs. It became impossible to have them around, and Estelle was forced to banish them to her dressing room.

"All I have to do is mention her name," said Estelle, moved by the romance, "and they howl most soulfully. They're always peering out the window for a glimpse of her, poor babies. I do so hate to lock them up like this."

The count was less moved. "That's what you do with rapists," he said, "you lock them up."

For though not rapists in *fact,* the two mutts were ("apodictically," said Cockleburg) rapists in intent. Only their physical limitations (and not their moral scruples, as Estelle insisted) had restrained them from committing

that basest of crimes. In the days before their imprison-
ment, Cockleburg had taken to walking the Queen on the
road instead of across "the swards," as he put it, surrounding the house. For the swards were the mutts'
stomping ground, and here Her Majesty was most vulnerable to attack. Cockleburg had hoped by this stratagem
to baffle her pursuers. His hopes were cruelly shattered
when, one morning, a mile down the road, the two suitors
plunged out from behind some box trees—and mounted
her ("not even on the side of the road," the count recounted in a trembling voice, *but in the middle of the
road!*). Had he not made violent use of his walking stick,
he shuddered to think of the damage that might have been
done. The attempt alone reduced the Queen to "hysterics,
fits, and fantods." He spent the rest of the day soothing
her with readings of his own poems belted out in his
uniquely penetrating tenor.

"There ought to be some kind of service," Lisanne said,
"where you can hire bitches to satisfy these carnal
needs."

"You mean, canine call girls?" Ellen said, thinking,
She ought to know.

"Why not?" Lisanne said.

"I don't think they'd go for just any old bitch," Estelle
said. "It's the Queen they long for, the Queen they
dream of."

The count agreed. He said, "No dog, having once seen
her, could ever forget her."

The attempted gang rape was the only jarring note in a
week of sunny days that slid serenely into balmy nights.
Estelle spent all her free afternoons with Cockleburg.
They read Proust by the pool. They perambulated across
the swards. They groomed the shih tzu, Estelle mascara-
ing the Queen's lashes while Cockleburg lovingly trimmed
the hairs around her anus. In the rowboat, they circled the

pond. (Estelle rowed; Cockleburg reclined, like an Edwardian maiden, one hand dangling in the water.) For long hours, they closeted themselves in Estelle's bedroom. Ears pressed to the door, Ellen and Donald heard the clacking of the typewriter. "What in God's name is going on?" Donald asked. Ellen didn't have the guts to tell him about the romance novel.

On the days her mother was at the hospital, Ellen searched her room for the manuscript—in vain. Where could her mother have hidden it?—she who had never before hidden anything in her life? All Ellen could find of it was this tormenting fragment, typed on a flap of paper left in the Smith Corona (Ellen's gift!) on the desk by the window:

> she closed the door and immediately was grabbed by strong arms and thrown across the room he came closer to her hot lust boiling in his eyes he had a piece of paper in his hand she started to scream he held her mouth open and forced her tongue to the top of her mouth with the piece of paper he sliced a paper cut across the bottom of her tongue the pain was excruciating. . . .

And so was Ellen's pain upon reading this. *A piece of paper?* What a bizarre choice of weapon for a ravishment! Ellen detected in this perverse twist, clear as day, the hand of the pedant. She wondered what they were planning to call this opus of theirs, this stream-of-consciousness romance. *A Pedant's Proud Passion? The Linguist and the Lady?*

By Wednesday, desperation had driven Ellen literally to her knees—in front of Estelle's dresser, in her dressing room, the two lovesick mongrels looking glumly on. Rifling through her underwear drawer, among the innocent white bras and matronly cotton briefs, Ellen was sickened and shocked to unearth this *garment of sin:* a black lace Merry Widow, obviously brand-new, still wrapped in tissue and fluttering a price tag.

10

Lady Perdita Phyllida Camilla Victoria Montresore-Wolfe debouched from the limousine Estelle had sent to meet her at the airport. With all the majesty that her five-foot, 165-pound frame could marshal, she swept across the yard and into Estelle's arms. "Dear sweet little Stellie," she said, "how divine to see you." Her head rested on the mantel of her bosom like a pumpkin. It gave an impression of great weight and rootedness, for it almost never moved, neither to nod nor to tilt nor to swivel (though sometimes to shake). Perhaps to compensate for this cephalic immobility, Lady Perdita made dramatic use of her eyes, which rolled and darted and swerved in their deep sockets; and of her glabella, which creased and quivered; and of her nostrils, which flexed and flared; and of her tiny sphincteral mouth, now unpuckering from its salutatory air kiss.

Estelle surveyed the yard over the stiff pinkish cone of Lady Perdita's coiffure. "But where is Dave?" she asked.

"Oh, I should think he's probably found his way to Grand Central by now." Her ladyship fluttered plump fingers in a gesture of ennui.

"To Grand Central—?"

"Yes. I left him waiting in line with the luggage. You know I can't stand to go through customs, so humiliating, all those vulgar little men with their nasty little eyes and dirty poking little hands." Lady Perdita shuddered. Her great fear in life was of being strip-searched by "Negro" customs officials. "Dave was a dear and said he'd handle it. Although, frankly, it was the least he could do for me, having made an utter *ass* of himself by vomiting throughout the flight. And anyway, I daresay there wouldn't have quite been room for both of us in the car, what with the luggage and all."

"I should have sent two cars, then—"

"Next time." Lady Perdita smiled magnanimously. "But I forbid you to fret, Estelle. He'll call from the station when his train gets in." She took a deep, snorting breath, exhaling a glittering spray. "Ah! How fine and bracing your American air is! I commend you Americans on your air!"

Estelle blushed as though her sister-in-law had paid her a personal compliment. "I hope it will help you to recover," she said gently, "from the catastrophe."

"The catastrophe?" Lady Perdita repeated, having clearly forgotten the excuse she had given Estelle for her visit: that one of her spaniel pups, while lounging in the garden, had been carried off by a large bird right in front of her shocked eyes, and that she needed a vacation to get over the horror of the predation. As excuses went, it was a bold and imaginative one—perhaps too imaginative, Lisanne thought. Estelle had fallen for it hook, line, and sinker.

"The poor, poor little pup," Estelle now prompted.

"Oh yes, of course! A most dreadful business," her ladyship said, with appropriate lugubriousness. "Never shall I forget the look of anguish on that lovie's face when those cruel talons seized him."

"What a tragedy." Estelle had tears in her eyes.

Although Lisanne and Ellen had been flanking their mother all along, only now did the noblewoman acknowledge their presence. "Hello, gels, you're looking rather well. You may give your Aunt Lady Perdita a kiss." She stood rigidly as the sisters did so, then clapped her hands. "How about some tea?"

"Yes, do come in," said Estelle. "There's someone I'm very eager for you to meet."

"Indeed. . . ."

Cockleburg had been thrown into a tizzy by the news of the noblewoman's visit. He professed himself most anxious to make a favorable impression. Estelle had tried to reassure him. "I know she's going to adore you, Coco," she said. "You two have so much in common: your noble birth, your passion for literature, your love of dogs, your knowledge of Europe, your cultivation, your refinement. . . ."

Still, the count spent all of Tuesday afternoon frantically trying on outfits—his satin knickers, his seersucker suits, his silk shorts, and linen trousers and tunics—and discarding them in despair. "I've gotten so fat," he wailed, "nothing fits anymore, except for my ninja's robes, and I can hardly greet her in those!" He was inconsolable until Estelle suggested that they go into New York on a shopping expedition. "Oh, could we, dear lady? Could we?" He smiled at her tremulously.

"We could, and we will, Count! We could and we will!"

So Estelle took a rare day off from work and went with him on Wednesday to Brooks Brothers, Armani, Sulka's,

Bergdorf's and Bloomingdale's, Ralph Lauren and Dunhill tailors. They returned to Bedford that evening with a half dozen large shopping bags.

"And who do you think paid for it all?" Ellen asked Lisanne.

Estelle told Lisanne later that he hadn't wanted to accept more than a single pair of slacks and a matching shirt—and these as a loan only—but that she had insisted. Absolutely insisted. Insisted on forcing the new wardrobe upon him. After all, his birthday was coming up soon (September 28) and Christmas, too.

Cockleburg had laid out his new finery on the sofa and chairs in the living room for Lisanne and Ellen to admire. "Your mother has such exquisite taste," he exclaimed, burying his face in a blue silk shirt, "she really helped me make some tough choices. This jacket, for example!" he said, dropping the shirt to grab up a pink jacket. "I didn't think it suited me at first, but she convinced me." He rose, holding the jacket to his chest, and regarded himself tenderly in the mirror. "And how right she was! But she is too extravagant." He pirouetted round to face Estelle. "Aren't you, dear lady? You spoil me! I don't deserve all these beautiful things."

"Oh, but you do," Estelle said. "And they deserve you."

Cockleburg was now awaiting the noblewoman in the den off the dining room. For this, the all-important first meeting, he had arranged himself in a contemplative pose, a pose suggestive of the man of letters, the philosophe. Uncharacteristically understated in his new cream-colored Dunhill suit, he was wedged into the windowsill, curled up with his head on his knees and a copy of *Great Expectations* open at his side. (So Estelle had told him of Lady Perdita's passion for Dickens.) His face was contorted in literary rapture: mouth agape, eyes half-closed, brow furrowed. Thus transported, he did not (or affected not) to notice the quartet of women when they came in.

"Cocovich?" Estelle said.

With a sharp crepitation, turning a page, he did not look up. He cocked his head. He pursed his lips.

"Cocovich?"—louder—the repetition of the hypocorism bringing an ominous frown to her ladyship's lips.

With a start, the scholar dropped his tome, unfurled himself, and lurched toward them with arms outstretched. "Dear lady—dear lad*ies*, I should say, for I see to my delight that the plural is called for here! Forgive me, I beseech ye, forgive me my Dickensian reverie!"

"Coco, this is Lady Perdita, Lady Perdita Montresore-Wolfe." Estelle stood between the two aristocrats. "And Lady Perdita, this is my—my dear friend, Dr. Count Francesco von Cockleburg."

"*Enchanté.*" Cockleburg bowed so deeply that his head disappeared between his slightly spread legs. He held this bow a good fifteen seconds; his cheeks were blazing and pouched with blood when at last he began his laborious ascent.

Lady Perdita inclined not her torso, not her head, but her lower lip, baring her tiny teeth. The tip of her nose seemed to lengthen and sharpen. She sailed to the sofa. Estelle sat down beside her. Lisanne and Ellen pulled up chairs. Cockleburg sank into a plump, engulfing ottoman. There was an awkward moment when, compressed by the mighty weight of his nates, the cushion sighed flatulently. Poor Cockleburg blushed to his blue-white roots.

"The von Cockleburgs," Lady Perdita said musingly. "I know all of the old noble families of Europe, but oddly enough, I've never heard of yours. Is it a *new* title?"

"C-c-c-c-c-c-c-c-c-c-c-c-c-cock—" Cockleburg was

spared having to complete his reply by the loud, clattering entrance of Mrs. Nipe with the tea tray. Estelle rose to take it from her (the cook being too obese to lower the tray to the coffee table). Lady Perdita regarded the varlet with frank horror. Nipe returned her stare boldly.

"Thank you, Mrs. Nipe," Estelle said.

With a sullen nod, the cook shuffled from the room.

"Heavens, that woman grows more rude and slatternly with every passing year!" Lady Perdita said. The flaps of her jowls leapt like smacked jelly. "I feel compelled to tell you, Estelle, for I know how naive you are in these matters, that your choice of servants does not reflect well on you. Not at all! No decent English family would ever employ such a female. Why, you should see the head cook at my-uncle-the-duke's country seat, Montresore Palace. A neater, trimmer, cleaner, humbler spinster you'd never hope to meet! And such a fine way with mutton, too!"

Estelle sighed and dropped sugar cubes in the teacups.

"I've heard so much about the glories of Montresore Palace," Cockleburg ventured, "its architecture, its legendary gardens."

His choice of subject was felicitous. Lady Perdita launched into a fervid paean to the palace, guiding her audience verbally through the great entrance hall, the grand dining and ballrooms, the many salons, the bedroom where Queen Elizabeth I had slept, and, after a brief but poetic stop in the scullery, out into the gardens, and the vast oak-lined park.

"*Mon Dieu,* how you make it come alive!" exclaimed Cockleburg. "I believe I should die a happy man if I could see it but once!"

Lady Perdita gathered herself up. "Well, it's open to the public every Tuesday and Thursday," she said.

Cockleburg shrank into his ottoman. He gave Lisanne

a sad, helpless look. She had never seen him so cowed.

"The count is a wonderful tympanist, Aunt Lady Perdita," she said, breaking the silence.

"And poet," said Estelle.

"You should hear him play sometime," Lisanne said.

"And you simply must hear him read," said Estelle.

Cockleburg gave them both grateful smiles.

"I'm afraid I prefer the silent arts," Lady Perdita said.

At six o'clock, the same group regathered around the porch for cocktails. Donald had a business dinner and was spending the night in town. Dave had still not arrived. His lady was peevish, despite a long nap. "Knowing him, he got on the wrong train. He's probably halfway to Miami by now!"

At eight o'clock Dave finally called—from Metuchen. He had gone to Penn Station instead of Grand Central, and that one misstep had led to a dozen others. He was exhausted; he was dehydrated from vomiting; he was spending the night at a Holiday Inn. Estelle wrote down the address, saying she would send a car for him first thing in the morning.

"Didn't I tell you?" said her ladyship, with the pride of an accurate forecast.

They went into dinner. Emboldened by the presence of her ally, Ellen was relentless in her grilling of Cockleburg. She asked him where his poems had been published. Where he had gotten his degree, and when. Whom he knew in Paris. Whom he knew in America besides them. ("Surely we are not your *only* friends?") Where and how he had met Harry. If he—by any chance—had any plans—of any kind—for gainful employment—at any time.

Cockleburg answered her questions evasively but with

a steady, mild courtesy that Lisanne silently applauded. The only time he grew defiant was when Lady Perdita launched a sudden volley at the shih tzu—not just *his* shih tzu, but the entire breed, which she contrasted unfavorably with her own chosen breed, the King Charles spaniel. "The shih tzu," she said (mispronouncing it "*shee* tzu," her noble tongue unable to shape the vulgar syllable *shit*). "Aren't they those ludicrous little creatures with the beards and the smushed-in faces?"—ironically, describing herself. "Now, the King Charles, as I'm sure you know, as indeed the name suggests, has been beloved by English royalty for hundreds of years." Flushing, Cockleburg argued that the shih tzu (he pronounced it "*shit* tzu," with a perhaps unnecessarily loud and guttural emphasis on that final -*t* sound) had been beloved by Tibetan royalty for *thousands* of years. "*Tibetans*," Lady Perdita said. "I should hardly think that's an endorsement."

"Sh-sh-sh-sh-sh-sh-sh-shit—" Cockleburg choked out.

Lisanne waited for him to continue, but to her surprise, he fell silent. Denigration of the shih tzu was to Cockleburg as the red cape is to the bull. Yet even from this most extreme of provocations, he backed away, with a visible effort composing himself, opening and closing his mouth, then opening and closing it again. The effort cost him. He seemed suddenly exhausted—disoriented, even. He barely touched dessert (hot apple pie, his favorite), and his eyes clouded over with what struck Lisanne as dumb confusion. He suffered like a dog, patiently, without knowing why.

Estelle was quiet that night. Several times, she reached out and seized Cockleburg's hand across the table.

And she did not touch a drop of wine. Refilling glasses, Ellen asked her more than once, "Mom, don't you want some wine?" Estelle just shook her head. Each time she refused, her gray eyes sought Cockleburg, his smile and his nod, a subtle, silent exchange. It was an old habit of Lisanne's, counting her mother's drinks. She had never known Estelle to go a night without one.

"He's every bit as bad as I thought he'd be—and worse!" Lady Perdita was saying.

Ellen heartily agreed.

For over three hours now, aunt and niece had been huddled together in the guest cottage. It was clear from their flushed cheeks and restless pacing that the fever of hatred was still too strong upon them to allow them to carry out the stated purpose of their powwow—that being calmly, coolly, rationally to strategize. So far the ladies had been unable to advance beyond frenzied vilifications.

"I fear that my upbringing at the ducal palace did not prepare me to confront so low, so cunning, so *common* a foe," her ladyship remarked.

"But is it not true"—Ellen tried to rally her—"that the noble blood that courses through your veins is the blood of warriors, of conquerors?"

" 'Tis true," her ladyship confirmed. "And conquer I will—you can be sure of that."

Just then, from outside the cottage, there came a panting—a shuffling—a snorting—as of some great approaching beast—and then a series of thuds.

Lady Perdita started. "Who *dares*—?"

Ellen rose. "I *swear*."

Then, in unison, the ladies sang: "Who's *there?*"

In one agile broad jump, Ellen was at the door. She swung it open. There was no one there. She looked to the left. She looked to the right. She looked down.

Curled upon the stoop, in a womb of suitcases and

portmanteaus, lay Dave Wolfe, her uncle, her ladyship's lord.

"Why, Uncle Dave!" Ellen reached down to help him to his feet. He lifted a hand—then let it fall.

"Let me handle this." The short but powerfully stout noblewoman elbowed Ellen aside, then clamped her tiny hands beneath her husband's shoulders and, arms rigid, heaved him to his feet. Her face purpled with the effort.

"There was no one to help me," Dave gasped.

"You don't intend to leave those there, do you?" Her ladyship pointed to the suitcases just outside the open door. "Bring them inside, and be quick about it!"

"Can't it wait, milady? I feel the headache coming on."

"I said, *Be quick about it!*"

It was nothing less than a ducal command. Dave scurried to obey.

"Here, Uncle Dave, I'll help you," Ellen said.

"Thank you, sweetie, bless your heart."

Under the regal eye of her ladyship, now comfortably reseated, Ellen and Dave staggered and groaned beneath the vast load of luggage, all of it stamped with the Montresore coat of arms. Dave was wanner than Ellen had ever seen him—the lingering aftereffect of yesterday's emesis, she guessed. At one point, reeling inside with milady's hatbox, he looked as though he was about to faint. As always, Ellen found it impossible to believe that this weak, soft, timid little valetudinarian was her father's brother. He was inches shorter than her father had been; inches narrower; shades dimmer. Dave had none of her father's bright electric charm, none of his power, grace, and carelessness. "He's the kind of guy who can't decide between a Snickers bar and a Hershey bar—and both are too expensive," was how Donald summed him up. "You just *look* at him and you're pissed off."

As soon as the luggage was shuttled inside, Lady Per-

dita ordered her husband to bed. "Take two aspirin, darling—and stay out of my sight."

The exhausted helminthologist was only too happy to
comply.

No sooner had this first interruption been dispatched
than a second swelled at the door.

Nipe.

"Is it too much to ask for a bit of privacy around here?"
her ladyship demanded querulously.

"Ya better come quick, Ellen," Nipe panted. "Ya better come quick."

Ellen sighed. "What is it now, Mrs. Nipe?"

Turning sideways and sucking in her great gut, the
cook—just barely—squeezed herself through the narrow
doorway. She was wild-eyed and trembling with excitement. "Boy oh boy—have I got a tale to tell!"

"Tell it," Ellen said curtly.

"Man oh man! I never thought I'd live to see—" The
cook's mouth opened vastly, then snapped shut. Her eyes
darted back and forth between Ellen and Lady Perdita,
who had both leaned forward at this tantalizing pause.
"But maybe it ain't my place to be tellin' tales," she said,
with a coy smirk.

Ellen lacked the patience to humor the cook today. She
said, with quiet hauteur, "If you have something to say,
Mrs. Nipe, please say it. *Our* time, at least, is valuable."

Lady P., who was clearly torn between her animosity
toward the varlet and her appetite for gossip, however
unsavory the source, added, "If you have witnessed anything improper, Goody Nipe, anything improper at all, I
command you to reveal it. Painful though it must be for
us to hear, our duty demands it—for duty rules us, as the
monarch rules the serf."

At this rather garbled mandate, Nipe cast all scruples
aside. She shrilled forth: "Improper? I'll say, improper!

Why, I just saw, Miz Ellen, I just saw your"—she hissed
the relation—"sissssstah"—she hissed the name—"Lisssss-
sssanne"—she hissed the sin—"kissssssssannne"—drool-
ing with each sibilation.

"Who?" Ellen said.

"The caretaker, that's who!"

"Mrs. Nipe," Ellen said, "don't you remember what
Mother told you about spying?"

"There's nothing wrong with a bit of spying now and
then," said her ladyship stoutly.

"Oh, but I wasn't spying, I wasn't, I swear it!" said the
cook. "I couldna missed it, not if I'd been blind, deaf,
dumb, and mute! Ya see, I just happened to be passing by
the caretaker's cottage on my way down to the big house,
mindin' my own business, like I always do—" Here,
Goody Nipe was forced to abandon her narrative, to
cough, hawk, hack, wheeze, spit.

Ellen stared at her, aghast.

"Do get on with it," said her ladyship frigidly.

Gasping, the cook continued: "Well, I went walkin' on
by as fast as ever I could when I heard this *sound*"—Nipe
recreated it, with a ghastly pornographic puckering and
smacking of her lips—"and that's when I looked up again
and saw *it*, sure as I'm standin' here. I woulda screamed,
except it—"

"—t'weren't your business," Ellen finished wearily.

"Exactly!" said the cook.

"And then what?" said her ladyship.

"Well, then it just went on and on and on," said the
cook, "I betchya it's *still* goin' on, if you ladies'd care to
come and take a look for yasells."

Lady Perdita rose instantly. "Let's *go!*"

"Lady Perdita, I think it's highly unseemly of us—"
Ellen began.

"Unseemly of *us?* Unseemly of *us?*" In her fury, her ladyship's eyes bulged alarmingly. "Not one vulgar misalliance in the making here, but two! I can see I've arrived in the nick of time." She raised her arm in a strong, ducal gesture. "I said, let's *go!*"

Mrs. Nipe was already out the door, waddling ahead of them.

"Don't look now," Adair said, "but she's back. In the bushes behind you. And she's not alone."

They were sitting on the porch. Ever since the Day of the Birds, as Lisanne now thought of it, they had been meeting here at noon, by unspoken agreement, for iced tea. They hadn't acknowledged this as their secret until they'd been discovered, half an hour before, by Nipe.

"Come on," Adair said, flinging himself on top of her. "Let's give them their money's worth."

"Adair, not again." Giggling, Lisanne tried to push him away.

"Stop laughing," Adair said. "You're ruining our show."

"I can't help it. This is ridiculous. You're going to get yourself fired."

Lisanne could hear the whispers of Lady Perdita and Nipe, as loud as anyone else's speaking voice: "Absolutely shocking! Beyond anything!" And beneath them, another voice, raised now in warning: "Be quiet, for God's sake!"

Ellen? Lisanne went still in Adair's arms.

"That's better." His eyes slid off her, to the right. "Don't look now, but Nipe is coming closer . . . she's out of the bushes. She's at the edge of the yard. . . ."

"Let me up," Lisanne said.

"Chicken," he said. "Not until you cluck like a chicken."

"I said, let me up. I'm serious, Adair. I can't breathe."

He shifted on top of her, but kept her pinned. He said, "Hold still, just a minute longer. I believe they are in retreat." He lifted his head. "Yes, I see them, bouncing away through the trees." He started to ease off her. He was laughing himself now. Then he looked down at her, and made a startled sound. "Don't look so scared," he said. "Why do you look so scared?"

Lisanne felt a stab of something deep in her, hot and sharp, that could have been disgust—that should have been disgust—only it was desire. It was easy to confuse them. She saw she'd been confusing them for years. They hit you in the same place, the lower stomach, only desire hit harder. It rose like disgust, only it rose faster. It sickened your heart, like disgust, only the surrender it demanded was more abject.

> "*. . . but most she loathed the hour*
> *When the thick-moted sunbeam lay*
> *Athwart the chambers, and the day*
> *Was sloping toward his western bower.*
> *Then, said she, 'I am very dreary,*
> *He will not come,' she said;*
> *She wept, 'I am aweary, aweary,*
> *O God, that I were dead!' "*

Estelle was used to tears by now, and didn't raise the hand that could have flattened them away. Her eyes ached and her skin stung in the usual way, but the taste in her mouth was sweet. Her heart had carved itself into these ripe slices. She clipped a lily and laid it, long and slim, in the basket by the others.

"Dear lady, have I—? You are—?"

"I'm happy. That's all." How could she explain it? Where would she begin? Once upon a time, there were things in the corners of my room I didn't dare to look at too closely. . . . "Read that again, will you? You read it so beautifully."

He floated on a lawn chair in her garden's lake of sun. He raised the volume, and in a deep, canorous voice, began at the beginning:

> "With blackest moss the flower-plots
> Were thickly crusted, one and all. . . ."

Estelle moved past the spider flowers. Tall, feathering Joe Pye weeds blew her purple kisses.

> "Unlifted was the clinking latch;
> Weeded and worn the ancient thatch
> Upon the lonely moated grange.
> She only said, 'My life is dreary,
> He cometh not,' she said. . . ."

Estelle paused. She was turning to ask why he had stopped, when she saw two heads, and the tip of a third, bobbing above the garden gates.

Estelle sighed, and closed her eyes, and willed the heads away. She heard the gate creak. When she opened her eyes, her cook, her sister-in-law, and her daughter were fanning out before her, their backs turned to the lounging count. For a long, dreadful moment, they stood in silence, and then abruptly, they all began to shout.

"Ladies, *please!*" Estelle said. "One at a time."

Perhaps in deference to her superior rank, Ellen and Nipe allowed Lady Perdita the first solo. The Kiss: her ladyship spared Estelle not a single shameful detail. Exposition was followed by commentary, the noblewoman segueing into a lecture on sin the likes of which had not been heard in any garden since God confronted Adam and Eve in Eden.

Her ladyship stepped back, handing the floor over to Ellen.

"Mother, I demand that you dismiss the caretaker." With these words Ellen snapped her fingers and whirled about in a brief but stunning flamenco. "For though Lisanne doesn't know any better, surely *he* does. And to take advantage of her, in the way that he has, constitutes a violation of your trust that *must* not go unpunished."

And now the spotlight swerved to Nipe. Nipe spoke: "I always knew that gal of yours was tetched in the head"— in vivid illustration, Nipe touched her own head—"but I didn't know she was a hussy, too."

At the word *hussy,* Estelle stopped listening—though Nipe went on for twenty-three minutes, developing her argument with Euclidean rigor.

When all three ladies had stated, and restated, their case, they exchanged nods and began, bizarrely, to circle Estelle.

"So, Estelle?"

"Well, Mother?"

"Whadya say, Miz Wolfe?"

Over this swirl of shoulders, Cockleburg rose and steadied Estelle with his smile.

"What do I say?" she said. "What do I say? I say you're interrupting, ladies, that's what I say! The count was reading 'Mariana' to me. Count, read on! Read on, Count, read on!"

Loath to waste even the second it would have taken to grab up his volume, the count threw back his head, as if to gargle the words, and recited from memory:

"Old faces glimmer'd through the doors,
Old footsteps trod the upper floors,
Old voices called her from without. . . ."

. . . in a voice that soared above the protests of Ellen, Nipe, and Lady P.

". . . She only said, 'My life is dreary,
He cometh not,' she said;
She said, 'I am aweary, aweary,
I would that I were dead!'"

11

As the days went by, and their forces made no headway, Ellen wearied of the battle—or, rather, wearied of her ally. The companionship of her aunt began to seem too high a price to pay even for victory. And victory grew more remote with every passing hour. Despite the efforts of her ladyship (or, perhaps, because of them), it looked as though Cockleburg was here to stay—but better he, thought Ellen, better he than Lady Perdita. Not only was this a case of the cure's being worse than the disease—the cure wasn't working.

Though a proud and imperious matron in her own right, Ellen had been forced by her aunt into virtual slavery (having replaced Dave as that goddess's hierodule of choice). Command followed command, all trumpeted out in that foghorn bray. Not to obey was somehow not an option, and soon Ellen was shuttling back and forth to town on an endless series of errands: hemming her ladyship's dresses, dry-cleaning her ladyship's turbans, reheeling her ladyship's pumps, restringing her ladyship's beads. One dismal Wednesday, she spent eight hours scouring the gourmet shops of Westchester for a certain brand of imported British marmalade ("If you expect me to eat your domestic pap, you're daft, my gel!") only to slink home empty-handed and be sent out again the next morning.

In the meantime, Lisanne was growing ever more ardent in her championship of the count. Who was to say he wasn't for real? Remember how they'd all scoffed at his claim of being a ninja? As soon as his buttock had healed, hadn't he expressed his reluctance to impose on Estelle any further? Didn't Ellen see that it was only Estelle's pleading that kept him staying on here? Did Ellen know that it was thanks to him that Estelle had stopped drinking? Hadn't he, by this amazing feat alone, earned his bed and board and wardrobe, and at the same time proved his honor? For if he were a fortune hunter, wouldn't he have preferred her drunk? *All women are tight except the drunks,* didn't their father used to say?

"How did he manage that?" Ellen asked. She was ashamed to admit that she hadn't even noticed Estelle wasn't drinking.

"He told her he was depressed about his weight gain," Lisanne said. "Then he upped the ante by saying he'd been having chest pains. He confessed that he'd tried several times to diet on his own—and failed miserably. Of course she said she'd do anything. So he suggested this: a buddy system. No alcohol for her, no sweets or fats for him."

"Are you saying, then, that the depression, the chest pains, were all just a ruse?"

"Brilliant, don't you think?" Lisanne said.

"Brilliant, yes," Ellen said, and then added with a trace of her old fighting spirit, "and a chilling illustration of his guile. Doesn't it scare you how easily he manipulates her?"

"Mother brings out the guile in us all," Lisanne said. "But there's good guile and there's bad guile. Let's not kick a gift horse in the face."

So now he was a gift horse, was he? Ellen was willing to concede some of Lisanne's pro-Cockleburgian points, but this was going too far. She said, "A gift horse who may well trot off with twenty mil!"

"Oh, Ellen! They haven't even fucked!"

"*Fucked?* Honestly, Lisanne, how *disgusting!*"

"Look at it this way," Lisanne said. "The sooner we accept Coco, for better or worse—"

"For richer or poorer," Ellen said, "more likely poorer."

"—the sooner Lady Perdita will go home."

This was a well-timed, well-aimed thrust. Ellen had just spent the entire morning at the post office shipping presents to Alaric and Oribel.

By the fourth week of her aunt's visit, Ellen was not only prepared to accept defeat, she was eager for it—so eager, in fact, that she caught herself rooting for Cockleburg. Yes, there were moments now when she actually longed to see him stand and fight like a man and beat back the berserker, Lady Perdita.

And then one night—one sweltering night at the end of July—he dropped the A-bomb. Or rather, Lady Perdita, in a series of tactical errors, dropped it on herself.

They were having a barbecue on the back porch. Donald presided over the grill, flipping steaks and drumsticks. Lady Perdita sat ramrod straight in a thronelike wicker chair, her child-size legs dangling. The rest of them—Ellen, Lisanne, Dave, Estelle, and Cockleburg—slumped about in various stages of heat prostration. Estelle's mutts and Cockleburg's Queen were locked away upstairs, Dave being violently allergic to all dogs, the base-born and the high—spaniels alone excepted. Every now and then, a faint piteous howl wafted down to them.

"Don't you find it odd," Lady Perdita began, addressing Donald (for it was Donald who now accompanied her in these nightly anti-Cockleburgian duets), "terribly, terribly odd, Donald, when a man hasn't married by the time he's forty?"

"You're damn right I find it odd." Donald caught this ball and ran with it. "Odd—and *queer,* if ya know what I mean, and I think you do. If a man hasn't hitched himself by the time he's forty, I'd say he's one of two things: a fag or a gigolo." And he grimaced over at Cockleburg, the grimace dislodging from the groove in his upper lip a droplet of sweat, which splashed onto the grill with a hiss.

"Why, that's utterly preposterous, Donald," Ellen roused herself to say.

"Name one over-forty bachelor who ain't a fag," Donald said, "or a gigolo."

Ellen thought. She was aware of the seconds ticking by, as though she were on a game show. She was silent so long, Donald sneered in triumph.

"Mr. Sneed in 7-A!" she burst out. "That nice white-haired gent who works at the Fashion Institute."

"*At the Fashion Institute,* Ellen," Donald said. "I rest my case. Old Sneed's a fag as sure as I'm standing here with this fork in my hand!" He raised high the giant fork. In this pose, redder than ever by the light of the fire, Donald looked like a suburban Beelzebub. "Why the hell do you think men get married?" he asked. "Not for sex, that's for damn sure! They can get that from any hooker." His gaze landed on Lisanne. "No, men get married for one reason, and for one reason only: so people won't say they're a fag." His eyes swerved to Cockleburg.

"A fascinating thesis, Donald," Lisanne said. "You're

on to something publishable here." Her mocking laugh would have put a lesser homophobe in his place. How beautiful she looks tonight, Ellen thought, even in her plain white shirt, her plain old jeans. How terrifying her beauty would be if it ever got a worthy setting—a red dress, say, like the Norma Kamali hanging in the back of Ellen's closet. Ellen had bought it wishing she were someone else. She couldn't carry off that red. But Lisanne could. Should she lend it to her? Give it to her? No.

"Your uncle-the-duke didn't marry until he was forty-four, did he, milady?" Dave ventured in a voice muffled by the white gauze surgical mask he wore at every barbecue to protect himself from the carcinogenic fumes of burning fat. Ever since Harry's death, a morbid obsession with his health had replaced worms as the ruling passion of Dave's life.

Milady swung her shoulders round to face him in a violent movement that dislodged her turban. "But he *did* marry. My-uncle-the-duke *did* marry. Didn't he? *Didn't he?* That's the important thing, damn you!"

Dave cringed on his stool. With tiny trembling hands, his helpmate rearranged her turban. And then she sprang at Cockleburg. "How old are *you*, Doctah?" (As a symbol of her contempt for his "ludicrous pretensions to nobility," Lady P. pointedly addressed Cockleburg by his academic title only.) "If you don't mind my asking."

"Not at all," said Cockleburg. "Fifty-one."

"I would have said sixty-one," said milady.

"I would have said forty-one," said Estelle—her first words of the evening.

"I would have said thirty-one," said Lisanne.

If milady's feet had reached the ground, she would have stamped them. "Why is it that you've never married, Doctah? If you don't mind my asking."

There was a silence. The meat snapped, and sizzled, burning on.

"I'd like a drumstick, please, if they're ready, Donald," Estelle said in a high, thin voice.

"I mean, it's rather odd, isn't it? Rather queer, isn't it? That you never married, I mean. If you don't mind my saying." Milady's nostrils quivered. She scented something—something good.

Cockleburg was silent—dreadfully silent. His blue head bowed. He was rather pale around the mouth. Everyone was staring at him now—except Lisanne. Estelle's eyes held to him as though tracking something in a fall. And for a moment, the bright blue eyes he raised to hers were reproachful—but for a moment only. Ellen's heart turned tightly with him in his corner. He had been attacked and taunted for weeks now, and she had believed that mask of easy patient amiability to be his true, his real, face.

"I suppose you just never found—" Lady Perdita began.

"As a matter of fact, I was married, Lady Perdita," Cockleburg said. "Since you ask. For twenty-one years."

Milady's cheeks consumed her jeering smile.

Estelle slid her chair closer to Cockleburg's. Her hand disappeared beneath the picnic table. Ellen imagined its blind, batlike flight through the darkness there—to his.

It was obvious that Lady Perdita was regretting this tack but was determined to brazen it out anyway. "So you're a—a *divorcé*, then," she said. "My word, Doctah, how secretive you've been about your sordid past. Ha ha," she laughed bravely.

"No—not a divorcé," Cockleburg said.

"Not a—"

Don't make it easy on her, Count, Ellen thought.

He didn't.

"Not a—*widower?*" Lady P. at last blasted out.

"I'm afraid so," said Cockleburg. "It's an awful word, isn't it? That's why I call myself a bachelor."

"When did she—?" Donald, with uncharacteristic delicacy, did not complete his question.

"Sandrine," said Cockleburg. "This winter. In Paris." Cockleburg's face was set and his voice steady. Only this rare brachylogy betrayed the depth of his emotion.

"Of?" Dave said eagerly.

"Cancer."

"Sweet Jesu." Dave blanched. "What kind?" he began. "What were her symptoms?"

"Shut up, for God's sake!" Milady abruptly terminated the ghoulish inquiry. She turned stiffly to Cockleburg, though she did not meet his eye. "I'm terribly sorry to hear that, Doctah."

On her mother's face, Ellen saw something like love. It started in the eyes, then rippled out in widening circles. "Here, dearest Count," Estelle said tenderly, holding out to him a napkined basket—"have a baked potato."

The count inclined his head in silent gratitude. He parted the folds of the napkin. The movements of his slender hands were beautiful, and dignified. Ellen would always remember how humbling he was at that moment: this absurd little man, with his deep sadness, gracefully spearing a baked potato.

After the barbecue, Lady Perdita retreated to the guest cottage. She was reeling from Cockleburg's revelation. Her parting glance at Ellen grimly conceded the shattering blow it had dealt her. She had to get Dave to bed—he was on the verge of a panic attack—but she insisted, in a whispered aside, that Ellen and Donald meet her in half an hour. Reluctantly, Ellen agreed.

Passing through the kitchen on his way out of the house, Dave paused by the medicine cabinet and downed a dozen pills: two aspirin, two vitamins from a jar clearly labeled "For Pre-Menstrual Tension," minerals, amino acids, and—before Ellen could stop him—one of the dogs' heartworm pills.

Arriving at the guest cottage, the Prawls were deafened by an aria of rage.

"I don't believe it for a minute!" Lady Perdita shouted. "Not for a second!" Her glabella, her dewlaps, even the bristles of her giant moles—every square inch of that ducal epidermis was twitching with malevolence. "Actually, I did believe it for a second," she emended. "That second has passed."

"What are you saying, Aunt Lady Perdita?" Ellen asked warily.

"What am I—? Heavens! You're as big a gull as your mother—that poor simpleton." Her ladyship gave a rare shake of her massive head. "Don't you see?"

"No, I don't," Ellen said.

"By God, I get what she's driving at!" Donald nodded in agreement as the embattled dame disgorged her appalling thesis: "*He never had a wife—dead or alive! I'd bet Dave's life on it!*"

Ellen had not expected quite this pitch of viperous cynicism. "To be frank," she began—

"Please be frank," said milady.

"To be frank, I think it's incredibly low of you to suggest that."

"Low of me?" said her ladyship. "*Of me?* So you're under his spell, too!"

"Hardly," Ellen said. "I just can't imagine anyone making up such a thing."

"You can be so goddamn naive, Ellen," Donald said.

"People will do anything for money. Lie, steal, cheat, shoot themselves in the buttock, kill—"

"Kill!"

"Yes, kill!" Donald himself looked easily capable of killing at that moment. "Cockleburg's a fraud—and for all we know, a murderer, too!—but one thing's for certain: he's no fool. He's hit upon the most potent aphrodisiac in the world as far as your mother's concerned—a dead wife! Oh yeah! One dead wife is worth a thousand words—a thousand friggin' poems! A dead wife! He knew that would open your mother's heart to him—open her heart, her legs, *and her bank account.* So he produced one!"

"I doubt he would have mentioned her if Lady Perdita hadn't wormed it out of him," Ellen said. "He could have *produced* her, as you put it, weeks ago—but he didn't, did he?"

"I daresay he's just been waiting for the right moment," Lady Perdita said. "And I gave it to him, yes, I did. Score one for Cockleburg."

"Come to think of it," Ellen said (with every word warming to Cockleburg), "the first time I met him, he said something about Paris becoming painful for him. This must be it. Poor Cockleburg."

"Poor Cockleburg?" Donald repeated in disbelief. "Poor Cockleburg, *my ass!*"—which was, by the way, now quivering with pyrophoric intensity. "That only confirms that he's been planning this all along, the dastard!"

Donald would have railed on, but just then, Lady P. lifted a finger to silence him. They heard a gasping. Then a scream—"*Aaaaaarg!*" Then rapid footsteps. The door to the cottage's living room crashed open, and Dave weaved into view. He stared at them with popping eyes. "I'm having an aneurysm!" he panted.

"You naughty boy, you've been reading the *Merck*

Manual again, haven't you?" Lady Perdita turned to the Prawls in exasperation. "Every time I take that dreadful book away from him he goes right out and buys a new one."

"Help me, milady!" Dave slid to the floor.

"Oh, for chrissakes!" Donald ejaculated. He had no patience for Dave's hypochondria, which he regarded as extremely unmanly—just a step above sodomy, in fact.

"Darling, you're just having a panic attack." Lady Perdita went over to the writhing helminthologist, knelt, and lifted his head onto her lap. It disappeared there between her lowering breasts. She looked over at Donald and Ellen. "This always happens when he hears about someone dying of cancer—real *or* fictitious!"

Dave's voice (muffled by her cleavage) rose in a plaintive wail. "I know panic! I live with panic! And this is not panic! I tell you, I'm dying, milady! I'm dying!"

"Get a grip on yourself, man!" said Donald.

Ellen's initial nervous amusement had sharpened to alarm. What if he'd poisoned himself with the heartworm pill? Ellen felt compelled to mention it.

"Maybe it's not an aneurysm, Uncle Dave," she said. "Maybe it's that heartworm pill you took."

"The *what?*" Dave now struggled into a sitting position.

Behind him, Lady Perdita mouthed, Shut up!

"The heartworm pill," Ellen said falteringly. "I saw you swallow it on your way out of the house. . . ."

"Call an ambulance, milady," Dave whispered.

"If they're good for dogs, darling, I'm sure they're good for humans."

"*Call an ambulance right now!*"

Lady Perdita rose to her feet. She looked exhausted. Ellen almost pitied her.

Dave slumped to the floor. He appeared to have fainted.

"I should never have married a commoner," milady said wistfully. "You know, the Earl of Curle almost made me an offer . . . almost." She sighed. "You two go on. I'll take care of him."

Back at the big house, Lisanne informed them, with a smile, that Estelle and Cockleburg had retired to her bedroom. With a wrenching groan, Donald lurched off to eavesdrop. Ellen considered joining him at the bedroom door, but her heart wasn't in it. To Ellen, dead Sandrine had done more than doom their cause: she had removed it altogether. She saw Cockleburg now for what he had always been, beneath the pedantic humor, the courtliness, the ludicrous affectations and mannerisms: a wounded man.

Wearing a long white nightgown, staring at herself in the mirror over the bed, Estelle remembered the night, long ago, when she had felt death for the first time—felt it buried in her happiness. The terror had driven her out of bed, to the armchair by the window, where she had watched Harry sleep on, watched only seconds before he cried out, "I'm scared." The next day, he said he'd dreamed of a ghost—an old woman in white.

She told Harry now: Every hateful word I never said is my love letter to you. How disciplined her love for him had been, after all. Now she wanted freedom from it, vengeance, just one minute of vengeance for all those years of love.

The count reached for her. He said, "You remind me of someone."

Always, she wanted to know, Who? Who?

He said, "Someone I've been waiting for."

This pleasure, it seemed, she'd been earning all her life.

She lay down beside him to comfort him, the way she comforted her dogs when they whimpered in their sleep: Yes, yes, my darlings, you're safe now, kissing eyelids, noses, lips, wondering about the lives they'd lived before she found them, before she saved them.

"Dearest, what do you think of this as a possible theme?" Estelle read aloud: " 'Theme number forty-nine: Be a Character! Plan a merry, memory-creating, theatrical evening for two! Design and sew period costumes for both of you! Whatever character you choose, spend the entire evening seducing him as that character! Some engine-revvin' possibilities: You could be Anne Boleyn and he could be lusty King Harry. Or you could be Marie Antoinette and he could be King Louis XVI.' " Estelle paused. "The second one's better, don't you think? Because of the French angle. I've begged Coco to speak French to me, but he's so shy about it. Maybe role playing would free him."

"Three out of those four characters were beheaded," Lisanne pointed out.

"Don't be so literal. Dare to dream, for goodness' sakes!" This was, in fact, the title of the chapter: Dare to Dream, Pick a Theme. One of the more mundane of the fifty-two themes was "Give Him a Massage: Use a musk-scented massage oil and spend at least three hours massaging him! Save the best for last—and listen to his engine give a monster-truckin' roar!!!" Rather than buy a book, Estelle had asked Lisanne to teach her. To which end, Estelle was now stretched out face down on her bed, with Lisanne's hands clenched around her pale, slim calves. Lisanne had been demonstrating the long, smooth strokes of Swedish massage when Estelle had reached for *Rev His Engine: How to Make Your Man Your Slave,* conveniently placed, as always these days, on her bedside table. Estelle had underlined whole pages in yellow, Lisanne saw; she had written notes in the margins, little phrases like, *How true!* and *This is me!* and *Yes—compliments are so important!* At first Lisanne had dismissed the book as ridiculous, but very quickly she had come to fear its grip on her mother's imagination. *Rev His Engine* had become Estelle's bible ever since Ellen had passed it along to her, two weeks ago.

What could Ellen have been thinking? For to give Estelle such a book, it struck Lisanne, was like giving sleeping pills to the suicidal.

"Frankly, Mom, I don't think Coco needs period costumes—period. Let's face it: his wardrobe is more than flamboyant enough as it is."

"And then, of course, there's always Rhett and Scarlett," Estelle went on.

Lisanne was trying to imagine Coco's face upon being handed a black mustache and a Confederate pistol, and told to dress up as Rhett. Probably the same gallant expression with which he had popped the fifty-two balloons tied to the handlebars of his bicycle to free the love notes inside them. The same gallant expression with which he had looked up and read, I LUV YOU, COCO, printed in white plumes across the sky. The same gallant expression in which Lisanne had tried fearfully, and to her surprise, failed to detect the slightest trace of irony, or impatience, or even bafflement.

By midnight that night, Harry had said, *I wanted to get in a car and drive ten thousand miles.*

Lisanne looked on in a kind of terror, as her mother bravely lit her candles and screwed her new red light bulbs in the lamps beside the bed.

"You know, Mom," she said, "it's pretty clear that Coco's engine is already revved—already roaring—like a rocket taking off! What I'm saying," she went on "is, *you don't have to do all this stuff!*"

"I know that." Estelle sounded impatient, but when she turned around and sat up, Lisanne saw that her eyes were amused. Lisanne's eyes lowered away from her mother's and clung to the safe curve of lips. It was mercy and fear that had always kept her from looking her mother in the eye, that old mercy and fear that followed her like years, and that now kept her from looking any creature in the eye—even a dog.

"Let me show you something," Estelle said.

Lisanne allowed Estelle to lead her into the dressing room and sit her down at the vanity table before the mirror.

"Let me try something," Estelle said.

Lisanne closed her eyes. She felt herself floating in a slow, melting flow, away from some familiar shore. As if from a great distance, she heard her mother's hands tapping out notes on the glass jars and pots of paint lined up on the table.

When Lisanne opened her eyes, Estelle was reverently removing the top of a golden tube of lipstick. The glistening blue-red head emerged.

"This is your red," Estelle said. "*Trust me.*" Her hand trembled as it slid the bright wax through the air.

"Look," Estelle said. "*Look at you.*"

• • •

"Goddamn it!"

The blasphemy flung Ellen from a fitful sleep. With a sigh, she sat up in bed and looked down upon her sleeping spouse.

Donald was having another nightmare. Night after night, these last two weeks, he had rent the darkness with his cries of odium: a sequence of blasphemies, imprecations, and incoherent impeachments so unvarying it was as though his tortured subconscious were reeling them off from a script, the lines of which he never recalled come morning. Ellen couldn't help but be nostalgic for the tepid "Thus's" and "By the same tokens" of the boardroom dreams he had dreamed in the past.

The blasphemy was usually followed with a plea—or was it a command?—to the same Lord to damn the sworn foe. As if on cue, the curse came now—*"Goddamn him!"*—and Ellen sighed again.

If there had been any doubt in her mind as to the identity of the nemesis to whom the pronoun referred, that doubt would have been dispelled by what invariably came next: a name, stuttered out in a dozen fragmentary variations, in a voice so curdled with hatred it made Ellen's blood run cold.

"Cocka-clocka-clugabug—"

In a sudden upward heave of his buttocks—a sort of butterfly stroke—Donald seized another square foot of the bed for himself, and Ellen teetered on the edge left to her. Night after night, these last two weeks, she had been kicked clear onto the floor as Donald thrashed beneath the weight of his incubus.

In these last two weeks, Donald had stood alone upon the battlefield, deserted not only by his quondam allies but also by his victorious enemy. And yet still he fought on until Ellen began to fear for his sanity—*and* for his poor buttocks, which worked a double shift now, quivering by day and by night.

Why doesn't he give up? she wondered. Even so valiant a warrior as Lady Perdita had known enough to cut her losses, and withdraw (though not without a few last impotent Parthian volleys). Estelle's radiance at the breakfast table, the morning after the fateful barbecue, had quite simply withered milady where she sat (before her, uneaten, a piece of toast smeared with the British marmalade Ellen had at last managed to procure at the cost of thirty dollars per jar—and, temporarily, her own sanity). That very afternoon, Lady Perdita commanded Estelle to purchase two first-class tickets to London on a flight leaving the next day. The noblewoman gave as an excuse for the abrupt departure Dave's urgent summons by the Society of British Helminthologists, which august body (she claimed) had begged him to replace a keynote speaker in an upcoming conference called "The Tapeworm Scolex." "I would never forgive myself," she told Estelle, "were I to deny the Society in this dark hour of their need." The desperation of the British helminthologists notwithstanding, it was a retreat. Ellen knew it, and Lady Perdita knew it.

But Donald did not give up. Just this evening, he had returned to Bedford from the city apoplectic at yet another outrage. Although, come to think of it, perhaps he had raved about this same one last week as well (the nightly jeremiads had begun to blur in Ellen's mind). He had been informed by his alarmed accountant that Estelle had lately been withdrawing large amounts of cash. "Cash!" Donald screamed several times. "Cash!" Thousands upon thousands of dollars in crisp, new cash. "What the hell does the old dame need with all that cash?" he screamed.

"Donald, lower your voice!" Ellen pleaded, fearful that his maddened howling would penetrate through the ceiling to Estelle's bedroom just upstairs.

Her plea was ignored. At the utmost power of his stupendous lungs, Donald ranted on: "I repeat—what does the old dame need with all that cash? She has credit cards, don't she?"

"But she never uses them." This was true. As many times as they had shopped together, Ellen had not once seen her mother employ plastic. Credit cards made her uneasy, Estelle said. She preferred the literalness of cash.

"Why does she need so much of it?" Suspicion had narrowed Donald's close-set eyes to slits—Ellen marveled that he could see out of them. "What the hell is she hoping to buy, god*damn* it? A husband?"

"Oh Donald!" Ellen tried to reason with him as he stamped about the room. "You know all too well that money confuses Mother. It always has. She probably just lost track—"

"When it doesn't add, it doesn't add!" Donald's voice now quieted to a rasp more ghastly in its dark threat and purpose than even his fiercest roar. "But you can bet that tight little ass of yours—"

(Even in the extremity of the moment, Ellen was not ungratified by this tribute.)

"—that Cockleburg's behind this! And I'm gonna get to the bottom of it! Oh *yeah!* No matter what low brand of knavery he's involved in—and I have my suspicions—"

(The wildest of these, Donald had already shared with the incredulous Ellen: drug dealing!)

"—I, Donald Patrick Prawl, am gonna get to the bottom of it if it's the last goddamn thing I ever do!"

(As it well might be, Ellen thought, with a worried glance at the dangerous venous swellings at his temples.)

It was ten of two in the morning. The clock's luminous

eye shed a faint green glow onto Donald's mottled cheek and twisted mouth; onto his fists, clenched upon the pillow; onto his *anger*. With another sigh, Ellen reached down and smoothed the matted hair back from the hot, damp brow. Then she lay down on her sliver of mattress. But her mind was racing, and she couldn't sleep.

Ellen took a deep breath and tried to think of something peaceful. She pictured herself lying in a meadow, combing the grass for four-leaf clovers. She saw herself walking across that grassy meadow. She saw herself running across it. She saw herself riding across it. Then she saw a close-up of her face, contorted in terror, as the horse threw her to the ground.

Ellen started. She felt she was choking. She couldn't bear to breathe this air. Donald's anger seemed to fill the room, like the smell of roasting meat.

"I've got to get out of here," she said aloud.

It occurred to her that in all the thousands of nights she'd spent in this house, she had never once walked out into one. And it was so easy, after all: the generous night just opened and received her. The darkness was at its deepest hour. Ellen could sense all the unseen, secret lives it held, swelling and thickening close beside her. She could feel all the silent multiplying. Only the grass was cool. Passing beneath her mother's window, Ellen glanced up and saw the pale curtains shudder against pure black. The red light of the red light bulbs, the red teardrops of the candles—all extinguished now.

In a last spasm of spite, Ellen had given Estelle *Rev His Engine: How to Make Your Man Your Slave*—figuring that if anything could stop the new romance dead in its tracks, it was that book. But so far this particular slave had borne, without so much as a whimper of protest, each new lash of the O'Boylean whip. If anything was needed to convince Ellen finally of Cockleburg's sincerity, it was his grace under the onslaught of balloons, and love notes, and picnics beneath the stars.

Then again, Ellen reflected, not every man was like Donald.

Ellen walked toward the pond. She skirted the hedges and circled past the tennis court. She was about to go back inside when she caught a floating scrap of laughter. Waves of silence rippled in its wake. And then again, she heard it—laughter. And faintly—taunting—music, too.

It was as if the night had swung shut before her.

Creeping close by the bushes to hide herself, Ellen moved forward, her progress so painful and so slow she might have been climbing ropes toward the sounds.

At last she reached the caretaker's cottage, rising on its hill. From where she squatted, Ellen had to tilt her head to see them: Adair and Lisanne, framed high above her on the porch. Lisanne was in the hammock; Adair watched her from the sofa, holding a guitar on his knee. He strummed a few chords, and sang a few lines from a song that must have been a joke from the way Lisanne was laughing, laughing with a purpose Ellen had never seen in her before, laughing as she lifted a hand to her hair in a movement that was both shy and vain. She seemed brand-new to Ellen—brand-new, and readied for ruin.

Something flowed between them, and spilled out into the darkness, into Ellen's eyes.

For long minutes, Ellen watched them. Her mind emptied.

She must have fallen into a trance, she realized later. Because when she at last became aware of the rustling and the panting in the bushes close behind her, it was too late: its source was virtually upon her.

Oh God. Was it some large animal?

Yes. She could feel its breath upon her neck.

Nipe!

Ellen froze. Her heart tipped over, like a bottle, and in a hot slide its shame poured out.

Just outside her mother's dressing room, Lisanne hesitated.

Last night, when she had met him on the porch, the first thing Adair said was "How pretty you look."

It was for this, of course, that Estelle had wanted her to leave the lipstick on.

And it was for this that she had allowed herself to be persuaded.

He looked right at her lips and said, "How pretty you look."

And immediately Lisanne had lifted a hand and dragged it across her mouth.

It must have seemed to him a childish gesture—or worse: defiant, perverse.

He had looked right at her lips—for her lips had given his eyes no choice—and said it: "How pretty you look."

Lisanne remembered how her father used to say exactly this to the women who turned their faces up to him. His charm did not bury his contempt, or disguise it. It was contempt that gave his charm its bright electric charge.

The women would turn their soft painted faces up to his eyes, and his eyes would descend upon them like booted feet.

"One compliment," her father would say, "and they're on their backs." When he spoke of women, his face and voice had been voluptuous, not with passion but with disgust: the only emotion in which he truly could be said to wallow. He often would speak of women to Lisanne, and always as though she herself would not become one.

When Adair looked at her lips and said, "How pretty you look," he reminded her of her father, but only because she reminded herself of her mother.

And not just her mother. Her father's other women, too. And Ellen. All the women she had ever spied on at their mirrors. And not just mirrors—any shining surface that gave them back themselves. Women pausing before store windows to pat their hair. Women pulling out their compacts to powder their cheeks, or leaning over sinks in bathrooms and mascara-ing their lashes. Women browsing through cosmetics at Lord & Taylor, trying on new lipsticks, with the foolish, earnest, satisfied expressions of dogs scratching themselves.

Lisanne never wore makeup, but she liked to linger in Cosmetics just to marvel at these creatures, so lovely, so hopeful, so oblivious in their captivity.

This morning, though, she had found herself sneaking to the mirror—sneaking was the only word for it—behind her own back to her own face.

Her features seemed to pant in happy surprise. Her eyes descended on them, one by one: chin, mouth, nose, cheeks; rising slowly till they met themselves.

Lisanne backed away—first from the mirror in her bedroom, then from the mirror in the hall; from every mirror in the house, in fact, except for the mirrors in her mother's dressing room, at the threshold of which she now stood, hesitating. She wanted, had wanted all morning long, to try that lipstick on again. The surprise of this small vanity almost made her turn away, would have made her turn away if it hadn't occurred to her that her reaction to the vanity was far more vain than the vanity itself.

Lisanne swung open the door of the dressing room and marched down the three stairs into the eye of the mirrors, aware with every marching step she took of every marching step she took, aware of herself being aware of herself, until she was her own jeering audience of thousands.

She approached herself in four different mirrors, from four different directions.

All her eyes were on her now.

It must have seemed forever to him, she thought later, all that time he waited to be seen.

Although, actually, it couldn't have been more than fifteen seconds before she saw him, kneeling on the floor beside the dresser—saw him, and almost died of shame. She felt as though he'd caught her in some dirty, furtive, private act—as, perhaps, he had. And later, it was easy to imagine how he must have interpreted the disgust upon her face in that moment, in the agony of her inflamed self-consciousness.

But Lisanne recovered herself with a smile. It didn't seem at all odd that she should find him here, in her mother's dressing room, on his knees before an opened drawer. After all, he was sleeping with her mother in her mother's bedroom just beyond the open door. Nor did it seem odd when, drawing closer, she saw that the drawer was full of bras and cash, tangled in a crazy growth—cash curled up in cups of bras, climbing over lace, sprouting from satin. Not even when she saw from the neat green stacks beside him on the floor that he'd been counting it—not even then did it seem odd. Not even when that face she thought she knew swallowed itself and disappeared—all stretched jaw, and mouth, and teeth, and glistening throat—not even that seemed odd. And when she looked into his eyes, and knew that he was stealing, that was the least odd of all.

PART
III

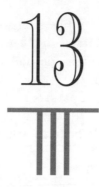

13

Lisanne turned and ran out of her mother's dressing room, out of the bedroom, out of the house.

Most people never ran; most people never had to. Only criminals and mothers ran like this—to escape someone, to save someone—because they had no choice. We have spent the last ten thousand years giving ourselves that choice. A human being running is ridiculous—threatened and shamed by every other creature on the earth. Start with fear and shame, Lisanne thought, and ten thousand years later you get people on the moon. And yet this was what she'd been after her whole life: a state of movement so perfect, and so pure, that mind, memory, imagination, years, all fall away.

"Hi, Mom. How was the hospital?"

"Wonderful! Ian's walking without a walker. And how was your afternoon?"

"Fine."

Ellen had had a miserable afternoon. She had spent it with two strangers: herself and Donald, as preserved in "the Donald File," which she had disinterred from her bottom bureau drawer.

"Well, I guess I'll go upstairs and change my things. It was so hot in the city." (Read: I guess I'll go upstairs and find Cocovich. I can't bear to spend even seven hours away from him.)

"Fine."

"Nothing's wrong, is it?"

"Of course not."

"You seem so—"

"I'm just tired," Ellen said. In her sadness, Estelle had looked anxiously for sadness in everyone around her. Happy, she looked anxiously for happiness. Now, anything less than a show of ecstatic high spirits elicited from her a frantic and unbearable tenderness. "Didn't get much sleep last night," Ellen said.

"You mustn't drink so much Tab! All that caffeine—" Estelle wrung her hands.

"It's not the Tab, Mom." Ellen waved an arm in dismissal.

Estelle followed her wave to the foot of the stairs beyond the kitchen door. "I'll be down in just a bit, then," she said, hesitating.

"Take your time, Mother."

With one last worried glance (as though Ellen might hang herself in the interval), Estelle went upstairs.

Ellen had begun "the Donald File" the morning after her first date with Donald. In the three and a half years that led up to his proposal, hardly a day had passed in which she had not added to it, updated it, or referred to it. The file consisted of four manila folders filled with letters from, and pictures of, Patti Jean, his old girlfriend (which

Ellen had with great stealth and cunning pilfered from Donald's drawers); monthly graphs plotting out his moods in different-colored inks; a Phone Log, keeping track of his calls; a Date Log, keeping track of their dates: pages of research on his interests (the Civil War, Napoleon, Winston Churchill, golf, Alexander the Great, and, briefly, whittling); lists of Donald's Favorite Songs, Sports, Games, TV Programs; anatomies of arguments they'd had; not to mention yearbooks, scrapbooks, and assorted diaries.

During their courtship, the File had been a solace to Ellen. And it had been a secret—not only from poor Donald, but from her closest friends, and even from Estelle. After their wedding, it became a secret from herself. In the early years of their marriage, Ellen never thought of it—the File had served its purpose. And later she tried not to think of it. She had grown to enjoy other people's desperation too much to want to be reminded of her own.

In the thirteen years since she had emerged in a shower of rice from the Church of the Heavenly Rest—Mrs. Prawl at last!—Ellen had not once looked through the File . . . not until this afternoon, when, on her knees in her locked bedroom, she had lifted the folders from the back of her bottom bureau drawer and opened them one by one.

She remembered how she had thrilled to these old yearbooks of Donald's: to his golf-team photos, to the fond inscriptions from his friends. ("Dear Donald, It was nice to share Latin Class, at least now I know about brown-nosing. . . .") She remembered the grim concentration with which she had plotted out the mood graphs and logged the dates and phone calls. She remembered the forensic fervor that had kept her up nights filling legal pads with word-for-word transcripts and deconstructions of their arguments. She remembered with what fury she had collected all these data, how she had laid her love down and cut it open, and how it had withstood her science to the end.

She remembered all this the way she remembered the pain of a toothache: only the fact of the experience, not the sensation.

Sitting at the kitchen table now, Ellen knew what she had feared to find in the File—because she'd found it. Not so much shame in the old yearnings as shame in the life that had fulfilled them.

And she knew what she had hoped to find, because she hadn't found it.

Meantime, everyone was falling in love around her. Ellen thought of Lisanne and Adair, how they had looked at each other on his porch last night. She felt closer to their love than she did to her own—wherever it was. And Estelle and Cockleburg—humping away two flights above her at this very moment! Was this, then, how she was destined to live out her middle years—a spy on love, a waiter in the honeymoon suite?

"Ellen—?"

Ellen looked up. Her mother stood in the doorway. She had not changed her clothes or her worried expression.

"Ellen, darling, have you seen Coco?"

"Not since breakfast," Ellen said. "But then, I haven't seen a soul. I spent the afternoon in my bedroom."

"I can't find him," Estelle said. "I can't find him anywhere." As she spoke, her face shuddered. Ellen wondered, What is she so afraid of?

"Where's Lisanne?" Ellen said. "Maybe they went into town together."

"The cars are all here," Estelle said.

"Have you looked outside? I bet he's just giving her a ninjitsu lesson."

Estelle turned away. Ellen joined her on the landing over the lawn.

"I have a bad feeling," Estelle said.

"I'm sure he's around somewhere. In fact, he's probably taking a walk in the woods." Ellen gestured vaguely.

"In the woods?" Estelle said. Then: "Call the police!"

"Since when is it a crime to walk in the woods?"

"What if he's been shot?" Estelle said. "Oh God! He's been shot!"

Was it only her imagination or did Estelle sound almost hopeful?

"The odds of that are one in a million," Ellen said.

"It happened before!"

"Well, the odds of it happening again are one in *two* million," Ellen said. "And the odds of the bullet striking the same area—in this case, the buttocks—are about one in a billion. And of striking the same cheek—in this case, the left cheek—" Ellen broke off with a laugh. As Estelle turned to her in bitter reproach, the laugh veered out of control.

"Something's happened," Estelle said. "Something's happened to him."

"This is Bedford—not Beirut. Coco will turn up by dinner, I assure you."

Estelle dashed down the dim hallway.

Ellen followed, and found her upstairs in his bedroom.

It was empty and cool and still. Estelle glanced once at his desk and then sat down carefully on the edge of the bed and folded her hands in her lap.

She said, "He's taken all his papers."

Ellen stared at her for a moment before she understood. Then she tiptoed over to the wardrobe (as though Coco might be hiding inside) and, in a sort of pouncing leap, flung wide its doors.

"Look!" she said. "There's his Dunhill suit, his pink jacket, all his new shirts . . . everything you gave him. He can't have gone anywhere."

"But where is Her Majesty?" said Estelle.

When the trees beyond the pond stopped her, Lisanne sat down and leaned back against a rock. In Puerto Rico, twenty years ago, she had run beside the sea, from one end of the resort to the other, to fetch the hotel doctor for her father. But when she returned with the doctor to her father's room, the patch of shirt over her father's heart had turned pure white, and he was laughing. And Ellen and Ellen's friend were laughing. When Harry explained, with apologies, that the blood was fake—a party trick!—and that he had tried to call his daughter back, the doctor started laughing too. Feeling her mother's eyes on her, Lisanne made herself laugh with them. Harry squirted more blood onto his shirt, and everyone laughed, watching the red flowers bloom, and slowly fade—everyone except Estelle. Lisanne saw her mother's sad, still mouth, and it was as though she had been falling into this hatred forever. It would always unfold, like a net, to catch her just in time.

If only it had lasted, that run between a vacationer's green sea and bright flowers; between fear, because her father's life depended on her, and joy, because her father's life depended on her.

Looking back, it was easy to see how the happiest moments can make the worst memories.

Right beside this rock, for example, in this exact spot, her father had buried a treasure chest for her to find. He drew up a map of the paths she'd named—Mermaid Lane, Witches Walk—and Lisanne spent her sixth birthday hunting X. She had been so happy, so triumphant, when she found it. She had trusted in the gold of the gold coins, and in all that a small pond might conceal: pirate ships, for example, and polished pirate bones.

Looking back, Lisanne could always find the innocence that curled like a worm through all her happy moments.

She thought again of the count on his knees beside the opened drawer. She ought to feel angry, she supposed. She ought to feel betrayed. She didn't even feel surprised. For so long she had believed in this inevitability: that anyone Estelle loved must sooner or later steal from her. The love she gave gave you no choice. Its riches wore you down. First, you could not resist them, then you could not refuse them. But it was only in loving her that you learned you could not repay them. Because it wasn't just the ones she loved who stole—Lisanne knew this now—it was the ones who loved her back.

It is always better to give than to receive. And sometimes, it's better to steal.

Lisanne thought of all her little meannesses, all the lies told, and secrets kept—every one a theft, and every one a proof of love. She would be the last to judge what she had seen this morning. She only blamed herself for having seen it. What she had stolen in that moment was the theft she counted as a crime.

Here was a sign—the drawer left open. In all the mirrors, her eyes were calm—distant spectators to the heart clinging, dizzy, to its ledge.

Ever since she met him, she had been like this: filled with longing and generosity and fear.

Estelle knelt down to count her money. Fifty, one hundred, one-fifty, two hundred. She licked a finger, as she had seen clerks lick their fingers in banks. Two-fifty, three hundred, three-fifty, four. . . . The numbers slid away from her, and she had to start again. Fifty, one hundred, one-fifty, two hundred, three hundred, four—in the thwarting slow motion of those dreams in which it takes forever to do the simplest things: dial a number, pack a suitcase. To think that such a small amount should take this time to count.

To her it was simple: She was a woman who had not had to work for her money, or marry for it, or think of it, or count it.

Lisanne wandered the paths behind the pond for hours. Walking back toward the house, she saw her mother's station wagon in the yard. So she was home from the hospital; then it must be after five. A massive shape filled the kitchen window. . . . Nipe! already engaged in preparations for their dinner. Soon they must all gather round the porch once more for cocktails, Donald, Ellen, and Estelle. . . .

Lisanne turned around. She walked past the bushes, up the hill and toward his porch.

She waited outside the sliding doors that led into the house, her nose pressed to the glass in the furred cloud of her own breath.

He stood with his back toward her in the kitchen off the living room, dropping ice cubes into a cup.

His braid *was* ridiculous. And what was he doing with his life? A failed musician, with a crippled son and no knowledge at all of shrubbery.

As soon as he saw her, Lisanne sensed his suspicion and shrank from it. Not because she was its object, but because she alone was not. She felt, gathering behind her, all the dangers his love for her had conjured: things that fall without warning; things that crash, crush, cave in, cut; things that burn.

She knew the way it worked: when you want to protect someone, when, worse, you think you can.

He slid open the glass door.

"What happened to you?" he said. "What's wrong?"

She started to say, "Nothing—"

He went on: "Cockleburg seems to have disappeared. Your sister just came by here, looking for you, to see if you knew where he had gone. All I could think was, Oh no, she's taken off again."

She said, "I was walking those paths behind the pond, the ones you've cleared. It's like a maze to me back there. And I used to know those paths so well when I was a little girl."

" 'When I was a little girl,' " he said. "Now there's something I've never heard you say before."

He raised his cup to her lips. He said, "Have a sip of this. This will make everything easier."

She swallowed. "It tastes like . . ."

"Grapefruit juice. Pure healthful fresh-squeezed grapefruit juice!" He handed her the cup. "Drink up, sweetheart. I'll get some for myself."

Lisanne took another sip and watched him lift a pitcher from the fridge. She took another sip as he drew the curtains closed over the glass doors and another as he sat down on the couch.

"Come sit down." He patted the place beside him. "Let's enjoy our juice together like civilized people."

She sat down.

What amazingly good juice!

Adair poured her more.

Lisanne leaned her head back and closed her eyes.

"Look at your poor legs," he said. "Next time you walk in the woods, Lisanne, let me spray you with my bug spray."

His thumbnail traced circles around a scab above her knee.

"I was mean to a musician once," she said. The memory had been falling through her mind for years, it seemed, landing suddenly in these words.

"Should I be worried?" Adair said. "Is this some kind of pattern?"

"He used to come to this restaurant where I worked," she said. "Percival. Yes, Percival Mobley. That was his name. He worked as a security guard in a mall, I think. And he couldn't have been a day under fifty, or a pound under two-fifty. But he played the banjo—and *Percival Mobley was gonna be a star!* I hated him," she said. "I hated him for his aftershave—I had to hold my breath to take his order. For weeks that aftershave was everything I loathed but had to live with anyway. I used to think, There ought to be laws against the stuff! I hated him for being so kind and leaving such big tips. But most of all, I hated him for being so goddamn hopeful. I used to think, You fat old, blind old fool. *You*—hopeful? *You*—happy? I was amazed that he hadn't slit his wrists ten years ago. But there he sat, night after night, enjoying his scampi."

Adair poured her more juice.

"Am I boring you?" she asked.

"On the contrary," he said.

"Well, anyway," she said, "he'd saved up his money to make this demo tape. And he carried it around with him everywhere he went in a Walkman. He used to listen to it while he ate. He'd tap his feet, and sway, and smile. And if he wasn't listening to it himself, he was making someone else listen. The busboys, the bartenders, the waitresses, the other customers. He'd clutch their arms, and *make them listen.* I made a promise to myself: He wasn't going to do it to me. A hundred times, he said, Hey, Lisanne! When are you gonna listen to my tape? And a hundred times I put him off, until finally, one night, he waited till my shift was over. He seemed to be gathering himself up for some final terrible effort—and so I slipped out through the kitchen. And would you believe, he ambushed me in the parking lot! He sprang out at me from behind my car. At first I thought he was a rapist. And in a way, I guess, he was. Because there was just no way out, no way out. The smile he gave me might as well have been a knife at my throat. So I just stood there as he snapped the headphones on. And then he leaned against my car, and tapped his feet, and watched me listen, with that stupid smile splitting his face."

"Was he any good?" Adair asked.

"It was a ballad," Lisanne said. "A folk song. Three chords. About a thousand verses. It just went on, and on, and on. And the chorus was, 'I wish I'd never met you. I wish I wish I wish I wish I wish I wish I'd never met you.' Adair, it was the worst song I've ever heard in my life."

"So what did you tell him?" Adair asked.

"I said, 'This is great, Percival.' I said, 'You've got a hit here.' I said, 'Percival, you're gonna be a star.' "

There was a long silence. Finally Adair said, "I don't get it, Lisanne. Where's the meanness here? As far as I can tell, he was a pushy, talentless bore, and you were nothing but kind."

She looked at him, amazed. "It's what I thought," she said. "You know—it's the thought that counts. This was years and years ago," she said, "the summer I first left home. I moved again soon after."

"I'm flattered that I remind you of Percival Mobley," Adair said.

"There's always a reason," Lisanne said, "why these

memories lie in wait for you. Because, I remember now, as I listened to that voice howl out, 'I wish I'd never met you,' I found myself wondering: When's the last time I did anything for anyone? And the answer was—years ago. Years ago, when I was a little girl, when I danced naked for this voyeur who lived in the building across the street from us. A few pliés," she said. "That was the last thing I'd given to anyone that I could think of. And it made me so ashamed. It was the first time in my life that I'd ever felt ashamed. I have Percival Mobley to thank for that."

"Shame is about thank-you notes not written," Adair said. "It's about not calling your grandmother on her birthday. It's about dropping the ball in gym class. Shame is something the guilty don't bother with."

"I believe in shame," Lisanne said.

She rose unsteadily.

"Where are you going?" he said.

"It's late," she said. She stood swaying in the middle of the room and said, "I feel so funny."

He was smiling. "You do?"

His face was right above hers, lowering. She smelled the alcohol on his breath.

"You tricked me," she said. "You're trying to get me drunk."

"You are drunk," he said. "But that's not what I'm trying to do. It's just how I'm doing it."

14

One thing Ellen looked forward to was the arrival of her mother's mail. Over the summer, she had gotten into the habit of loitering in the kitchen every morning, starting around eleven, to watch for the mail truck, while drinking coffee, perusing the paper, and bringing the kettle to a boil in preparation for steaming open envelopes.

In the last week, a secret hope had lent this ritual a new urgency, a hope that now sent Ellen across the yard to seize the day's delivery out of the postman's hand.

If there was a letter from Cockleburg, Ellen wanted to be the first to find it. She wanted to be the one to bestow it on her mother.

There was no letter.

Instead, a deft shuffling of the epistolary deck revealed a dozen bills, which Ellen set aside, and the inevitable requests from assorted godchildren, relatives, and "dear old friends." These—so wretched, so reckless was her mood—Ellen ripped open, not bothering to steam them.

Freddy Keck, a second cousin once removed, wanted Estelle to co-sign a bank loan. And Buddy Bulber, a spry young man of sixty-five, was thinking of buying a yacht on behalf of his bladder (thus, bizarrely, did Bulber phrase the petition): "The clean salt air, the wind and sun, are just what my urologist orders," he wrote. Gwendolyn Pluff, in memory of their childhood friendship, offered Estelle the first opportunity to invest in the crockery shop she was planning to open. Lilly James, one of the godchildren (a minx of nineteen whose apple cheeks Ellen always itched to slap), needed help with the insurance payments on the car Estelle had given her as a graduation present. And that unctuous eunuch Tiger Sprague-McHay (another cousin) wanted a trip to Europe financed—his third trip this year, as though antiquing in Europe were some kind of birthright.

Trembling violently, Ellen dispatched these supplications to the trash.

The rest was just the usual junk: the announcement of a sale at Bloomingdale's, a couple of magazine subscription renewal forms, and—*wait!*—tucked between these, an envelope of the manliest shade of royal blue, addressed to . . . Cockleburg.

The name was scrawled in that dear, round, childish hand that was scrawled upon Ellen's heart (though never once upon a letter to *her*).

If the letter had been from anyone else, Ellen would have opened it without hesitation.

But she found she could not open this—this letter from her son. She wasn't sure what held her back, but something did, something stronger than the usual scruples, which were, after all, so easily dismissed.

She could lift the letter to the light, though, to see if she could make out any words. This she instantly did.

In the week since Cockleburg's disappearance, Ellen

had wanted—tried—and failed to believe her mother's explanation: that he had been called away on "sudden business." The idea of business of any kind affecting the unemployed pedant one way or another was, sadly, laughable—*risible,* the count would have said. Lately, Ellen had caught herself lapsing into the same plethoric diction she had reviled in Cockleburg. What began originally as a form of mockery had now become a habit: it was as though her tongue had been possessed by the vanished pedant!

At first, Ellen had suspected Donald of being somehow nefariously involved in the flight of his Belial. Had Donald bribed the nobleman? Blackmailed him? Abducted him? Threatened him in some way? Appalling and improbable as these possibilities were, anything was better than the alternative: that Cockleburg had simply walked away, leaving her mother just when he had made her most happy, just when he had let her love him. Once Ellen had believed the count to be a fraud, a cad, a small-time villain. She had *wanted* this. But to have walked away from her mother now went beyond any of the mundane meannesses in which Ellen might have been able, still, to take a certain spiteful satisfaction.

In the last week, she had seen her mother's face—so hopeful, so brave. It was the only face her mother let be seen. But it was like a statue of bravery and hope. She had seen her mother's face, for the first time, invent itself for the sake of human eyes. It was worse than any suffering Ellen had ever seen there: because it was generous, and because it was final. When she looked at her mother's face, Ellen saw it close like a door upon something quietly dying, and she felt no satisfaction, none at all.

Her mother's happiness had been ridiculous to Ellen, her mother's love more ridiculous still, her mother's lover most ridiculous of all. But there was nothing ridiculous about Cockleburg now. Because if he had done this, he had done it for no reason Ellen could name. If he had done this, he had done it for nothing, and he had managed, in spite of himself, to do an evil thing.

So Ellen had hoped that somehow Donald was to blame; and when she told him the news of Cockleburg's disappearance, she left many artful little openings for a confession to that effect. But it was impossible to doubt the sincerity of Donald's bafflement. After the initial taurine snorts and stamps and bellows of surprise, he launched into a series of the most offensive speculations.

"He must have found a dumber, richer widow!"

Ellen did not have a chance to respond to this hypothesis before Donald himself dismissed it as "*Impossible!*"

Gamboling round the room in his excitement, Donald abruptly turned to Ellen and yelled in odious, gloating triumph: "*I've got it!* The feds have caught up with him, by golly! Yes, that's it! The feds are on his tail, god*damn* his black and twisted soul!"

"The *feds?*" Ellen said. "I saw Mrs. Larson in town yesterday, and the Reverend and Mrs. Prisslerpiss, and a number of other upstanding suburbanites, Donald, but I saw no one who even remotely resembled a federal agent."

"You can be so naive, Ellen," said Donald, shaking his head. "It wouldn't surprise me in the least to find that damnable face of his—and I *do* damn it!—smirking out at me from a Most Wanted poster. In fact, I'm going to the post office first thing tomorrow to see for myself. Heck, I shoulda done it weeks ago!"

"Donald, spare yourself that trip. I've been to the post office almost every—"

"Or maybe he's gone to Miami to pick up a drug shipment!"

Ellen could only stare in horror as Donald went on in this vein for the next hour.

Finally, Ellen could stand it no longer. She rose from the bed, and, with a look of scorn that reduced even this maddened man to mutinous maxillary mashings, quoth: "I forbid you to mention Cockleburg to my mother," adding, staccato, "*in any context whatsoever.* And I categorically forbid you," she went on, taking a deep breath that swelled her bosom to its most majestic amplitude, and unleashing now, in all its Cockleburgian glory, her new pleonastic magniloquence, "*I categorically forbid you* to utter to her a single one of the preposterous words, the vile traducements and embittered obloquies, with which you have besmirched, besmeared, bespattered, bemired, begrimed, befouled, and befooled yourself here tonight!"

Clearly bewildered by this stunning rebuke, Donald stood stock-still in the middle of the room.

"And if I do?" he said slyly, recovering after a long silence.

"If you do, I'll—" The threat she had not deigned to articulate rose in the air above them like a blimp, beneath which Ellen glided to, and out, the door, stepping rather high, with pointed toes, and holding her long skirt away from her feet, as if performing a *pavane.*

Donald's got it backwards, Ellen thought now, as she laid aside (with a painfully acute sense of her own virtue) the unopened letter. He keeps focusing on Cockleburg's guilt. What about ours?

Guilt was there, though Ellen could not name the crime.

It occurred to Ellen now that Donald Jr. might be able to shed some light on the mystery. He had been corresponding with the count on a weekly basis ever since he'd left for camp, the royal blue envelopes arriving for Cockleburg, and Cockleburg only, with a regularity most galling to the slighted mother.

Ellen seized the phone and dialed the number of the tennis camp. At first the supervisor refused to summon the child from the court. "He's drilling right now, Mrs. Prawl. Couldja call back later?"

Ellen was speechless for a long moment, during which the supervisor popped his gum (and it must have been, if the volume of these pops was any indication, among the largest wads ever stuffed into the human mouth). When Ellen found her voice again, it was shrill with rage. "It's urgent."

The supervisor dropped the phone. After ten minutes (Ellen clocked them), her son at last picked up.

"Mommy?"

"Donnie!"

Ellen was forced to endure another ten minutes of suspense as the budding champion regaled her, in exhaustive detail, with the catalogue of his recent victories.

"And then I beat Chris Shlunk, who's ranked twenty-two in the ten-and-unders in the East. At thirty–love in the first game, Shlunk serving, I hit this incredible overhead smash, even though the sun was right in my eyes. . . ."

"Fabulous," Ellen said, finally bursting into this triumphal narration, two sets later, mid-tiebreaker, "but I was wondering if I might ask you a question."

"A question?" repeated the boy.

"Yes, darling. A question." Then, amplifying in falsetto: "Just an itty bitty question for my itty bitty kitty kit."

"Jesus, Mom! Get a grip—and get to the point!" Donnie spoke now with all the manly gruffness of his sire.

"All right, then," said his mother, stung. "I was wondering if you happened to have heard from Cockleburg."

"Cockleburg?"

"Cockleburg."

"Cockleburg?"

"Cock-el-burg," Ellen said, enunciating aggressively.

"Not recently," said Donnie.

"Not in the last week?"

"Not in the last week."

"Not at all in the last week?"

"*Not at all.*" He paused, breathing heavily. "What's it to you, anyway?"

"Well, he seems to have disappeared, I'm afraid," Ellen said. Hoping to astound the child into some revelation, she made no attempt to soften the blow. "And of course Grandma's terribly upset, as are we all. I had thought you might be able to tell us where he might have gone."

It was the child who now astounded her—by bursting into tears.

"Cry it out, darling," Ellen urged him. "Let it go. Release the pain. Don't be afraid of your emotions. It's healthy to cry"—shuddering at what Big Donald would make of this heresy—"it's *manly* to cry."

He went on. "I feel so bad about it!"

"We all do."

"You don't understand," he sobbed.

"But I do," Ellen said. And then suddenly—completely—*she did*. The realization sickened and oddly satisfied her; and did not in the least surprise her: Her son had shot Cockleburg. And Cockleburg had known this all along.

Estelle went late to the animal shelter that summer. Lisanne drove her into the city and waited in the car while Estelle went inside to pick up her two new pets.

"Two?" Donald had said that morning at breakfast.

"My dear Estelle, I thought the deal was one new dog a year. And that's one too many, as far as I'm concerned."

"But that would make thirteen, Donald," Estelle said. "That would be unlucky."

"Stuff and nonsense!" her son-in-law expostulated. "If thirteen is so unlucky, then why isn't every thirteen-year-old on this earth struck dead? Why doesn't every couple split up after thirteen years together? Look at me and Ellen! Thirteen years last May, and we've never been happier"—askance at Ellen—"eh, little woman?"

But the look of husbandly affection was wiped off his face by what the little woman then said: "If Mom wants fourteen dogs, or a hundred and forty, Donald, what's it to you?"

"Half of 'em look like they're about to croak at any minute anyway," he said vengefully. "Gettin' on in years, those two big black ones, ain't they?"

"Don't say that, Donald, don't say that," pleaded Estelle.

"Don't say that, Donald, don't," said Ellen.

He immediately said it again: "Gettin' on in years, those two big black ones, ain't they?"

Lisanne looked up now to see two new black mongrels surge through the door, straining at the leash that attached them, by coupler, to their new mistress, who seemed about to be dragged off her feet and lofted like a kite into the air behind them.

"Just open the car door, darling," Estelle panted.

Following Adair's example, Lisanne attempted to whistle the dogs into the vehicle.

"Get the biscuits, darling," Estelle instructed between gasps. "Now drop a few on the seat there. Oh, see how intelligent they are!" she said, as the animals lunged upon these dainties.

Estelle climbed into the car after them.

Reseated behind the wheel, Lisanne was, within minutes, assaulted by an unmistakable odor.

Swinging her head around, she nearly swerved into a taxi.

"Watch where you're going, Lisanne! If anything should happen to either of these animals . . ." Estelle could not complete the thought. "Poor things, they're just excited," she said, "and who wouldn't be, in their place? Going out into a brand-new world. . . . Nice big poo poos," she told them. She scooped one up with newspaper and waved it in the rearview mirror. So Lisanne could admire it, too?

"Lovely," Lisanne said. "But what's that long white thing?"

"Just a worm," Estelle said. "They always get worms in the shelter. Worms, and mange, and all sorts of parasites." She reeled off a list of canine ills—concluding exultantly: "All, *all* curable!"

Lisanne pulled over so that Estelle could throw out the soiled newspaper.

The dogs tracked her with anxious, golden eyes as she walked away from them to the trash can.

Once Lisanne had hated her for loving like a dog, for being faithful as a dog.

But what could be more noble, and more dangerous, than loving like a dog? As if there were something wrong with loving that way.

"They already adore you, Mom," Lisanne told her when she returned.

Estelle deluged them with kisses and biscuits. "Do you, angels? I adore you, too. And I would never leave you, not for all the money in the world. From now on," she promised them, "you will never be left behind. From now on," she said, "you will always be included."

A line from a Joy Williams story Lisanne had read years

ago came back to her: "Many things that human words have harmed are restored again by the silence of animals."

It's not so much what they can't say to hurt us, Lisanne thought. It's what we can't say to hurt them.

"Tug toys, tag, catch, wrestling, walks in the woods, swimming in the pool," Estelle was saying in the backseat, "we're going to do something fun *every day!*"

Junellen used to say to her little dog, I'm madly in love with you, little dog, and I'm bigger and stronger than you, too.

Lisanne remembered everything Adair told her about Junellen.

"Who could fail to love creatures so beautiful and good?" Estelle said. "And yet people fail all the time."

"By the way, Mother, this came in the mail for you," Ellen said.

Estelle had just returned from the city, laden with exotic herbal teas—it was part of her campaign to get Ellen off caffeine. Mother and daughter were sharing a pot of Serenity Mint (which tasted to the latter like boiled Listerine).

"It looks so official," Ellen said, as she slid the pink envelope across the kitchen table. "I wonder what on earth it could be!"

The return address read Amoretto Press. Ellen had, of course, steamed the letter open within minutes of its arrival.

On pink stationery, beneath the Press's logo (a naked and salaciously grinning Cupid of repulsively overdeveloped physique who looked to be about fifty-seven years old), were four typed paragraphs, which Ellen had rapidly skimmed, and which sent her reeling to the liquor cabinet for a rare matutinal potation.

Estelle's romance novel, *Priapus Erumpent,* had been accepted for publication.

"Dear Mrs. Wolfe," wrote the editor-in-chief, Ms. Aurora Randeleigh:

> We at Amoretto are most eager to publish your spellbinding medieval romance, *Priapus Erumpent* (though not, perhaps, under this title, which seems to us a bit obscure).
>
> Your hero, Marmaduke the Magnificent, has captured every heart in the Amoretto office. So fiercely male, and yet so tenderly vulnerable, too. That he is a bard, a potter, and an accomplished zitherist, as well as a man of war, gives him an extra dimension, a modern sensitivity, which our contemporary readers will be sure to appreciate. (We do like the musician angle, though you might want to give Marmaduke a different instrument on which to display his talents—did they even have zithers in the Middle Ages?). Mariana, with her playful high spirits, and warm generous nature, is just the sort of inspiring, sympathetic heroine we at Amoretto look for.
>
> There may be too many descriptions of the castle dogs, particularly Marmaduke's seven shih tzus, a breed which seems an odd choice, frankly, for a fortress guard dog. (Wouldn't mastiffs be more appropriate?) We will need to work with you on punctuation—for we do insist on *some*. Also, the language is at times rather more literary than our readers are used

to. For example, in that thrilling scene where the troop of migrant barbers come upon Lady Mariana bathing in the brook, you use the word algolagnic in describing the ensuing attempted gang rape. Wouldn't bestial do just as well?

But these are mere quibblings, Mrs. Wolfe. All in all—a tour de force! Please contact us at your earliest convenience to discuss a possible contract.

Ellen's first impulse had been to hurl this missive into the trash (along with a second plea from the now frantic Freddy Keck). She said to herself: *my mother, the romance writer*—and did not think she could bear it. She thought of how she had sneered at these writers gazing heavenward (or heroward) in their back-cover photographs—lifted eyes glistening, bright crimped tresses frothing up from incongruous matronly brows, glossed lips parted as if in ecstasy, Chihuahuas cradled in their arms. She imagined her mother posed in this way (although in Estelle's case, substitute a pack of obese mongrels for the Chihuahua).

But then (pouring herself a second shot of vodka), Ellen thought of her mother's sadness growing like a pearl within the hard calm that enclosed it and did not think she could bear that.

Slowly, an alternative vision began to take shape in Ellen's imagination: her mother, wearing a suit; lunching with Ms. Randeleigh; her mother, fêted, courted, the triumph of Amoretto, the toast of the romance-reading public; Cockleburg, wandering into a bookstore, wherever he was (some dreary and polluted burg, she hoped), and limping through the romance aisle on his way to

Nietzsche; how a certain book-jacket photo, prominently displayed, would shame him as he passed.

Two vodkas and five hours later, Ellen found herself sliding the pink envelope (deftly resealed) across the kitchen table to Estelle.

She watched now as her mother opened it and unfolded the pink paper. She watched her mother's eyes travel those lines that she, Ellen, had practically memorized over the course of the afternoon. She watched and, affecting a carelessness that she was very far from feeling, said, "So what is it? Do tell."

Estelle laid down the letter—and burst into tears—the first tears Ellen had seen her shed since Cockleburg's disappearance. Ellen sat there, flabbergasted. This was a far cry from the exultant smile she had expected.

Finally she said, "Mother, what's wrong?"

Estelle shook her head.

"Please," Ellen said. "I can't stand this. You must let me comfort you. How can I comfort you if I don't know what's wrong?"

Estelle steadied herself with a sip of Serenity Mint. "Only if you swear you won't laugh."

"I swear I won't."

"Coco and I wrote a romance novel this summer," Estelle intoned, doloroso. "We finished it, and sent it out, just before he got called away on sudden business. And it seems"—looking down at the letter—"a publisher called Amoretto Press is interested."

"But how secretive you've been," Ellen exclaimed, "how sly!"

"Yes, well, I wanted it to be a surprise," Estelle said. "I made Coco promise not to breathe a word."

"It certainly is a surprise," Ellen said. "*And a marvelous one!* So why such a sad sack, Mother? You ought to be bursting with pride. I know I am." She paused. "My mother, the romance writer!"

Estelle shrugged. "I never could have done it without Coco," she said. "I never *would* have done it without Coco."

"What do you mean?" Ellen said. "This was a dream of yours long before you met Coco."

"I wouldn't have had the guts to do it on my own," said Estelle. "And anyway, the whole point of it was *to help Coco.* You see, he had no insurance, and so Sandrine's hospital bills wiped him out. And though I didn't know that till later, I knew he was struggling, I knew he was broke. Not that he ever complained, mind you. It was just painfully obvious to me that money was on his mind."

"I imagine it always is," Ellen said, "when you don't have any."

"I tried to make it clear to him," Estelle said, speaking rapidly, "that if he ever needed help—help of that kind—he had only to ask. But he never asked. Then I made the mistake—I couldn't help myself—of offering outright, a loan. I said a loan, though of course I meant a gift. I practically begged him to accept it. I *did* beg him, until he threatened to go away if I mentioned it again. And though he was kind about it—he was always kind—and gracious, and gallant, I realized then I'd been insensitive, I realized I'd hurt his pride. Because he had so much pride, Ellen," she said, "so much."

"Where does the romance novel come in?" Ellen said, hoping to curtail this swelling eulogy.

"It occurred to me," Estelle said, "that the only way I'd be able to help Coco was if he believed he was helping me. And so I racked my brains and came up with this: I told him I wanted to write a novel—a romance novel—and I implored him to be my editor. And Ellen, I will never,

never forget the generous words with which he responded to that plea."

Ellen braced herself.

"He said," Estelle said, with swimming eyes, "he said, bowing low, you know, in that graceful way he had, he said, 'Dear lady, from this moment on, until I slide into the silent tomb, I pledge myself to be, not merely your editor, but your most humble, your most grateful, your most honored and adoring Erato.' "

God, he could really lay it on! Ellen thought.

"And so we began to work on it almost every afternoon," Estelle said. "Mostly he would dictate, and I would type. What a flair, what a God-given gift he had for the genre! All the best ideas, the most lyrical passages, are his." Estelle bowed her head for a long moment in (to Ellen, blessedly wordless) remembrance.

"And so you offered to pay him for these labors?" she prompted.

Estelle nodded. "And again, he wouldn't accept. Absolutely would not accept. But I did finally get him to agree to split the advance with me, should our little project ever meet with any success. And now it has," she said, "thanks to him, thanks only to him. It just breaks my heart that he isn't here to share this moment with me—let alone to share the advance. You see, he was called away so suddenly"—she began to cry again—"that I don't even know where to send him whatever money he's earned."

Ellen rose, and went round the table, and laid her arm across her mother's shoulder. "Don't cry," she said. "I'll find him for you, Mother. I promise I'll find him."

15

Every night now, after dinner, Lisanne went over to Adair's. They watched TV. When the beer commercials came on, Adair would point to the prettiest blonde on the beach and say, "There's Junellen."

The first night they had sex, Junellen afterward bent down and struck a match to firecrackers she had threaded through the grass. He watched in awe, the darkness burning. Then she said, Now get out of my yard.

She was seventeen years old.

He said she had a laugh that made him want to kill her. They never fought. She let him say what he had to say, her eyes averted. When he had finished, she would set free that soaring laugh, and he would see it had been rising in her all along. Then he would have to leave the house to keep from hitting her. It was as if her flesh existed only to contain this laughter. To bury the laughter, you would have to break and bury the vessel. He said,

"Something about it invited violence. Something about the way it belittled violence." He said, "At the end of the world, when all life has been destroyed by man, that laugh will ring out over the scorched earth."

Donald was not contacted for information by the feds, nor did he find the face of his foe among the Most Wanted at the Bedford post office. His initial blast of excitement at the count's disappearance quickly subsided; and Donald plunged headlong into what Ellen came to think of as the Post-Cockleburgian Void. This was a state marked by a profound hebetude, asthenia, inappetence, listlessness bordering on despair—a state almost as alarming to Ellen as the volcanic wrath it had displaced.

It was all Donald could do to habilitate himself in the morning for work—muttering as he moved from the bureau to the closet to the sink. How he managed to get through his grueling twelve-hour days at the Firm, Ellen had no idea. He spent the evenings in bed, his face turned to the wall. In vain did Ellen ply this former glutton with caviar, pâté, hecatombs of beef. Dish after dish was wanly refused. Most pitiable of all these data of decline was, perhaps, *the complete and total stillness of his buttocks*—a stillness that chillingly presaged, for Ellen, the stillness of the grave.

Donald himself believed that he had the flu, and even managed to croak out a weak curse or two against the man from whom he thought he'd caught it ("Jack Drake, in Mergers and Acquisitions—the bastard!"); and though he had no fever, no sore throat, not a single swollen gland, not a drop of nasal discharge, Ellen tenderly indulged him in this delusion.

Hovering by the hour over her fallen spouse, she could

only hope and pray that after this painful transition period, Donald would be restored to his pre-Cockleburgian
equilibrium.

Two weeks after Cockleburg's disappearance (and ten
pounds thinner), Donald at last surged up from the
shores of apathy on the swelling tide of a new outrage.

It was a Saturday afternoon. Leaving strict instruc-
tions that Donald was not to be disturbed, Ellen had gone
into town in search of strawberries (his favorite berry).
During her brief absence from the house, Nipe—Ellen
pieced it together later—had disobeyed the interdiction
and penetrated the sickroom. Her excuse: a restorative
bowl of cream of egg yolk soup for the invalid. Infinitely
more restorative, however, than this, or any other soup in
the cook's repertoire, was the news she served up with it:
Lisanne and Adair's romance. Ellen returned from the local fruitery to find Donald rearing about in his bathrobe,
beneath the billowing folds of which his somewhat atro-
phied glutei were quivering (she observed in dismay) with
all their attenuated might.

"God*damn* it!" he yelled, as she stood in the doorway.
"Can't a man even get the flu without the whole world
goin' to hell in a hand basket?"

"What are you talking about, Donald?" Ellen asked,
fearing that he'd had news of Cockleburg.

"You know goddamn well what I'm talking about!" he
said. "And I damn you, Ellen, I do damn you, for not
telling me what in hell's been goin' on here!" He pointed
at her now the index finger of his right hand—the digit of
damnation. "I'm talking about that *whore*," he said,
"that sister of yours, and that *whoreson,* her paramour!"

Ellen sank into the armchair.

"Spending every night together, eh?—as soon as my
back is turned."

"Donald, I don't think you, or your turned back, had

anything to do with it," Ellen said. "I think they love each other—truly love and honor each other."

"Love and honor? *Love and honor?* You dare, Ellen, you *dare* to invoke the rhetoric of matrimony to dignify this unholy union?"

"For goodness' sakes—" Ellen began.

"I will not have it, I tell you! I will not have it, d'y'hear? I will not allow it in this house!" And the arm he waved as he spoke these words seemed to encompass not merely the house and its surrounding grounds but the whole moral and spiritual sphere of his patriarchate.

"But Donald," came a quiet voice in the doorway—

Donald wheeled round. It was Estelle.

"Donald," she said, *"this is my house."*

Adair and Lisanne were walking through the woods. The cook, in the lull before her prandial preparations, often paused on her way to the kitchen to squat behind the vegetation outside the caretaker's cottage. (She had lately taken to wearing green muumuus to intensify the camouflage.) To thwart this espionage, the lovers had made a habit of hiking. Several times the cook had followed them (ponderously tiptoeing in their peripheral vision) as far as the pond, but being allergic to poison ivy, she had not dared to venture out into the treacherous flora beyond.

Tomorrow, Adair was taking Lisanne to the hospital to meet Ian.

"So what did Junellen say," she said, "the first time you asked her if she wanted children?"

"She said, 'Children? Children just make me hungry,' " Adair said. "She said she had always identified with the witch in 'Hansel and Gretel.' And I thought she was just trying to shock me." He shook his head. "I thought all women loved children."

"Love of children," Lisanne said, "like fear of snakes. Just one of those facts of female nature."

"That's right," Adair said. "So I didn't believe Junellen when she told me she hated them—told me like it was something she was proud of. She loved to think of herself as being different from other women. She always set herself apart."

Adair held the branches back for Lisanne, as though they were doors.

"I didn't believe her," he went on, "even when I saw the way she looked at them. She would stare at them in supermarkets—like *they* were what she was having for dinner. And you could almost see her nose lengthening," he said, "and the hairs sprouting from her moles. "The mothers sensed it—they would wheel their kids away down the aisles. And Junellen would laugh, and say, 'If the little fuckers are going to stare at me, I'm going to stare right back.' She said that if she came upon an unattended child, it took a great effort of will to keep from pinching it."

"Maybe she didn't really hate them," Lisanne said. "Maybe she was only scared of them. Some women love snakes and fear children. I know I fear them."

"It's their judgment, isn't it?" Adair said. "And their innocence."

Lisanne thought of Mrs. Rainey and Mr. Lumkin. She thought of the old people she had seen outside the shopping malls in Florida, looking to the left and looking to the right with every step they took, as they crossed the parking lot on their way to the drugstore. She had studied them, trying to figure out what it was that made them seem so innocent. It was all their years of living, it was life that made them innocent.

Lisanne had never believed in the innocence of children.

"I didn't believe her," Adair was saying, "when she told me she wanted an abortion. I thought, even if she hates kids, she'll have to love her own, right?"

The air was so moist you could almost drink it. It seemed to stir and swirl like water.

"Later," he said, "she used to say, 'You didn't believe me, did you?' "

It was midnight again.

Estelle looked up from her desk by the window. She was in the process of punctuating *Priapus Erumpent* before her lunch with Ms. Randeleigh the following Wednesday (a truly monumental task, for, as written, the 450-page manuscript had not a single period, comma, or colon). It had become impossible to concentrate, the dogs all round her having abandoned themselves to a final burst of play before bed. All except the two new ones: Cyd and Charisse. They had been with her almost a week and she had still not discovered their special talents, their game of choice. Tug, tag, catch, wrestling—none of these had as yet struck a chord. They were sitting on the sidelines now, thrilled by the antics of the others, but too shy to join in.

Estelle laid down her red pencil and went over to them. They thumped their tails and looked up at her with eyes that seemed to say, *Life is fun now.*

Estelle sank to her knees between them. "Don't be shy," she said. "Don't you want to play?"

Charisse still cradled in her jaws the rawhide bone Estelle had given her after dinner. The gift had seemed to fill her with equal parts joy and anxiety. Perhaps it was her first gift ever, Estelle thought. She apparently found it too precious to chew. She had spent the last four hours looking for a safe place to hide it—under the pillow, in the potted plant, at the bottom of the trash can in the bathroom—no place was safe enough.

"I won't let anyone take it away from you," Estelle said, kissing the cool, uplifted nose.

Sometimes it seemed to Estelle that all the beauty in the world was, if not limited to, then at least contained in her fourteen dogs.

Since their arrival, Cyd and Charisse had, between them, broken all the screen doors in the house. They had done this by bursting through them in pursuit of Estelle. They would not let her out of their sight. Estelle was deeply moved—she was *thrilled* by their devotion, though she imagined that less devoted dogs were probably happier. They are safer, too. Twice now, Charisse had escaped and followed her down the road when she went to the hospital, down the dirt road as far as the highway before Estelle noticed the black shadow receding like a memory in the rearview mirror.

They were all like this when she first rescued them. The devotion was not why she did it; she would go on rescuing them, she knew, even without it.

But perhaps she enjoyed the devotion too much.

Estelle rose and went back to *Priapus Erumpent*. Her heart was no longer in the project, and she would have abandoned it, except for this: it was the last thing she might ever be able to do for him. She read again the brief dedication she had written out that night—"For Coco, wherever you are, in love and gratitude"—and crossed out the *wherever you are.*

She thought it might seem reproachful.

An hour later, Estelle, in her white nightgown, one by one kissed all fourteen dogs goodnight. As she turned out the light and climbed into bed in the middle of them (it was like climbing into a fort), it occurred to her that tomorrow they were due for their heartworm pills again, and she closed her eyes, almost happy.

She felt a small but perfect joy in that moment when she gave the dogs their monthly heartworm pills. Yes, this was one thing she could make sure of: none of her dogs would die of heartworm. The fact that she could trick them so easily, just by rolling the pills into cream-cheese balls, made her love them all the more.

At the end of her life, someone would be able to say, She made fourteen dogs happy.

It was a disease of the nervous system. Too many signals got sent from the brain.

Some people who had it were also retarded, Adair said. Ian was only quiet. "You'll see," he said.

Through revolving doors, he flowed into the lobby, Lisanne following. This was not the same wing where her father had died, but it was the same hospital with the same hospital smell.

Recreation wasn't due to begin for another ten minutes. A candy-striper directed them in a piercing soprano down the hall to Physical Therapy. This was a large room, with a ramp descending along one wall. Herded along by therapists, the children rolled and crawled across rubber mats. The air smelled of urine—spreading puddles of which an orderly grimly stalked with mop and pail.

A cross rose in the middle of the room. A small boy hung from the burnished boards strapped by the arms and legs. He was naked except for a pair of Jockey shorts.

Lisanne guessed this was Ian, because Estelle was sitting on the floor at his feet, a storybook open on her lap. His head was twisted down at an odd angle.

Estelle looked up as Adair and Lisanne approached.

"He's been waiting for you," she told Adair.

The child looked up. He was ashamed, Lisanne saw, ashamed—of being almost naked? of being alive? of being seen?

"Dada," he said.

Lisanne tried to imagine, as Adair lowered himself to the child's eye level, what this word meant to him. She was suddenly dizzy, thinking of her own freedom, that desperate freedom from all ties that had once seemed like her life's achievement. Now it seemed like the empty air through which her life had fallen, and disappeared.

16

At five o'clock, Ellen emerged from the house with a lounge chair, which she unfolded on the front lawn directly overlooking the road. Estelle was due back any minute from her lunch with Ms. Randeleigh, at that editor's chic midtown eatery of choice, and Ellen couldn't wait to hear how it had gone.

Estelle had left for the city that morning in a navy blue Oscar de la Renta suit. Her first choice had been a flowing flowery gauze sundress, which Ellen had vetoed as being "most inappropriately jeune fille"—not to mention *completely transparent.* While authoresses were no doubt allowed sartorial liberties denied their professional sisters, appearing naked in public was *not* (Ellen supposed with a grimace in her lounge chair now) among them.

By six, only two vehicles had stirred the dust of this dead-end road. The first of these (its approach heralded by ghastly tintinnabulations) was a Good Humor truck, manned by an unsavory individual, muscular in a mesh tank top, whose leering offer of a free Fudgsicle Ellen haughtily refused.

The second vehicle, a black Volvo, Ellen recognized from afar as the chariot of her lord, who paused just before the driveway to yell out this observation: "Ya look like white trash loungin' there, Ellen!" Then, with an outraged glance at her legs, bared in a bikini: "Cover yourself, goddamn it!" flinging at her, along with this imperative, the means to obey it: his jacket, violently doffed for exactly that purpose.

By seven o'clock, Ellen was on the edge of her lounge chair. Where on earth was Estelle? Surely—barring the most unholy gluttony on the part of the editor—they weren't still at lunch! And yet, according to Nipe, she had not called in to explain the delay. This was unlike Estelle, very unlike her.

At seven-thirty, Ellen abandoned her post for a quick supper. At eight, reseated roadside in the thickening darkness, she abandoned herself to Panic and Despair.

"I'm sure she'll be here any minute," Lisanne said, pausing for a moment on her way to Adair's. "She probably just got caught in traffic."

"But what if she drank at lunch," Ellen said. "God knows, she's a bad enough driver stone-cold sober. But drunk—! Oh, I knew I should have chauffeured her in and back myself."

"She's stopped drinking," Lisanne pointed out.

"*As far as we know.*" Ellen paused. "What if she stopped to give money to some homeless maniac and was murdered?"

"Oh Ellen," Lisanne said. "And you always say you have no imagination."

Twenty minutes later, at the exact millisecond Ellen was rising to call the police, two snouts of light poked through the darkness. Headlights! Thus arrested, Ellen stood with one bent knee held high, like a statue of a curveting horse.

Thank God! It was Estelle's old Chevrolet! Ellen lowered her leg and raced round to the front yard.

"What took you so long? I've been out of my mind with worry."

But the sight of her mother's sad face, illumined by the porch light, vaporized her wrath.

Wordlessly, Ellen followed, as with faltering steps Estelle mounted the three stairs into the kitchen.

"You look like you could use a pot of Serenity Mint, Mother," she said, setting the kettle to boil.

Estelle sat down and laid her head on the kitchen table as Ellen prepared the tea.

"You're so good to me, Ellen," she said.

"Nonsense!" said the daughter briskly. "Now, tell me, Mother, for I'm all agog. How did your lunch go?"

At the first detail Estelle offered, Ellen went from agog to agape.

"They're giving me fifty thousand for it."

And at the second detail, from agape to aghast.

"And I've decided on my pseudonym: Francine Cocklette."

"Cocklette?" Ellen said. "It's not very melodious, is it? Why not Ashley Vespertina or Gwendolyn Cloudburst?" For these were the typical noms de plume of her mother's chosen genre.

"Well, Aurora liked it," said Estelle.

While Ellen endorsed the idea of a pseudonym for Estelle, this choice struck her as pathetic. She let it pass. They sat for a while in a silence broken only by the smackings of their lips upon the steaming mugs.

"So what time did you finish lunch?" Ellen said.

"Oh, a little before three. Afterward—"

"Yes?" Ellen fixed upon the widow a gimlet eye.

"Well, afterward I walked downtown."

"And?"

"And I went by *his* apartment."

"*Jesus!*" Ellen said.

"And he's gone, Ellen. The count and his Queen. Just vanished. He was subletting the apartment from some professor, Professor O'Reilly, who's on sabbatical in Ireland—studying leprechauns, I gather. His lease doesn't run out till January, but there's no way to know if he's still paying rent, because it's O'Reilly who sends in the checks. Apparently, he spent one night there early this month. And no one in the building has seen him since."

Ellen could have told Estelle all this. She had covered this terrain early on in her own search—a search she'd secretly been pursuing these last three weeks.

"My goodness, you've been busy!" she said now. "What did you do, Mother? Lurk on the stoop and bushwhack the poor tenants as they emerged?" (This had, in fact, been Ellen's method.)

Estelle looked sheepish. "Well, I did rest there for a while," she said, "being tired from my walk. One kindly red-haired lady—"

(Kindly? Ellen knew exactly the redhead to whom Estelle referred; she had not found her kindly in the least. On the contrary, she was one of the rudest viragos Ellen had ever had the misfortune to encounter in her life.)

"—took the trouble to rustle up Dr. O'Reilly's address for me," Estelle was saying. "I thought I might drop him a line and see if he's heard anything."

(Ellen had already dropped this scholar a line and had as yet received not a single syllable in reply. Too busy with his leprechauns—the quack!)

"I've been so worried, so frantic," Estelle was saying. "If only I knew he was okay, I wouldn't have to know where he was, I wouldn't have to see him. Just to know he was safe would be enough."

"I'm sure he's safe," Ellen said.

"You really think so?"

"Absolutely," Ellen said. "Most people live a long, long time. And don't forget—he's a ninja! He can take care of himself."

"I wish I could believe that." Estelle reached across the table to clasp Ellen's hands. "I want you to know I appreciate it," she said, "your listening to me like this, Ellen. You're the only one I can talk to."

Ellen knew this to be true. Lisanne seemed to have taken a vow of silence on all subjects Cockleburgian, and with everyone else Estelle felt bound to maintain the pitiful fiction of "the sudden business"—not to protect herself but to protect Cockleburg.

Still, Ellen was ashamed by her mother's gratitude, by what it betrayed: that she had never listened to her mother like this before.

"Don't be silly," she said. "It's my pleasure."

Ellen thought of all their morning phone calls over the years, of all those hours she had talked about herself. She thought of the rare chances she had let go by, long ago, when her mother used to call her late at night. Just to chat, she used to say, just to kill an hour, because your father isn't home yet.

"My divorce is final today," Adair said. "Do you want to get married?"

Lisanne thought she must have misheard. But then, from the bushes below them, to the right of the porch, there came a long sibilation, as though a water sprinkler had been turned on.

"Married?" she said.

Again, even before Adair's confirming nod, there came that hissing exclamation.

"Married," Adair said. Then, turning his face toward the bushes, he cupped his hands around his mouth, and shouted: *"I'm asking you to marry me!"*

Now they heard the sound of thrashing movement— twigs snapping, leaves rustling.

Lisanne smiled and tapped Adair's arm. "Don't, honey, don't taunt her."

He turned back to her. "I'm serious. I want to marry you."

They had cut short their walk this evening because of an approaching storm. You could almost see the seeds of rain spilling down in the distance from the dark slit clouds.

"You mean, you want me to be your *wife?*" Lisanne said.

"Yes, that's what I mean, that's what men usually mean when they ask that question."

"Bit sudden, ain't it?" said a scornful voice to their right.

Lisanne and Adair ignored this. Now and then, Nipe lost control of herself, and muttered out some comment from the gallery—comments that Adair and Lisanne obligingly pretended not to hear.

"Bit sudden, ain't it?" she said, smiling until she saw from his face that he was serious.

She said, without thinking, "But I don't want to be a wife."

The first time her father asked her to lie, she was nine years old. He said, "I was in the car with your mother last night and there was a tape of Frank Sinatra love songs playing. Your mother knows I don't give a damn about music, so she asked who gave me the tape. I told her, 'Someone you love very much," and she said, 'Who?' and I told her you gave me the tape, okay? *You* gave it to me."

Her mother mentioned it a week later. "That was a nice present you gave Daddy."

Lisanne had been practicing what she would say. She said it: "Oh yes—Frank Sinatra, he's one of my favorites."

She hadn't felt guilty in the lie. She had felt strong and proud.

"Look, I'm sorry I asked," Adair said. "I guess it is sort of sudden. Why don't we just forget it?"

He stood up and went inside.

Lisanne sat there for a long moment on the sagging sofa.

Then she followed him in.

She said, "You don't understand."

"What's there to understand?" He was standing over the sink—washing dishes!

She went over to him. "Sit down," she said.

He wouldn't look at her.

"Look at me," she said. "I have to tell you something, something I've never told anyone."

"You don't have to tell me anything."

"I want to." She tugged his arm.

He sat down.

I was my father's alibi, she thought.

"I was my father's alibi for years," she told him, "and I enjoyed it."

Although she never wanted to be a wife, she had thought, for a while, that she might want to be a mistress. Gay, charming, contained, and cruel, like the mistresses she admired from history class. Barbara Castlemaine, Lillie Langtry, Madame de Maintenon. She admired them for the things they wanted: titles, palaces, money, jewels, power, even marriage. Mistresses wanted things before they wanted love. Love was just the currency of the transaction.

She had been jealous of her father's mistresses, she remembered, until she learned how much better, how much safer it is, being a daughter. The mistresses she knew in real life waited, and were lied to, and were in love, just like the wives.

In the first week of September, four things happened— four things that Ellen jotted down in her Filofax (which served as a sort of diary) in order of ascending importance (also chronologically correct).

(1) *Donald, Jr. returns from tennis camp.*

. . . To the boundless joy of his father, who took a day off to meet him at the airport, and who had hardly slept the night before, so great was his excitement. The only jarring note in the reunion was the pink tank top in which the revenant deplaned—but this offensive garment ("Fit for a mincing queen," as Donald described it) being immediately stuffed into a trash can in Baggage Claim, the father abandoned himself to pure, unalloyed—indeed, boisterous—merriment. Thus bare-chested did Donnie make his way across the airport parking lot to the waiting Volvo, and thus bare-chested did he greet his weeping dam on the porch steps of the Bedford manse. With bursting pride Donald fondled the brand-new thews bulging about the boy's shoulders, and with bursting pride he pointed out to Ellen the boy's new swagger, and his deepening voice (imperceptible to Ellen). "He left home a lad," rejoiced the father, "but, by golly, he's come home a youth!"

As Ellen had hoped, Donnie's return had an assuasive effect on Donald, who spent hour after transported hour courtside, watching his Pride and Joy hit backhand cross-courts with a local pro.

(2) *Lester Lipp apprehended in Tempe.*

Wreathed in smiles, Nipe summoned Donald from the dinner table with these words: "It's the feds, sir—on the line for ya." Cheeks flushed with triumph, Donald returned to the table and proclaimed the news of that larcenous groundsman's downfall: "They caught his ass—and it's about time, too, by God!" Triumph quickly gave way to outrage, however, for Estelle refused to press charges. With quivering buttocks and dartling tongue, Donald denounced her decision. Never in the history of the human tongue did a tongue dartle as fast and as furiously as did Donald's tongue dartle that night! By turns cajoling, pleading, and bullying, he exhorted the obdurate dame to let justice take its course.

Lester Lipp was never tried, the paintings and silver—never returned.

(3) *Patsy calls from Paris—COCK'S FOR REAL!*

With O'Reilly, the leprechaunologist, turning out a dead end, Ellen had been forced to explore other avenues in her search for Cockleburg. One of these avenues, so to speak, was her friend Patsy, who upon being dumped by her husband for a Ford model, had moved to Paris and embarked on a sexual odyssey the lurid chronicles of which made Ellen's head spin. Slithering her way up and down those famous boulevards, Patsy, it seemed, had not passed a single busboy, bellhop, waiter, or cabby without a proposition. For Ellen's sake, the democratic Patsy had turned her hot, lascivious gaze a little higher—to the capital's philosophes and aristocrats. It was from one of the latter that Patsy heard (while flat on her back) this news of Cockleburg, which she relayed in a collect call to her dumbstruck friend: that he was, in fact, a genuine count, the title so ancient as to make the Montresores look like parvenus; that he was a published poet, and a respected tympanist who had performed at the Paris Opéra; and that he was the bereaved widower of a woman named Sandrine.

(4) *Lisanne announces her engagement to Adair.*

Ellen had to wonder: Is anyone ever really happy to hear that someone they love is getting married?

17

Summer traditionally ended, for the Prawls and for Estelle, with Donnie's birthday on September 15. That event was celebrated with particular extravagance this year, for not only did the date mark Donnie's entry into the double digits of age, it also marked the official end of the moratorium on presents. Trucks, trains, guns, swords, kites, games, sportswear, and tennis rackets—so immense was the tribute paid to the youth the Prawls had to hire a U-Haul to transport it back to the city! Donnie received forty-one presents in all: seventeen from Estelle alone; thirteen from Donald; five each from Ellen and Lisanne; Nipe bringing up the rear with one—a Bible.

The morning after this bacchanal, Estelle moved back to her Fifth Avenue apartment, and Donald, with Ellen and Junior, resettled on Seventy-eighth Street.

And Lisanne moved her big black suitcase—"For the last time, I hope," she said—across the yard to the caretaker's cottage.

But the Bedford house did not long remain empty, for the family reconvened there every weekend that fine fall—not only to revel in the beauty of the foliage and the joy of one another's company, but also to plan the upcoming wedding, scheduled for the last Saturday in October.

"Please, Mother, please," Lisanne kept saying, "nothing grand—just a small, plain, simple, family wedding, okay?"

"Small, plain, simple, family, yes, darling, yes," said Estelle. "But that doesn't mean we can't make it special." She would talk by the hour, if permitted, about flowers, tents, toasts, bands, balloons. . . . She met regularly for tea with the Reverend Prisslerpiss, who was to officiate at the ceremony, to discuss her plans for the great day.

"What is he? A wedding coordinator or a preacher?" Donald said in disgust. "Crawling up the driveway every goddamn weekend to kiss the old dame's ass! Shouldn't he be writing sermons or visiting the poor? I'm of a mind to boot him back to his rectory, by golly!"

"Please, Donald!" said Ellen, shocked. "He's a man of God!"

"He may be of God," said Donald, "but he sure as hell ain't a man! Reverend Prisslerpiss, my ass! Reverend Sisyphus, that's what I call him, the sissy. Sisyphus," he repeated, majestic in his scorn—and ignorance of mythology.

Outraged as Donald had been over the unholiness of Adair and Lisanne's union, he was even more outraged by their decision to make it holy. Estelle made it clear, however, that she would not brook a word of protest against the engagement. Thus the river of Donald's outrage was rerouted, so to speak (for it could not be dammed), and it poured in all its mighty torrents upon the head of the holy man.

Though Ellen deplored this scapegoating of the Reverend, she had to admit that some of his ideas were a bit outlandish. For example, it was Prisslerpiss who suggested to Estelle the Elizabethan theme (which she enthusiastically embraced). The guests were to arrive in horse and buggy, dressed in jerkins and stomachers and hose. . . .

"I will not wear hose," Donald said. "He cannot make me wear hose."

There was also to be a giant suckling pig, roasted out on the lawn on a spit; and, immediately following this feast, readings of Elizabethan poems. (Donald didn't mind the pig, but, needless to say, he heartily denounced the poems.)

"Wouldn't it be lovely," said the Reverend one Saturday afternoon, sucking down his tea, "if the immediate male family—say, Mr. Prawl and his son—were to dance a spirited jig in honor of the Happy Pair?"

It was this suggestion, even more than the Elizabethan costumes, that cemented Donald's enmity toward the clergyman.

"I will not dance," Donald said. "He cannot make me dance."

"Jigs? Pigs? Jerkins and hose? My wedding is turning into a farce," Lisanne said to Ellen.

"Don't spoil it for her, darling," Ellen said. "She's having such a good time."

"That's what Adair says," said Lisanne.

"You know, I planned this all along," Estelle told Ellen, "Lisanne and Adair. I knew they'd be perfect for each other. I knew it," she said. "I just didn't dare to dream."

Two days before the wedding, Lisanne, husking corn at the kitchen counter, glanced out the window and saw

Adair passing by with a black garbage bag slung over his
shoulder, on his way to the trash cans in the back garage.
She dropped the golden ear, its silky skirt half lifted, and
ran outside to stop him.

"You don't have to throw them out," she said.

Because she knew, with a flash of intuition too sure to
be a guess, that this was the garbage bag filled with photos of Junellen.

He set the bag down on the gravel. "It's like having
something dead in the house," he said. "It's starting to
smell."

The mouth of the bag was gaping open.

"You want to see them, don't you?" With the toe of his
boot, he nudged the bag, so that the glossy faces spilled
out.

There were hundreds of snapshots. Lisanne knelt down
and arranged them in fans at his feet. In some, the
woman was casually posed, smiling for the camera, in
doorways, on windowsills, in swimming pools, in fields
of daisies. In others, she seemed caught unawares, rising
from the tub with soapy shoulders and a violated look;
sitting nude and coiled and combing out her hair like
Circe. In several shots, she was laughing, head tilted,
mouth slanted, eyes blood red in the light of the flash. In
all the photos, she was alone. She was not as beautiful as
Lisanne had feared, had hoped—no woman could be—
but she was beautiful enough, in a hard, bright, burnished way. She wore a lot of makeup. Although Lisanne
knew she had no right to it, she released it at last—the hot
flood of jealousy. She knew his love had been obsessive.
He must have stalked her day and night, behind the camera's small glass eye.

He had not once—not yet—taken a photograph of her.

Reading her mind, Adair said, "I didn't take them,
Lisanne. She did. Every single one. She had a tripod, and

one of those cameras with a self-timer. When you're through with them, throw them out."

Lisanne heard him walk back to the house. She was glad he'd gone. She did not want to see Junellen through his eyes.

As she studied the photographs, Lisanne felt her jealousy shift into something else: envy. She had dreamed of Junellen many times—as many times, she was sure, as Adair dreamed of her. Lisanne imagined them now, their two dreams, rising night after night over the bed they slept in, and laughing at each other. She had been fascinated with Junellen from the beginning. She didn't want to touch her, necessarily, or possess her. Her fascination was a kind of love, but not the lover's kind. What she'd wanted was to get to where love's object looks out at the world—at me, Lisanne thought now, *at me.*

She had wanted to become her. She had recognized Junellen, from the beginning, as what she had been trying to become her whole life.

Here was a woman who had walked away from husband and child—walked out into the desert! A woman prouder of her cruelties than her kindnesses. A woman protected by that disgust that is the true luxury of the loved. Here was a woman who had betrayed everyone who loved her—betrayed them without love and therefore in perfect innocence. The loveless betrayals seemed to Lisanne like random slashings of tooth and claw: there is no meaning, beyond damage, in the damage that they do. If love is the richest, the only source of shame, no wonder Junellen had none.

Lisanne envied Junellen her freedom. In the end, she had not had the stomach for it. In the end, it was easier to be kind, to return the calls and write the letters, to tell the truth and love the ones who love you.

• • •

In the weeks before the wedding, there were reports of rabid coons in the area, scuttling down chimneys in the dead of night and attacking old women in their beds. Ellen had feared that she would be bitten; that she would develop rabies just in time for the wedding; that she would, in effect, go down in infamy as the Rabid Matron of Honor in the gossip columns of the local paper.

But she was not bitten, and she was not rabid, and no displays of rolling eyes and foaming mouth marred the Elizabethan merriment of the celebration—not even from Donald, whose outrage had been known to manifest itself in rabious ways. The humiliation of wearing hose kept his upper cheeks pallid and his nether cheeks, for the most part, sepulchrally still.

"You have such a magnificent leg, dear," Ellen said, trying to jolly him the morning of the wedding, as he completed this most painful toilette. And indeed his big calves swelled majestic in white tights over his pointed, high-heeled Elizabethan pumps. "You ought to be, if anything, thankful," she said, "for this opportunity to display it."

This suggestion elicited a muffled groan of anguish.

"Look at it this way," Ellen said. "Sir Walter Raleigh wore hose—and surely no manlier man than that knight and navigator exists in all the annals of history! Why don't you just pretend you're Sir Walter?"

Another muffled groan. Then: "I'm just thankful I don't have to wear a goddamn periwig!"

For this final indignity had been rather self-servingly suggested by the bald Reverend. In deference to Donald's feelings, however, Estelle had decided to make this embellishment optional.

At the sight of Li'l Donald, Big Donald cast off his dumb despair.

"By God, it's not right!" he cried. "It's just not right!"

For already in the distance the brisk clip-clops of approaching horse-drawn buggies, laden with guests, could be heard; and Li'l, who had been hiding in his room, could hide no longer. He stepped forward now into his parents' chamber with downcast eyes still glistening with the tears that had moistened his pillow all morning, stepped forward in all the pomp and pageantry of the panoply chosen for him with such loving care by his grandmama, as morose an Elizabethan page as ever drew breath in this or any other century!

"Darling, don't you look wonderful!" Ellen exclaimed, scarcely able to restrain her laughter, for Donnie was the very picture of absurdity in his high, white, frothing collar, jeweled doublet, and billowing red velvet breeches that ended snugly mid-thigh to reveal spindly shanks sheathed in matching silk hose.

Sensing her silent laughter, Big Donald now shot Ellen a look of hatred and minced forward in his pumps to lay a lace-clad arm around the boy's bowed shoulders.

"Buck up, man," he said. "We'll get through it together."

"But the jig, Father, the jig," said the lad in a sobbing voice—for this hellish ordeal loomed darkly ahead.

"I re*peat*, my good man," said the father, shaking as with palsy, "we'll get through it together—*like men.*"

While sympathetic (up to a point) to the sartorial—and imminent saltatorial—humiliation of her husband and child, Ellen, whirling one last time before the full-length mirror, couldn't help but reflect on how well the archaic garb suited *her*—the low, square-cut bodice plumping up her breasts and the tight stomacher displaying the taut, aerobicized curve of late-twentieth-century waist and hip.

In the bridal suite across the hall, Estelle was kneeling—fastening Lisanne's garter.

"Are you nervous, darling?" Ellen asked.

"Not at all," Lisanne said.

Although Estelle had tried to talk her into panniers, feathered hats, and all manner of Elizabethan titivations, Lisanne had insisted on the simplest wedding dress she could find: a strapless cream-colored satin sheath that plunged down, clinging to her hourglass figure, from a deep heart-shaped bodice. It was almost austere—unadorned by a single ruffle, bead, frill, or scrap of lace—and it suited Lisanne's statuesque beauty to perfection. You could almost fasten her to the prow of a ship, Ellen thought. People like to say that all brides are beautiful, but Ellen, for one, had known many a homely bride in her day (Patsy, Sherry, all her best friends, in fact!). Lisanne was beautiful, though, so beautiful the sight of her made Ellen draw in her breath (already drawn in by the stomacher). That tribute she had never quite been able to bring herself to pay her sister burst from her now:

"You're so gorgeous, Lisanne."

Lisanne smiled doubtfully in the mirror.

"So gorgeous it almost makes me want to puke," Ellen said, in perfect truth.

Lisanne turned away from her reflection. "Thank you, Ellen, that means a lot to me," she said. "I've always felt so in your shadow."

"Stuff and nonsense!" Ellen said, pleased all the same.

She thought of her own wedding day, so long ago, and wiping away a swelling bittersweet tear, stumbled downstairs and out onto the lawn to help Donald greet the arriving guests—and not a moment too soon, either, for the hose-clad homophobe made a churlish host indeed. Pausing for a moment on the landing, Ellen saw several guests approach him, wreathed in smiles, only to reel back with stricken looks.

She rushed to his side: "Darling, do try and make an effort, won't you? I know it's hard—"

"Hard? Hard? *Hard?* You don't know the half of it!" And as he glanced now at Prisslerpiss, who was hovering by the bar, Ellen could actually feel the hatred rising off him. "Look at him, for God's sake! Look at him in that friggin' periwig!"

Ellen did look, had been looking. It would have been impossible, frankly, *not* to look. Ellen had known, of course, that the Reverend, in his alopecia, could not afford to scorn the periwig, but even thus prepared, she was stunned by the wealth of white sausage curls that rose up in a prodigious pompadour to dangle *halfway down his cassock!*

"It's a bit much, isn't it?" she said.

"I'll say it's a bit much," Donald said, his voice rising. "And I'll tell ya what else is a bit much—the amount of punch he's been swilling!"

And indeed the Reverend *did* look rather flushed.

"By God, it's clear ol' Sisyphus is no foe to alcohol!" And Donald lunged forward, the high heels of his pumps sinking into the grass, as if he meant to dash the brimming tumbler from the holy man's plump hand!

Even as Donald struggled to disinter his pumps, the ingurgitating clergyman, catching sight of Ellen, began to make his way toward them, his gigantic wife in tow. He moved in dots and dashes like a Morse code across the lawn, his curls streaming out behind him. Simultaneously Donald spoke.

"By God, the preacher's drunk!"

The preacher now pantingly arrived before them.

"Never has my sacred calling brought me more pleasure, spiritual or corporeal, than on this joyous day," he began, booming as though he were in the pulpit. "The weather so unseasonably mild, the sky so celestially blue, the pig so succulently plump—"

Donald cut through these panegyrics with this curt advice: "Lay off the sauce, why donchya, padre! From now on, I think you'd best stick to tea!"

There was enough here, certainly, to provoke repartee.

"Prithee mind your own business, me heartie," said the minister in his playful Elizabethan way, "and let the good Lord see to mine."

Donald was quick to resent this kind of comment from a man, cloth or no cloth.

"The good Lord doesn't seem to be doing a very good job of it," he said, making a grab for the preacher's glass.

Listing a bit, the preacher swung it from his reach.

Just then, Donald's attention was diverted by a spectacle infinitely more horrific even than the preacher's gross inebriation: Tiger Sprague-McHay, a known homosexual, dressed today like the Virgin Queen herself, *backing Li'l into the bushes.*

It was a scene straight out of any father's worst nightmare. With a string of expletives that made the minister cross himself in horror, Donald, at the utmost speed of which he was capable in his crippling footwear, raced to the aid of his cub.

"Quite the Harry Hotspur, eh?" said the preacher, watching his host stagger off.

There was a tense silence.

Then Mrs. Prisslerpiss began to declaim on the beauty of the flowers, the elegance of the guests, speaking in a mournful whisper that made everything she said seem like bad news.

Presently Lady Perdita waddled up, her immense train and headdress visibly stupefying the surrounding guests, and Ellen made the introductions. The preacher's wife was a full ten inches taller than the noblewoman, even with the headdress. After one quick upward roll of her eyes, the noblewoman ignored her.

"Rather shocking, isn't it?" she said. "Carrying on

with the caretaker and all—like out of Dickens—"

Lady Perdita seemed to think everything was written by Dickens.

"I think you must mean D. H. Lawrence," Ellen said.

"This kind of thing just isn't done—simply is not done—not among the fine families of England, certainly," said her ladyship. "But then I suppose there are no fine families in the colonies. I always said so, and this just proves it—"

"I adore your costume, Aunt Lady Perdita," Ellen said.

"It's not a *costume*," said milady, sneering up at Ellen's stomacher, "at least not in the vulgar, theatrical sense I'm sure you mean, dear. Why, it belonged to my great-great-great-great-great-great-great aunt, Perdita Margaret Catherine Elinor Louise, seventh Duchess of Montresore and esteemed lady-in-waiting to Queen Elizabeth herself!"

"They were shorter in those days, weren't they?" said Mrs. Prisslerpiss. "And quite a bit stouter, too, I should think. Truly, milady, the dress fits you perfectly."

Milady sublimely did not acknowledge this remark, not by word, deed, twitch, or quiver. She leaned forward and said to Ellen in a hissing voice that was meant to be a whisper but that carried like a shout, "I must say, I have never in all my life seen so many common-looking people gathered in a single tent. For example"—pointing a rigid dactyl—"who is that loutish midget over by the lutists?"

It was Gunter-the-doorman, whom Estelle had insisted on inviting. He was tap-dancing to an Elizabethan ballad, a bottle of scotch in hand; and though the festivities had barely begun, he looked but a quaff or two away from total unconsciousness.

"I suppose we should be thankful, at least, that the good doctah couldn't make it," Lady Perdita was saying. "Your mother told me he was called away—on sudden business—and I must admit, I was only too glad to hear it." The glint in milady's eyes boded a thorough interrogation on this subject.

Ellen smiled brightly. "I'll be right back," she said— and weaved away through the throng of godchildren, relatives, and dear old friends. There was Freddy Keck, looking anxiously about for Estelle (and her checkbook, Ellen was sure). And Buddy Bulber, the sickly viridescence of whose complexion suggested to Ellen that it was his liver, and not his bladder, that could use the yacht—or better yet, six months at Hazeldon.

These reflections were interrupted by Estelle, who appeared, breathless, on the landing. There was a sudden hush, and then a rustling of silk and satin as the guests made their way toward the benches ranged in rows outside the tent. A raised platform served as the altar. Here stood Adair, handsome in a severe blue suit (Ellen had to admit)—*and without his braid!* (So he'd finally done the decent thing and cut it off.) He was holding the hand of his little boy, who leaned against his walker, his twisted legs in blue knickers. The child, breathing loudly through his mouth, looked dazed with happiness. In what was the only act of generosity in his short life to date, Donnie had, the night before, showered Ian with dozens of his old toys. When the shock of this had worn off, Ellen had, for the very first time, wept the hot, sweet tears of maternal pride.

Then Lisanne emerged from the doorway, to a collective gasp of admiration from the seated guests. The lutists segued into the Wedding March. Arm in arm, Lisanne and Estelle walked down the gray stone steps, and down the aisle, Ellen tearful and tottering behind them.

Prisslerpiss began: "I intend to say to you toady—to-*day*—jush a foo shimple wordsh. . . ."

Foo became many, however, as the preacher lost control of his discourse, to wind through tortuous digressions.

("Nothing to say," Donald would say later, "and said it over and over again.")

Finally, Adair leaned forward and discreetly whispered a word or two to the rambling man of God. With a shake of his periwig, Prisslerpiss recalled himself to the business at hand.

". . . And if anyone present knows why this pair should not be joined in holy matrimony, let them speak now, or forever hold their peashe!"

All the ladies sighed as the groom bent his head and kissed the bride, all except one, resplendent in a velvet muumuu, who snorted. Nipe.

"And now," intoned the Reverend, "we have a special treat in store," And he stepped back, with the bridal party, leaving the platform clear for the jiggers, who at this cue shuffled forward, as if in a coffle, with bowed heads and agonized expressions, to stomp about.

In twenty seconds, the hymeneal jig—if movement so mournful can be called a jig—was over, and the guests rose as one and lurched toward the suckling pig.

"What a perfect day!" Estelle said to Ellen later. "I only wish you-know-who could have been here with us to share in all the joy."

"You mean—Daddy?" Ellen said.

"Oh, him too," she said. "But I actually meant dear Coco. I felt his absence so keenly today. Didn't you?"

If the truth be told, Ellen had. Among all the dandies gathered on their lawn that day, he would have shown the brightest. And of all the epithalamiums sung that day, his would have soared the highest. Ellen had half-expected he would show up unannounced, as was his fashion. She had half-hoped to see him limp out of the bushes in some

preposterously gaudy costume. She had a feeling, somehow, that he was around, hovering like a guardian angel,
or a criminal at the scene of the crime. Gunter swore he'd
seen him many times, sitting on a bench on Fifth Avenue,
across the street from her mother's apartment. "He was
wearing a hat, and a scarf, and big glasses," Gunter said,
"but I'd know him anywhere." Gunter was a drunk and a
fool, unquestionably; but then Ellen began to see, or
dream him, too. But when she crossed the street toward
him, he had turned into an old lady, a blue-haired old
lady, who looked a lot like Ellen's tenth-grade math
teacher.

Lisanne and Adair went to Paris on their honeymoon,
and stayed at the Ritz Hotel. Lisanne had not wanted a
honeymoon—or at least not such a lavish one—but Estelle had insisted.

"You've already been far too generous as it is," Lisanne
told her, "paying for the wedding and all."

"But that part's for me," Estelle said. "This part's for
you. Please, you must let me give this to you." She said,
"You're the only one who's never asked me for a thing."

Lisanne had spent the night before the wedding in her
old room at the big house.

"Here's a little something for you," Ellen had said,
dropping onto her bed a package wrapped in gold paper.
"Open it when you get to Paris—and think of me, okay?"

"I'd think of you anyway," Lisanne said.

"Now, Lisanne, you must promise me something," said
Estelle, who had been standing in the doorway.

"Anything," said Lisanne.

"You must promise me you'll go and see Femme—"

"Femme?" said Lisanne.

"It's a statue," said Estelle. "Coco's favorite statue in

the whole world. He used to speak of it to me all the time. He said that when he lived in Paris he went to see it almost every day. It's in the Hall of Greek and Roman Antiquities at the Louvre," she said, "on the way to the Venus de Milo. Think of Coco when you see it," she said. "And think of me."

18

A week after the wedding, Estelle did something she rarely dared to do. She listened to the tape of Harry snoring—snores saved all these years. She lay down on her bed, and pressed Play, and closed her eyes.

She used to think she would know his snores anywhere. . . .

("If someone dropped me down blindfolded into a room filled with snoring men," she told him, "I would be able to pick you out.")

"But why would anyone do that, Estelle?" he said. "Why would anyone want to drop you down blindfolded into a room filled with snoring men?")

. . . but really, they could be anyone's snores—or even any dog's, any sleeping mammal's.

For the first time, Estelle listened till the end of the tape—the whole hour of it. The last fifteen minutes, she discovered, was silence. He must have rolled onto his stomach. He had only snored when he was on his back.

For the first time, she listened to it without crying or forcing herself to cry. Before, she had forced herself to cry, just in case he was watching—or, perhaps, to summon him if he wasn't.

Because this was what she wanted when she had played this tape in the past: to summon his ghost. If any ghost would haunt her, it would be his. No other ghost would care. She had wanted to be haunted. She had wanted to believe that something flowed behind the skin of silence. Something evil, even. But something.

All these years, she had been looking for a sign. She had waited for his ghost to guide her from danger—or into it. She had looked for its pale glow above her bed each night, wondering why it is that people always look up for ghosts—as though ghosts couldn't, or wouldn't, creep along the floor.

Estelle opened her eyes when the taped silence snapped off. That's when, slowly, the smudges on the ceiling started to move.

Little Donald was at the movies, and the Prawls were enjoying a rare peaceful Saturday afternoon together.

The phone rang.

Ellen picked up, listened in silence for thirty seconds, and said, "I'll be right over."

Donald looked up from his *Wall Street Journal.* "What the heck—?"

"That was Mom," Ellen said. "I'll be back as soon as I can."

Donald glanced aggressively at his watch. "It's almost four o'clock. What about that roast leg o' lamb you promised me for supper?"

"Roast it yourself," Ellen said.

With an indignant shifting of his great rump, tightly

encased in an armchair, Donald said, "What's wrong with the old dame now?"

Ellen hesitated at the door. "There are worms on her ceiling."

"Worms!" Donald half-rose, then sank back into his skin-tight chair. "By God, now I know where you get your crappy housekeeping from! It runs in the family, don't it?"

"Better that than the heart disease that runs in yours, dear." Ellen had taken a step out into the hallway, when this husbandly maxim caused her to pirouette round on pointed toe:

"Let me suggest to you, dear wife, that extermination, like charity, begins at home. I'd advise you to see to your own roaches before concerning yourself with someone else's worms."

Ellen said, tight-lipped, "You can be impossible, you know that?"

Donald inclined his head, in a baronial manner—as if at a tribute.

Ellen again pirouetted round. Her lord's laughter lofted after her into the hall.

"Better worms," he cried, "better worms than Cockle-burgs, eh? Ha! Ha! Ha Ha! Ha!"

Outside, the sky was the unwholesome white of eye-balls. Running up to Park Avenue to hail a taxi, Ellen broke into a sweat in her light jacket. For November, it was weirdly hot—had been since the wedding—and the weather was starting to give Ellen the creeps.

Anything unseasonable was sinister to Ellen.

Estelle met her in the foyer by the elevator. Ellen looked up nervously as they walked into the apartment together.

"They're only in the bedroom," Estelle said.

The light seemed stale, as though it had not been

changed for days. It seemed to separate in swirls in the
air, like sour milk poured into water. Everything bleached
spectrally in it: the shabby furniture, the chandeliers, Estelle. Ellen glanced into the open doorways off the hall.
All the rooms were in order, she saw—in order, because
untouched. This tidiness was worse than filth in a way.
At least filth was a sign of life.

"I was thinking of your father," said Estelle, "when I
saw them."

"Pure, meaningless, random coincidence, Mother!"
Ellen said. "Of course they must have been there for
hours—even days."

Estelle said, "Yes, of course. I noticed them before, but
I thought they were smudges." She said, "The second
thing I did was check my body to make sure that's not
where they were coming from."

Ellen didn't want to ask what the first thing was. They
ascended the stairs in silence.

"I'll wait here," Estelle said, just outside the door.

As she walked into her mother's room, Ellen saw something rolling ahead of her on the bare floor, something
she must have kicked with her foot. At first she thought it
was a bead. Bending down, she discovered it to be a vita-
min. Dust coated its thin red skin, its hopefulness.

Through the glass doors, the dogs, out on the terrace,
saw her and began to howl.

Rising cautiously, Ellen looked up, shielding her eyes
as though from blinding light, with a hand over her brow.

It was true, they looked like smudges, innocent nicks in
the white ceiling. From the floor, they appeared black.
Climbing onto the bed for a closer look, Ellen saw they
were in fact yellow. You would have to track them for
hours to perceive movement, but they *did* move: in
plumpings and swellings that slid them along in minute,

stately undulations. Ellen shivered. She thought, Think of the reasons why you are frightened, and you will see they are not good enough.

She was frightened because the worms were so calm, and so steady, and so stupid. They had the strength of the utterly mindless. She reminded herself that she was larger than they, and that if she saw a single one of them on the ground, in the earth, where it belonged, she would not be afraid. But they were many, and they were not where they belonged. She was frightened of their ugliness, their oozing yellow fatness, their completeness. She was frightened by the way they ignored her. They were enough to make her think of her roach with something almost like affection! Her roach was intimidating—*he was so accomplished*. He could fly, he could dive into drains, and scuttle through pipes. He could outrun her. But though he defeated and defied her, he could not afford to ignore her. Compared to her roach, these worms were helpless. All she had to do was reach up—she had a human brain. She had human fingers with which to pluck them up and crush them. All these powers, and none of them a comfort. Because she could kill the worms, she knew, but she could never disturb them. In their obliviousness, they were inviolable.

Ellen bounded off the bed and into the hallway. She passed Estelle without looking at her and ran down the stairs and into the blue sitting room. She sat down by the phone and called the Montresore-Wolfes in England.

Estelle appeared, panting, in the doorway.

"Damn!" Ellen slammed down the phone. "No answer. Where's that helminthologist when we need him?"

"You mean—Dave?" said Estelle.

Ellen said, "You're damn right I do! Here's a chance for him to repay you, finally, for all those years you put him through worm school."

It still rankled Ellen that Dave had not even had the decency to dedicate his dissertation on parasites to Estelle. He had dedicated it to a spaniel.

"What shall we do?" said Estelle, tottering into the room and sinking onto her blue sofa.

Suddenly Ellen was furious with her. No one else's mother had worms on her ceiling.

"Obviously, we're going to have to call an exterminator," she said.

She looked under Pest Control Services in the Yellow Pages and dialed the number of one that was close to the apartment. A woman's voice answered, and it grew increasingly eager as Ellen explained the situation.

"I've seen more worms today than ever before in my life," the woman said. "I've seen so many worms today my eyes are like crossed-eyed. I've seen so many worms today *I'm doubting my own self!*"

There was a silence, and then the sounds of a struggle—a thud, a gasp—and then a man came on the line.

His was clearly the voice of reason here, the woman's the voice of passion.

"I'll tell you what," he said. "It's after five, but we'll stay open for you. I can tell how upset you are, and I can't say as I blame you. Same thing happened to us once. At least yours are still on the ceiling—for now, at any rate." Ellen begged him, please, just to send someone over, but the man said it was crucial that he know what breed of worm it was first. "There are more kinds of worms than you might think," he said menacingly. "What might get one might not get another." Ellen hesitated. The man was sympathetic but stern. He instructed Ellen to capture a worm, put it in a jar, and run it over to the shop. Simple enough on paper, but when Ellen hung up the phone, her hands were shaking.

She remembered when she didn't mind insects, when

they were just another potential proof of Donald's love. Every time she saw an insect, she would imagine Donald killing it for her. She would imagine the triumphant crunch of his booted foot, or perhaps even his naked fist.

But worms are a different kind of insect, aren't they?

It was only five blocks to the exterminator's, but Ellen had to walk by her old school. In the last couple of years, she had avoided it whenever possible—detouring around it, or cabbing past it on her way to Estelle's. Now she understood why. It was not that the memories themselves were sad, but that there were so many of them. It was what they said: that time had passed, is passing.

It began to rain, a soft spray like a last fetid exhalation. Worm weather, Ellen thought: warm, moist, juicy. She said aloud, "I walk through the rain with my mother's worm. . . ."

Lisanne had been wandering all morning, buying postcards. She ended up at a café in Les Halles called Au Père Tranquil. The name appealed to her. She sat down, ordered café crème, lit a cigarette. She wondered where Adair was, what he was looking at, what he was thinking of—right now. They spent every morning of their honeymoon apart, meeting back at the hotel for a late lunch. She loved that he didn't want to be with her all the time. She loved that he loved to be alone.

Their first night in Paris, they went to a bar on the rue Casanova. It was only a few blocks from the hotel, but Lisanne had to hold on to his arm to keep from falling. She was unsteady from looking up at the sky. She thought it was the color blood would be if blood were blue, dark, rich, and slowly flowing.

The bar was on a corner. The street was too narrow for tables and chairs, but the tall glass doors stood open, and people stood outside with their glasses of wine. They all shared the same unsuitability for the hours of day. Lisanne imagined them living bravely through difficult nights, and dying in peaceful dawns.

Adair led her to a table in the back and ordered a bottle of red wine. "I hope you'll have a glass of this with me," he said. "Even you have to admit, it's a special occasion."

"I'll have a glass with you," Lisanne said.

The waiter brought the wine, and opened it with a flourish. He insisted (to Adair's embarrassment) that monsieur sniff the cork.

"Cheers," Adair said. "I can't believe it. My first time in Paris—and I get to be with you. I don't think I've been this happy since second grade."

Lisanne said, "I don't think I've been this happy in my life." As soon as she said this, she regretted it.

It seemed dangerous to be so happy, reckless to flaunt it in words.

Lighting another cigarette, Lisanne spread her new postcards over the table. She had picked out the same one for Mrs. Rainey and Estelle: a painting in maroons and blues of an Edwardian woman with her dog. When she'd called Mrs. Rainey to tell her she was engaged, to tell her that she wouldn't be coming back to Florida, Mrs. Rainey had burst into tears. Mrs. Rainey had said, "I've been thinking of getting a new dog, but I'm afraid that when I die, Pamela will send it to the pound. I can't count on her for anything."

Lisanne had promised Mrs. Rainey that she would take the dog.

She turned over Mrs. Rainey's postcard and wrote: "Dear Mrs. R., I'm so sorry you couldn't make it to the wedding, but I'm thrilled you got Patrick. He sounds and looks adorable."

For Mrs. Rainey had written at great length about the

beauties of her new puppy, sending along, as proof, a dozen pictures of the puppy posed like a wedding ring on tiny velvet pillows.

Lisanne thought of Florida, her last few months there. She realized now that she must have been having some sort of nervous breakdown. Every time she went to the supermarket, it was like *Apocalypse Now*. The most innocent things had combined in her mind to create pure terror.

She remembered one night, walking out of Publix with a bag of apples, how even the clouds had scared her. They had looked planted in the earth, instead of set in the sky, rising up from the horizon in huge, dark mushrooms. Then, as she drove home on Albee Road, the toads kept leaping across the road into her headlights, leaping fantastically high—you could almost hear them go *boing!* The first one she saw, she thought, How sad. What a sad and lonely toad. But they were all down the road, and after about a dozen, it started to seem sinister. Bounding out of the bay, in some kind of mating ritual, probably, in a migration that was at once absurd, beautiful, and brave. They were leaping to their deaths, after all, under the wheels of Lisanne's car. Or some of them were. She had heard the crunch. But whatever was driving them across the road was worth the risk, worth dying for.

Lisanne reached for another postcard. She wrote, Dear Mother . . .

Estelle was at the Sky Rink with Ian. He had made her miserable this last week, asking for his father every morning at visiting hour. In desperation, she had pleaded with his therapists for this rare excursion: an afternoon of ice skating.

She bought the special skates for him. She laced him into them. She guided him out onto the rink with his walker. She had not been sure whether this new experience would excite, frustrate, terrify, or bore him. She stood over him, and steadied him, and studied his face fearfully as it reflected, in pinched frowns, the adjustment of his feet to the strange surface. Children were so tricky. You could only hope to give them moments of happiness. She loved her dogs not for what she could give them but for what they could receive.

Not until Ian had assured her, with tremulous smiles, that he was enjoying himself did it occur to Estelle: this was her first time on ice in almost fifty years!

She lifted her arms and tried a timid twirl.

Fifty years.

She skated in slow circles around the child. The circles slowly widened. Estelle began to go faster. She began to go fast—trusting in the memories of her muscles. She sensed the other skaters gasping: *Look at Granny go!* Among all the losses were the things that stayed: books, dogs, songs, oceans, ice. . . .

Adair and Lisanne had been walking all afternoon. The unseasonable beauty of the day saved them from having to have a purpose. This was enough: just to wander through its clear heat.

Then Lisanne remembered. She said, "Let's go to the Louvre."

Portrait da Femme rested on a pillar, impaled upon a thin metal neck. Her chin was deeply indented, her lean lips curved, as if just sliding out of a smile, her coils of stone hair serenely center-parted. The thickly lidded eyes rolled slightly upward, over and above life, unaware.

It was a beautiful face. Lisanne wasn't sure if its stupidity made it seem hopeful, or if its hopefulness made it seem stupid.

She knew where she had seen it before. It was Estelle. It looked just like her.

She called Adair over, wondering if he would see this too. He had wandered ahead of her through the crowd.

He looked the stone head up and down. He said, "She's beautiful."

"But the expression is so dumb, don't you think? So beautifully, hopefully *dumb*."

He said, "You're confusing the blankness of stone eyes with stupidity."

"Maybe so," Lisanne said.

She remembered her mother's face when she had told her about the theft. Lisanne had wanted her mother's anger more than forgiveness. She had known from the beginning that the count's disappearance was her fault. First she had stolen the husband, then the lover. To Lisanne, it had made such perfect sense: the second theft was her punishment for the first.

What Estelle said was worse than anything Lisanne had imagined. And the way she said it, with joy, with rapture, was worse than what she said.

"But don't you see, Lisanne? I left that money there for him. I wanted him to take it."

Lisanne had always believed her mother's love to be helpless against the violations it invited.

But to be so pure, so hard, so whole—

In her generosity, she was inviolable.

"Come look at the Venus de Milo," Adair said, "if you want to see a real woman."

Lisanne was disappointed that he hadn't noticed the resemblance that to her was so uncanny.

She thought perhaps that Coco had.

• • •

At the sound of footsteps in the foyer, Ellen struck a pose, facing the doorway: back arched, left leg slightly bent and angled in, left foot playfully pointed. She wore a black silk negligee with an underwire bra (this support being, unfortunately, crucial), and black satin mules. Donnie had been dispatched to a friend's for the night. Champagne was chilling on ice. Frank Sinatra sang in the background. Candles burned the length of the hallway. The fire extinguisher hung on the wall within easy reach.

For Donald had been away all week on a business trip, and Ellen, tearing a page out of O'Boyle's book, had vowed to give him a welcome he would never forget.

At last his key clicked in the lock. And clicked. And clicked and clicked and clicked and clicked. An angry oath, followed by violent knocking, confirmed that the lock had jammed. Ellen stepped forward, and then stepped back—in loyalty to her pose.

At last the lock gave, and the door swung open, and Donald burst into the hall.

"God*damn* it!"

He lurched toward her, shrugging off his jacket, which he slung over her shoulder as though she were a coat hook.

"What the hell are ya doin' standing' there like a statue, for chrissakes? Dinchya hear me knockin'?"

Ellen sighed, and slumped out of her pose, and went over to the closet to hang up his jacket.

"And what the hell's with all these friggin' candles? Oh no. Don't tell me. *Don't tell me!* You've blown another fuse, havenchya? How many times do I have to tell ya, El? You can't blow-dry your hair *and* heat your curlers *and* wash your dishes *and* listen to music at the same time. Choices, hon. Ya gotta make choices. That's what life is all about. Choices. Ay?"

Ellen felt her upper lip lift. She felt a snarl rise in her throat. She counted to ten slowly, and turned around. What she saw then, in Donald's embrace, sent her sashaying forward with arms outstretched.

An enormous box tied in blue ribbon.

"Darling!"

"Hey, son!" Donald shouted. "Hey, son!" He turned to Ellen. "Where's our fine youth this evening?"

"He's at a friend's house," Ellen said.

Donald's face fell. He set the present down on top of his duffel bag, and said sadly, "Well, I guess it can wait."

"How was your flight?" Ellen asked in a choked voice.

This question instantly revived him.

"An outrage, by God! An absolute outrage! Couldna been worse if it had *crashed.* I was sittin' between, Ellen, sittin' between"—Donald's voice here hushed, to build over the course of the next sixteen words to a barbarous howl—"the two fattest, smelliest broads I have ever *seen,* let alone *sat between,* in MY LIFE!"

"I'm sorry to hear that, darling," Ellen said. "Why don't you relax and have a glass of champ—"

"And I said, very nicely, to the broad on my left, 'Wouldja mind giving me your aisle seat so I could have a bit more room here?' And she said, 'Don't you be a fly in my ass!' And I said, 'By God, I bet your ass has seen many a fly in its day!' And then the broad on my right said. . . ."

Husband and wife had moved into the living room. Ellen sat down on a green velvet love seat and watched the minute hand of the grandfather clock as Donald repeated, *word for word,* every line of the violent brabbling that had ensued. Everyone on the plane, it seemed, had gotten involved: the other passengers, the flight attendants, even the co-pilot. And *no one* had taken Donald's side!

His re-enactment lasted almost as long as the actual flight: fifty-two minutes.

Finally, after a recapitulation that recapitulated the several recapitulations that had preceded it, Donald surged into this Churchillian coda:

"I will fight them in the airports, in the lounges and the gift shops. I will fight them on the ground, I will fight them in the air. I will fight them on the phone lines, I will fight them in the courts. I, Donald Patrick Prawl, frequent flyer and business traveler, *will never surrender!*"

With this last word—*surrender*—still ringing in the air, Donald wheeled round, to reveal buttocks ecstatically aquiver, and executed a flank march across the room to the phone.

"Operator, get me Continental's Customer Service Department!"

Ellen went into the bedroom to change into sweats. The thought of herself—crimped, painted, scented, silked—was so humbling, so reproachful.

It was almost as bad as the sight of herself.

Once Donald's rages had stirred her. He had gotten a bloody nose in a bar fight with a man who asked her to slow dance. He had shoved aside a couple who tried to step in front of her into a waiting taxi. In his rages, his bearing was still heroic—head held high, chest thrust forward, fists clenched—cartoonishly heroic, even: she used to imagine a Superman cape streaming back from his squared shoulders. But now the rages themselves seemed absurd.

And not just Donald's—the rages of the world. Ellen thought of all those people you see every day on the streets of New York, people pushing one another, cursing and screaming and shouting and shaking fists. And all it took was one person crying in a phone booth to put the angry crowd to shame.

Once Donald had seemed so brave, so strong, so manly. . . .

"I'm calling to report an outrage," she heard him yelling down the hall, "and to demand a free first-class ticket to anywhere in the U.S. of A., including Hawaii, on my next Continental flight!"

Of course the person you fall in love with is not the person who needs your love.

". . . the two fattest women I have ever seen . . . just ruined my flight . . . an outrage, I tell ya. . . ."

In the bathroom, Ellen bent over the sink to scrub off her makeup. Even over the splash of water, she could hear him *ranting*. . . .

"I'm not saying it's Continental's fault that there are fat people in the world, d'y'hear? I'm just saying, you might want to stuff 'em in a different cabin. . . ."

Even she could hardly see the lines yet—but they were there, uncoiling with the minutes. Ellen wished she had a photograph of herself for every day of the last thirteen years. She wished she hadn't stopped her journals with her marriage. Worse, even, than the things you can remember are the things you can't: years, for example, whole years.

Of course, the years would have gone by anyway.

"If I pay business class, by God, I believe I have a right to sit next to fat people who *don't* stink. . . ."

Ellen thought of those thirteen years, and all that they would not give back. She saw how tenderly thirteen years can take from you the life you hoped to live and leave you with nothing but the life you'd been living all along.

Thirteen years that could seem so innocent at the time.

"And where the hell do ya find your stewardesses, by the way? In the sewers?"

Ellen thought of the hot, slow stares of strangers, dust

rising on a road. She thought of the postcards she could send:

Because I am a crappy housekeeper. Because I ruin evenings. Because I can't make choices. Because I can be so goddamn naive. . . .

Estelle was lying in the middle of her enormous bed in the middle of her enormous dogs. It was the hour of the night that she hated most—eight o'clock—when she had just finished dinner. Just finished dinner — *and now what?*

She had decided at the end of the summer, with the acceptance of *Priapus Erumpent* (now retitled *Sweet Summer Seduction*), to lay aside her romances for a while and improve her mind. With this aim in view, she had started *The Norton Anthology of Poetry,* which she planned to read from beginning to end. In the middle of Popular Ballads, at "Johnie Armstrong" ("There dwelt a man in fair Westmorland / Johnie Armstrong men did him call, / He had neither lands nor rent coming in, / Yet he kept eight score men in his hall. . . ."), Estelle almost abandoned the project. She was glad now that she had struggled on. She had just gotten past Henry Howard's "So Cruel Prison" to Queen Elizabeth I's "When I Was Fair and Young."

When I was fair and young, and favor graced me . . .

The word *torture* kept appearing in Estelle's mind as she read, but she would check the page and it was not a word she could have read, it was not a word that was written.

Jimmy, her oldest dog, was stretched out, snoring, beside her, his head on her pillow. For comfort, Estelle leaned forward and kissed his speckled groin. It smelled oddly of cocoa butter, heavy and sweet. Up around his ears, his smell lightened and sharpened, making Estelle think of wet grass, white pants after a picnic. His long black lips smelled warm and nourishing, like chicken soup.

Estelle loved the smell of her dogs. It never ceased to amaze her that there were people out there *who actually thought dogs stank.*

In sleep, the dog's mouth worked furiously. The muscles in his jaw twitched, and his lips undulated, as though he were fighting back tears, or struggling to speak. Estelle laid her hand across his trembling mouth, she tracked the movements of his lips. She believed that if dogs could speak, it would not be to say, *I played ball today,* or *I chased a squirrel.* It would be some pure truth of the heart that would change everything.

> *How many weeping eyes I made to pine with*
> *woe,*
> *How many sighing hearts, I have no skill to*
> *show.*

The exterminators had arrived with their bombs, and their leering eyes, and the ceiling was bare and still again. The worms came from a box of dog food she had left out over the summer, the exterminators told her. Eventually, they would have turned into moths, and she would have been able, she imagined, to open her windows, set them free. Estelle wondered where the worms had disappeared to until she began to find them, stiff, dry, and curled as if in agony, on her bureau, in her drawers, on her dressing table, in all the corners of her room.

Saturday night, after Ellen left, there was a storm, and the temperature plunged thirty degrees. Estelle still heard the rain and the wind, now, days after it had stopped. All week long, she had been hearing things that did not belong in the silence. Half a dozen times a night, she would look up from her poetry, in a terror that was no longer expectant, but resigned.

Estelle's worst nightmare was not that someone would break in and kill *her,* but that someone would break in and kill her dogs. Lately, she had been haunted by this recurring scene: men in wet suits with stakes and ropes and axes burst into her bedroom and force her to watch, helpless, as one by one each dog is tied down (tied down like that pig in the military experiment), tied down and hacked to death. The men did this to her dogs simply to teach Estelle this lesson: that her love can't save or protect anything. It was an experiment to prove exactly how powerless love is.

Other images, images of suffering and betrayal, would come to Estelle out of nowhere and fill her with horror. And yet she knew: worse goes on and goes on every minute of every hour every day across the world.

Estelle looked down at the sleeping dog, down deep into the center of his half-closed eye, past the rim of glossy brown that contained the nacreous white—deep down into the slow-circling, glowing iris.

The movement of the soul, she thought, must be something like this—something like the movement of a sleeping eye.

Estelle had been reading for over an hour, through Gascoigne and on into Sir Walter Raleigh, when, abruptly, all fourteen dogs stirred from their sleep. They had heard something—something she hadn't.

All week long she had heard what wasn't there, and now she had missed what was.

For a second, Estelle believed this: that by acknowledging her worst fear, by imagining it, she had made it happen. Again, she saw her dogs tied down—the ax rising—only now she herself was wielding it. And the worst of it is this:

the love in their eyes as she kills them. Not the blood, not the suffering, not the death—the forgiveness.

Estelle began to tremble. *Get a grip on yourself,* she heard Donald's voice shouting across the caverns of her mind. Who would have thought that angry voice would come to her in these moments of panic and call to her as the voice of reason?

Slowly, Estelle's terror throbbed away as she registered the fact that none of the dogs seemed in the least alarmed. If anything, they were excited. They had lumbered off the bed and were gathered now round the door that was opened, just a crack, onto the hall.

If there was something evil out there, Estelle knew, they would be barking.

Suddenly, and with stunning synchrony, Marlon and Brando both attempted, unsuccessfully, to mount two nearby, outraged bitches. A chorus of adulatory yelping rose above a crescendoing percussion of thumping tails.

And now, soundlessly, through the crack in the door, there came whirling into the room, scattering the hounds, a small fluffy black-and-white ball—

Her Majesty!

—into the room, and in one amazing leap, onto the bed—

Her Majesty!

Estelle fell upon the shih tzu, and kissed her paws in gratitude. That the Queen should appear like this in her bedroom, out of the blue, in the middle of the night, was nothing short of a miracle. It did not occur to Estelle to question it. A miracle was all you could ask out of life. It did not occur to Estelle to ask for more.

On their last night in Paris, Lisanne inserted herself into the red Norma Kamali Ellen had given her the night before the wedding. The dress was made of pleated crushed velvet.

"I can't imagine Ellen in that dress," Adair said. "It's so, I don't know—"

"*Red?*" suggested Lisanne.

Redder than her dress, however, was the lipstick Lisanne wore to distract from her nose, which was redder than her lipstick.

Lisanne had come down with a cold.

All through dinner, she sneezed and sniffled and blew her nose—accumulating a wad of used Kleenex on her lap. When she tried to eat the food she couldn't taste, let alone smell, rivulets of mucus ran down her nose. She was disgusting—a fact confirmed by the glances of the other diners.

Lisanne apologized to Adair for ruining what should have been the most romantic evening of their honeymoon.

It wasn't enough that she didn't know how to dress, or how to walk, or what to say. It wasn't enough that she broke things and spilled things. Even her body had to conspire against her. Other women could create romance, other women could sustain it, other women could enjoy it. . . .

"And I can't even smoke," she said, stamping out her cigarette. "My throat is so sore I can't even smoke!"

Adair smiled at her tenderly, over the candles, over the single rose in its fluted vase.

Back at the hotel, the concierge stopped them on their way to the elevator. "An urgent message for you, madame!" And he held out to her a folded note.

"Adair, I'm scared," she whispered. "You read it."

Closing her eyes, she leaned back against the mirrored wall between the elevators. Urgent messages were always bad news. She thought of the ways people hurt themselves, and are hurt, of accidents and crimes.

She opened her eyes at the sound of Adair's laugh. "What on earth—?"

The elevator opened. He guided her inside. "Tell me, what is it? Not bad news?"

"I guess that would depend on your point of view," he said. "I don't happen to think so."

He held the note up, dodging her when she tried to snatch it. "Guess," he said. "You'll never guess."

He didn't give her the note until they got inside the room. Lisanne sank onto the bed to read it. He lay down beside her and watched her face.

Lisanne looked up at him. "No!"

Adair said, "Yes!"

The curt message ran as follows: *Stay on extra week. We will be joining you tomorrow.*

It was signed: The Countess von Cockleburg.

So he had come back.

Because he was broke? Because he was lonely? Because he loved her and could not live without her?

Lisanne said, "My mother—the countess!"

Adair said, "My father-in-law and slave—the count!" He said, "Is there any way the title might pass to me someday?"

"It would probably pass to Donald first."

"I wonder what Nipe will have to say."

" 'Bit sudden, ain't it?' "

"And Lady Perdita!"

"Your sister!"

"We'll have to unpack our bags. Maybe they've booked that empty suite next to ours."

"God, honeymooning with the in-laws!"

"Ten to one, they bring the Queen. . . ."

He came back.